"Aja, do you watch Channel 13?
Roxie asked out of the blue.

"What does that have to do with anything?"

"If you do, your date next Saturday won't be a blind one, at least for you."

"Date? What date?"

Roxie smiled mischievously.

"Roxanne Bingham-Daniels, I told you about trying to fix me up. I don't do blind dates."

"Hey, like I said, if you watch 13, it won't be blind."

"And just why is that?"

"Because, drumroll please . . ." Roxie began banging on the table. People were beginning to stare, but Roxie couldn't have cared less. "Your escort for next Saturday evening shall be none other than Channel 13 Eyewitness News sports anchor Charles Clayton. Yes, behind door number one is a luscious, deep chocolate colored, sexy, *working* man, who wants to take you out."

Aja stared in disbelief. "You've got to be kidding me."

"Oh my, are we interested? Could it be?" Roxie chuckled.

My Brother's Keeper

RESHONDA TATE BILLINGSLEY

POCKET BOOKS
New York   London   Toronto   Sydney

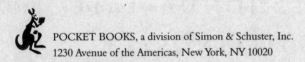 POCKET BOOKS, a division of Simon & Schuster, Inc.
1230 Avenue of the Americas, New York, NY 10020

ISBN: 0-7434-7713-8

First Pocket Books trade paperback edition September 2003

10 9 8 7 6 5 4 3

POCKET and colophon are registered trademarks of Simon & Schuster, Inc.

Manufactured in the United States of America

For information regarding special discounts for bulk purchases, please contact Simon & Schuster Special Sales at 1-800-456-6798 or business@simonandschuster.com.

To Mya,
My inspiration

Acknowledgments

I have been blessed, truly blessed, to have some of the most wonderful people in my life. And I have to take a moment to say thank you to all of them for helping my dream become a reality.

To my husband, Miron. We did it! Thank you for your emotional, financial, and spiritual support. Thanks for the nights you took the girls so I could write in peace, for offering feedback even when I didn't listen, for being my biggest cheerleader and my number-one fan. I am eternally grateful to you for pushing me to use my talents.

To my mother, Nancy Blacknell. Thank you for giving me those talents to use. You have always pushed me to be the best at whatever I do. I owe all that I am to you. (And don't worry, people are not going to think this book is based on our family.)

To my wonderful little sister, Tanisha Tate. Thank you for always supporting me, whether it's pushing my books as if they were your own or reading the rough draft and giving me your two cents, I know I can always count on you.

Of course, I need to give big, huge thanks to my agent, Sara Camilli, for believing in my story and being patient—even when I was not.

To my editor, Brigitte Smith. Thank you for helping me

shape my story into an even better one, and also for believing in the book.

I also have to give much love to all the people who helped make the self-published version of *My Brother's Keeper* such a success; all the book clubs who chose it as a book of the month and all the bookstore owners who welcomed an aspiring author with open arms. And while there are just too many book clubs and bookstores who have supported me to name, I have to give special thanks to: Circle of Friends, the Good Book Club, The Sistah Circle, Cydney Rax at Book-Remarks, Tee C. Royal at RAWSISTAZ, Yasmin Coleman at APOOO, Shunda Blocker at Booking Matters, The Cultural Connection, The Shrine of the Black Madonna, Jokae's, and Black Images.

And my gratitude remains the same for those who helped me get the self-published version of *My Brother's Keeper* off the ground: my sisters from Delta Xi, especially Jaimi Huff, Kristie King, Kim Patterson-Wright, Trina McReynolds, Clemelia Humphrey Richardson, Finisha Waits, Raquelle Wooten, Beverly Davis, Nikelle Meade, and Leslie Mouton . . . thank you for your advice/support throughout the years. You have always believed in me.

To my brother-in-law, Joseph Davis, for being the one person we can count on no matter what (and for the advice on what life is like for an aspiring basketball player).

To Deidre Lodrig, for making it happen with me. Good luck with your books! To my longtime mentor, Marilyn Marshall, for teaching me what a good writer is. To Sonny Messiah for giving me my start in journalism.

Thank you to my online family at Blackwriters.org, especially the one and only Tia Shabazz, for bringing us all together. Thanks for the endless feedback.

Much love also to Bruce and Helen Tate, my Smackover

family, Della Jones, Kysa Daniels, Shiral Gaines and the crew at Shiral's Ultimate Looks, Dr. Kit Givan, Dawn James, Terri Hurte, Beta Sigma Omega, Reggie Picou, Chris Francis, Cheryl Smith, Waleed Salim, Natalie Hughes, and all my former colleagues at KFOR-TV.

Stretching my arms real wide for a big hug to all the authors who let me pick their brains and encouraged me tremendously, especially Karen Quinones Miller, Tracy Price Thompson, Tijuana Butler, Troy Martin, Brian Egeston, Brandon Massey, and Zane.

That about covers it (I guess) . . . oh, how could I forget the most important people who helped me get where I am today— YOU, the reader. Thanks for the love! Enjoy!

Author's Note

This is a work of fiction. Any resemblance to actual people is purely coincidental. Neither the characters nor storyline are based on my family life. (There, Ma, are you happy?)

My Brother's
Keeper

Prologue

1986

There they go again.

It seemed almost ritualistic. He'd come home past midnight—high, drunk, or both.

Aja touched the award she won at the school history fair. How she had hoped to be able to show it to her father and watch him beam with happiness. But it looked like there would be no happiness tonight.

"Why does she put up with him?" Aja muttered.

Bam!

Now he was trying to break down the bedroom door. That shouldn't be too hard since it was hanging on its hinges from all the other late-night fights.

"Open this damn door!" Her father was screaming in a high-pitched, slurred sound, muffled only by his constant banging and kicking on the door.

"Stop it, Gerald!" Aja heard her mother shout. "You're drunk! Just go to sleep!"

"Don't tell me I'm drunk in my own fucking house! Open the door!"

Aja threw back the covers on her bed and got up. This was one fight she wouldn't be able to sleep through. She knew the commotion had woken up her brother, Eric, by the sounds of Run-DMC blaring from his room. As usual, he had turned up his rap music to try to drown out the sounds of fighting.

Her six-year-old sister had already retreated to the closet, her comfort zone when their parents fought. There, Jada would cry while holding and rocking Felix, her stuffed and tattered teddy bear. Felix was a gift from Daddy and a reminder of happier times.

"Open this door before I blow this fucking house up!"

At sixteen, Aja was used to the fights. She stopped praying that they would stop a long time ago since it was obvious God wasn't listening.

Wham!

She heard her mother scream.

He had made it in.

"Woman, don't you ever lock me out of my own bedroom! You hear me?"

Even though her parents' bedroom was on the other end of the house, Aja could hear everything like they were standing right next to her.

"Gerald, please don't do this."

Aja hated when her mother used that all too familiar begging-for-her-life tone of voice.

Whap!

A slap. Another scream. More cries. From her mother. From Jada.

Aja slowly opened her bedroom door and saw Eric's door swing open. She looked at her thirteen-year-old brother standing there in a pair of Batman boxers and a T-shirt. He looked aged beyond his years, his eyes red with rage, his light-freckled complexion turning crimson.

Aja's eyes made their way down to her brother's hands where he tightly clutched his prized baseball bat, signed by Hank Aaron. Eric kept that bat in a special case and never took it out for anything.

"Eric," Aja whispered. "Eric, what are you doing? You know better than to come out when they fight."

Eric looked Aja straight in the eyes, then turned and headed down the hall toward his parents' bedroom.

"Eric, don't."

He ignored her.

Aja began a silent prayer as she headed down the hallway after her brother.

Eric stopped at the entrance to his parents' bedroom while Aja remained just outside. The door lay on the floor. Their mother was in the corner near the bathroom. Her gown was torn. Tears were streaming down her face and blood was dripping from her nose.

"Leave her alone," Eric firmly said.

"What . . . ?" their father muttered after he spun around and noticed Eric.

Aja looked at the difference in sizes between her father and brother. At 6 feet 4 inches and 280 pounds, her father towered above her little brother. Standing in front of their father, Eric's frail body reminded Aja of David and Goliath. Aja noticed her father's appearance—his usually hazel eyes were bloodshot, the obvious effect of a night with Jack Daniel's. His broad shoulders that used to stand so proud were slumped over and his shirt was torn at the sleeve. He looked like a madman.

"What you goin' do with that bat, you little sissy?" As he spoke, drool trickled out of the corner of his mouth.

"Eric, please, go back to bed. I'm fine." Aja watched her mother try to get up off the floor.

"I said, leave her alone." Eric wasn't backing down. He was shaking, but determined. Aja hovered behind him, silently willing him to just walk away.

"Well, well, well. If the little piss-in-the-bed, sissy-ass son of mine ain't trying to have him some balls," their father laughed. "Boy, if you know what's good for you, you'll put that bat down and get your ass back to bed before I break you in half."

Again, Eric didn't move. He just clutched the bat tighter.

"Oh, so I guess you gotta see to believe." Fear gripped Aja's body as her father lunged forward and hit Eric in the chest so hard, his 85-pound body went flying out of the bedroom entrance. Eric hit his head on an antique table across the hall and slumped to the floor.

"Eric!" Their mother struggled to get up.

"Sit down!" Aja felt her heart drop as her father reached back and slapped his wife across the face. The impact knocked her back to the floor while out of nowhere, Jada came rushing in.

"Mommy, are you all right?" Jada cried, trying to clutch her mother's neck.

"Baby, just go. Go back to your room." Their mother tried to ease Jada off her, but before Jada could respond, their father had her by the neck.

"Get your ass back to your room!"

Jada began wailing. "Mommy!!! Mommy!!"

"Shut up!" Her father struggled to get his belt off with one hand; the other hand was gripped firmly around Jada's neck.

"I'll teach your little behind to mind!"

Jada continued to scream. The louder she got, the angrier her father became.

"Gerald, please, you're hurting her." Aja saw her mother stretch her arms toward Jada, but it seemed that she couldn't pull herself up off the floor.

Their father was out of control—this was one of the worst scenes ever: Aja stood in the doorway, still unable to move. Jada's tiny body dangled midair. Her long, black ponytails swung from side to side as she frantically tried to get away from her father. Eric lay unconscious on the hall floor.

"Gerald, let her go!" Aja continued to watch in horror as her mother—barely able to stand and her face covered with blood and tears—pointed a twenty-two caliber pistol at her husband. "Don't make me shoot you. Put my baby down."

"Has everybody in this house lost their fucking minds?"

Aja remained frozen as her father dropped Jada and stumbled toward his wife.

"Baby, don't." Her mother's beautiful brown eyes softened, pleading for this all to end. She backed up but kept the gun pointed. "I don't want to use this. I just want you to go get some sleep."

"You pull a gun on me and then tell me you don't want to use it?" Aja's father and mother were face-to-face. "Go ahead, shoot me," he laughed as he placed his chest to the gun's barrel. "Your little weak ass doesn't have the nerve."

Nervous and in tears, Aja's mother held the gun firmly and said, "Just go."

Their father laughed again and turned as if he were walking away. In a matter of seconds he turned back, knocked the gun out of his wife's hand, and pushed her to the floor. A scream started building in Aja's throat as her father grabbed the gun, grabbed their mother by the hair, and then put the gun to her head.

"Okay, Superwoman, who's bad now?" He laughed.

Aja wanted so much to help, but she couldn't move. She couldn't move to see if Eric was all right, or to come to her mother's aid. It was as if her feet were glued to the floor. Aja watched the tears pour down her mother's cheeks. She watched the man she had once loved so much hold her mother's life in his hands. Then she watched as Jada came running out of the corner, racing toward her mother, screaming, *"Noooooooooo!"*

Aja watched as the gun went off and her mother's blood splattered all over her little sister's face.

Part One

One

"If you could change one thing about your life, what would it be?" Aja read the question in *Cosmo* magazine out loud as she sat waiting for her sister.

"Well, that's easy," she answered. "I'd take the gun from my daddy and shoot him instead. Maybe my life would've turned out a whole lot different." Aja didn't realize she was talking to herself. The puzzled look from the elderly lady passing by made her snap out of her vengeful thoughts. She managed a slight smile at the woman as she imagined how she looked, sitting there talking to herself. *Probably like I belong here.*

Aja closed the magazine and glanced around the lobby of Memorial Greens. She hated coming to this place. It was heartbreaking to watch the people wander aimlessly about, some muttering to themselves, some in their own world, and others with no idea who they were or why they were even here.

If only I could get Jada out of here. If only things could be different.

But they couldn't. Aja had come to terms with that fact years ago. It had been six years since her sister was committed, and Aja knew it was for the best.

"Good morning, Miss Ah-jah. Your sister will be out shortly." Aja hated the commanding, bullish tone of Jada's primary nurse, Mrs. Overton. The fifty-nine-year-old, 220-pound woman looked like a prison warden. Her beady eyes seemed buried in her head and her thick, bushy eyebrows met just above the bridge of her nose, forming a V. She wore her long, stringy gray hair tied back in a bun. Her nostrils were permanently flared.

"It's A-ja, like the country, Asia, with a J." *Why must they go through this every time? It's like that woman was doing this on purpose.* The nurse shot a fake smile before spinning around to go back to her station.

Aja sat near the window that overlooked the large courtyard, where she and Jada had spent many evenings. They both loved the shade the sycamore tree provided from the hot summer sun. With the high humidity, it could get unbearable sometimes. But for the most part, it was always extremely soothing to sit outside.

Even though Jada seemed to be improving, it hurt Aja's heart to see her sister here. After their mother died, their father was sent to prison and Aja and her siblings were shipped off to different relatives. Aja stayed in Houston and finished high school, living with her father's sister. Jada was sent to Alabama to live with another aunt and Eric was sent to Chicago with an uncle. Their mother was an only child, so Aja, Eric, and Jada had to grow up with their father's family, which wasn't easy because all of his relatives thought he should be forgiven. And for Aja, that simply wasn't happening.

At first, everyone thought Jada was simply traumatized. After the shooting, she barely talked for months. At their mother's funeral, she sat emotionless and didn't shed a tear or say a word. It was a silence that had stayed with her, even through her horrible nightmares when the only sounds she made were screams in the middle of the night. She was withdrawn at school, speaking only when absolutely necessary. They even placed her in a special school after she refused to do her work. After a year, relatives started suggesting to Aunt Millicent that Jada get help.

"That child don't need to see no head doctor," Aunt Millicent would always say. "Ain't nothing wrong with her that time can't heal."

But time didn't heal her. In fact, as more time passed, the more Jada withdrew. Eventually, she just stopped talking altogether. When she tried to slit her wrists at the age of twelve, Aunt Millicent knew there was no other choice.

Luckily, Aja managed to convince her aunt to let Jada come back to Houston, where the mental health facilities were among the best in the world—not to mention that Aja could be close to her sister. In actuality, Aja thought Aunt Millicent was relieved. She didn't know how to handle Jada. Plus, she had already raised eight children and wasn't too happy about having to take Jada in the first place.

"You have exactly two hours." Nurse Overton's deep voice jolted Aja out of her thoughts. The nurse was gone before Aja could even say thanks.

Aja saw her sister, Jada, standing in the entrance of the hospital lobby. She looked like an angel in the white sundress Aja had recently bought her for her eighteenth birthday. Jada's long, golden brown hair was pulled back and tied with a matching white ribbon. Her caramel complexion was free of the acne that had plagued her early teen years. Had it not been for her eyes, Jada would have looked like a normal, pretty teenager blossoming into a woman. But her eyes revealed the real story—they were sunken and dark, like they were being swallowed by her face. The light that was there as a child had burned out long ago.

"Hi there." Aja walked over to hug and kiss her sister on the cheek. "You look great. Let's go to our favorite spot."

Aja took Jada's hand and the two of them walked outside to the bench under the tree. It was the same thing every Saturday afternoon—Aja seldom missed a week. Coming here was important to her and she felt to Jada as well. During their visits, Aja would recount her week, all the while trying to remain upbeat and as if nothing was wrong. Today, as usual, Jada said nothing and Aja continued talking. She knew she was rambling but she knew that sooner or later her weekly conversations would get through to her sister, so she never let up.

". . . and Mrs. Atkins, you remember her—she used to live across the street. She up and got married. Seventy-nine years old and she gets married to a fifty-six-year-old man. I can't buy a date and here she is getting married." Aja laughed. While she tried to joke about being dateless, it did bother her. She wanted a family of her own one day, but at the rate she was going, it would never happen.

Aja continued talking, stroking Jada's thick hair as she made conversation. People always used to tell them they had "good hair" because it was long and wavy—something they inherited from their father's Indian ancestors. Her great-grandmother was Cherokee, and although she never met her, Aja was sure that's where her butterscotch color and reddish brown hair came from.

Aja had taken pride in her hair when she was a teenager, until one day her mother got angry because Aja kept telling a friend she had "bad hair" because it was short and kinky. Her mother told her there was no such thing as "good hair"—that was just something society used to unfairly label people. Since then, Aja had worn her hair shoulder length and kept it dyed dark brown.

"Jada, did I tell you I got a cat?" Aja stopped rubbing her sister's hair and they were now face-to-face. "This guy at work gave her to me because he moved someplace they can't have pets. I named her Simba. She's a beautiful, gray-colored calico. I never in a million years thought I would own a cat. I'm a dog person myself. Remember that dog we used to have? The Labrador, Cooter?"

Aja looked at her sister to see if there was some sign that she was taking it all in. There was none. Aja continued her stories, telling Jada about her plans for the weekend and the leak in her kitchen sink. Through each anecdote, Jada sat with a blank stare on her face.

It was difficult for Aja to keep up her enthusiasm. As a child, Jada had been very talkative. She'd constantly gotten on Aja's nerves. Jada's response to everything had been "Why?" Aja smiled as she recalled how absolutely crazy it had driven her. Now what she wouldn't give to hear her sister say that one little word.

After another hour of talking, Aja got up to go. "Well, I hate to run, but I've got to stop by the office and check on some clients." Aja reached into her big DKNY tote bag and pulled out a plastic shopping bag. "But you know I brought you something." She pulled a long, light pink silk dress out of the plastic bag and held it up. "I got it on sale at this boutique when I went to New York last week. I'm so glad they let you wear your own clothes here. I know how you like to look pretty."

Jada slowly reached up to touch the dress. She gently ran her hand over the fabric. For a moment, Aja thought she saw a twinkle in her sister's eyes, but it passed so quickly, Aja wasn't sure if she had imagined the whole thing.

"Yeah, see how nice and soft it is. That's what sold me on it. I bet it'll feel good on you. Will you wear it for me next Saturday?"

Please God, let her say something. Jada just kept gently rubbing the dress.

"Okay, then," Aja said, trying not to let her disappointment show. "We'd better go. Nurse Overton will be calling out the dogs in a minute."

Aja put the dress back in the plastic bag and helped her sister up. Together they walked back up the path to Memorial Greens.

As Aja waved good-bye she yelled, "Next time, I'll bring Eric."

She knew that was a long shot. The last time he'd come, Jada had sat in a trance and Eric had left in tears. That was more than a year ago. He hadn't been back, saying he couldn't stand it. Aja had been working to convince him to come again, but he had problems of his own. Problems that were another story entirely.

Two

Ringgg!

The ringing telephone startled Aja awake just as she was dreaming about making love to Denzel. He had just slipped his hand up her back to undo her bra strap . . .

Ringgg!

Aja pulled herself up and looked at the alarm clock. Two-thirty.

"This had better be good," she muttered as she leaned over to answer the phone.

"Hello." Aja made sure the irritation in her voice was evident.

Aja heard what sounded like somebody crying. *Oh no, not a client problem.* That was the thing she hated about working with at-risk teens—drama happened twenty-four hours a day. It had already been a long day. After leaving Jada, Aja had worked at the office for three hours, so she was not in the mood to deal with a client.

"Aja?"

"Yeah?"

"I'm sorry to call you so late. I just didn't know what else to do."

It was Elise, her brother's fiancée. "Oh, hey girl . . . What's going on?"

"I can't take it, Aja. Why does he do this?" Elise cried.

Aja sat up, leaned over, and flipped on the lamp near her bed. She hated seeing Elise upset. Out of all her brother's girlfriends, she really liked this one. A honey brown–skinned girl with sparkling eyes and deep dimples, Elise had her head on straight. Not like all those other gold-diggers, hanging on to her brother because they thought he was going to go pro and wanting to be seen on the arm of an NBA player.

Elise was different. She stuck by Eric's side after he got kicked out of Michigan State University for fighting. He had beaten the crap out of one of his basketball teammates after they argued during a practice. Getting kicked out of school had destroyed his life, making him an even bigger and more bitter jerk than he already was. But Elise had moved home to Houston with him two years ago and she was still hanging in there with him, even though Eric's trifling ass hadn't found a job.

"What's wrong?" Aja asked.

Elise paused.

"Look, you called me, so talk to me."

"It's Eric. We had a fight and he hit me."

"He hit you?" That was the last thing Aja wanted to hear. Her baby brother could be as sweet as he wanted to be—until his temper took over. He had inherited that trait from their father. After Yolanda, Aja thought he was beyond hitting women.

Aja leaned her head back against her headboard. *Damn Eric, don't mess this one up like you did with Yolanda.*

Yolanda was her brother's girlfriend before Elise, and the only other girlfriend Aja liked. They went to school together and were such a great couple. But when Eric had gotten furious about some guy talking to her at a party, they'd argued, he'd slapped her, and it was all over. Yolanda hadn't had two words to say to him since.

"Aja, I love him to death. But you know me and I'm not going to have any man putting his hands on me."

"Elise, I'm sorry. I don't know what to say."

"I guess I really didn't expect you to say anything. That's your brother and I know you love him. I love him too. I just needed someone to vent to—someone who wouldn't tell me to leave him. You know that if I call my family, they'd never forgive him. But, Aja, he needs help. Right now, I don't even know if I can forgive him."

Aja could understand. Forgiveness was a task she had yet to master. She thought back to her childhood, to after what relatives called "the family tragedy."

"Aja, it's your daddy," she could still hear Aunt Shirley say as she held out the phone. Aja didn't move. "Honey, it's been three years. Please talk to your daddy."

"Baby, your heart won't be able to heal until you face your father," she'd tell her.

But nothing had ever worked. At first, Aja would just cry and run into the other room. Soon, she would just ignore her aunt when Gerald called. Finally he just stopped calling.

Aja shook away the memory. "Hey, don't ever hesitate to call me when you need to talk. I'm sorry, okay? I'll talk to him."

"Thanks, Aja. Like I said, I love him, but during my parents' forty-one years of marriage, I've never known my father to lay his hands on my mother in that way and I expect the same from any man I'm with," Elise sniffed.

"I understand. Talk to you later."

"Thanks again. Bye."

Aja placed the phone back on the cradle and flipped off her light. She lay back down and pulled the cover over her head.

She had never been one for religion, but Aja felt Eric needed a prayer tonight. *Dear God, please help my brother. Don't let him be like our father.* Aja lay in the darkness and hoped that sleep would come before more memories did.

It seemed that Aja had just fallen asleep again when the alarm went off. She grumbled in frustration—she didn't have any plans today, except to sleep in. But it was too late. Once she woke up, it was hard to go back to sleep.

"Might as well get up," she mumbled. She reached over, pounded the alarm clock, threw back the covers, and slowly eased her way out of bed.

Aja had planned to be a total bum today. Turn on the answering machine, order a pizza, throw on some sweats, lie around and watch Lifetime. They had the best movies for women. She wasn't even going to comb her tangled hair or put on a drop of makeup. Just brush her teeth because she couldn't stand morning breath.

But Elise's call had changed all that. She had to go see Eric before he lost the best thing that ever happened to him.

Aja popped in her Whitney Houston CD, turned the volume way up, and jumped in the shower.

After a long, steamy shower, she dried off and threw on a sleeveless denim dress. She surveyed herself in the mirror hanging on her closet door. *Ughhh. I look a mess!* The dress had a small hole in the bottom and desperately needed ironing, but Aja decided it was okay. She wasn't planning on making any more stops.

She brushed her hair back into a ponytail, slipped her feet into her favorite thong sandals, and headed to her brother's.

It took about thirty-five minutes for Aja to get to Eric's.

Maybe I should've called. Nah. Calling would give him time to make up an excuse about having somewhere to go.

Aja pulled up to the gate of her brother's overpriced apartment complex and punched in his code. Even though Elise lived with him and paid half the rent, living here was sure to eat up all the money Eric had gotten from their mother's life insurance policy. The money had been placed in a trust fund until they turned eighteen. Aja rarely touched hers, however, since Eric wasn't working, she knew he had nearly depleted his.

Aja drove in and parked next to Eric's red Toyota 4Runner but didn't see Elise's black Honda Prelude, which meant she probably had stayed somewhere else for the night. Aja rang the doorbell three times before Eric answered. He was wearing nothing but boxer shorts and obviously had been asleep. The lines from the bedspread still dented the side of his face.

"Hey, little brother. Can I come in?" Aja said through the crack in the door. Eric had opened it just enough to see who was outside.

"Hey yourself. What . . . time . . . is it?" He rubbed his eyes like a little boy.

"Time for you to get up." Aja pushed the door aside and walked in.

Her heart dropped when she saw the beer cans on the coffee table. He must have been drunk last night. Aja had to play it cool. She didn't want her brother to jump on the defensive. He was quick to do that whenever Aja tried to talk to him about his temper.

"Rough night?" Aja tried to joke.

"Something like that." Eric shut the door. "What brings you by?"

"I can't just stop by and check on my kid brother?"

"Yeah, right." Eric eyed her suspiciously. "Cop a squat, then."

Eric yawned, stretched, and then plopped down on the sofa. He grabbed the remote and started flipping channels, looking for a basketball game.

"If I can find someplace to sit." Aja picked a dirty T-shirt off the sofa. "Why don't you clean this place up?"

Eric ignored her and kept flipping channels. "What channel are the Rockets and Lakers playing on?"

Aja looked at her brother sitting there trying to act like nothing was wrong. She knew how much he loved Elise, what he struggled with, and *who* he struggled to keep from becoming.

"Hey, I need to talk to you."

"Yes!" Eric said to himself after finding the game.

"Did you hear me? I said, I need to talk to you."

Eric didn't respond. Aja looked at the television and noticed it was nearing the end of the second quarter. She would have to wait until halftime if she was going to get anywhere with him.

Aja sat back and watched her brother watch the game. He was truly a handsome man. At twenty-five, he was well-cut, 6 feet 5 inches tall, and 210 pounds with a bald head—which he said he sported long before bald was in—and features that looked like they were chiseled from stone. His butterscotch complexion was smooth and flawless. Thank God those reddish freckles had faded years ago.

Those freckles used to get Eric in so much trouble. Kids would always tease him and Eric would always get into a fight because of them. Aja's one and only fight had been with an older boy who had taken a red marker and lightly drawn spots on Eric's face as he slept on the bus on their way to a school field trip. He'd only gotten a few on before Eric had woken up. But Aja was still furious. She and the boy argued and he popped her in the eye. Aja and Eric tag-teamed the boy and he ended up walking away more bruised than they did. Their mother wanted to punish them for fighting, but their father talked her out of it, saying he was actually proud of his kids for standing up for each other.

The final four minutes of the half seemed to take forever, but finally the commentators took over and Aja seized her chance. "Eric, can I talk to you?"

"I knew it." Eric scowled at his sister.

"You knew what, Mr. Know-it-all?"

"Why you're here. Elise called you didn't she? Why she gotta be calling my people?"

"Would you rather she called her father and told him?"

A deep silence hung in the air. Aja could tell Eric really didn't want to hear this, but he knew with her he didn't have much choice.

"Look, sis." Eric got up and walked to the kitchen. "I know what I did was wrong." Eric opened the refrigerator and took out a Heineken. He snapped the cap off, took a sip, and walked back into the living room. "I'm sorry and I'll tell Elise I'm sorry. But don't go giving me no psychobabble about how I need help."

Aja knew this conversation would get nowhere. She had tried to talk to Eric time and time again about his temper, but he always jumped on the defensive and their talks were never productive.

"Eric, I'm just scared for you, that's all," Aja said solemnly. She shot a disapproving look as he turned up the beer and guzzled it down.

"There ain't no reason to be scared for me. I'm a grown man—I can handle my own business." Eric stood in front of the television, trying to focus his attention on the halftime commentators. He turned and saw his sister looking pitifully at him. "I'm fine, okay?"

"I just don't want you to turn out like him."

Suddenly Eric kicked over a side table. He thrust his index finger in Aja's face.

"Don't you ever compare me to that man! I had a little fucking argument that got out of control! That doesn't mean I'm going to turn into a murderer!"

"Eric, calm down. I'm not trying to say you are."

Eric glared at his sister before plopping back down on the sofa. Both of them sat silently for a few minutes.

"Why won't you ever talk about it?"

"What's there to talk about?" Eric sat the now empty beer bottle down, picked the remote up, and started flipping channels.

"Come on, Eric. We were all pretty messed up behind what happened. I hate him. I hate what he's done to us and I'll let the whole world know it. You, you don't say anything, bad or good. I'm the only one you even acknowledge his existence with. It might help to talk about it."

Eric turned his attention back to the game. "Look, I don't need to talk about it. I don't want to talk about it. And if that's all you have to talk about, then you can leave."

Aja rolled her eyes in frustration. "Okay then." She realized it would be pointless to push the matter.

"I saw Jada yesterday." Aja tried to change the subject. "It sure would make her day if you went to visit her."

"She wouldn't even know I was there," Eric mumbled.

Aja knew this was another pointless discussion. Something about visiting Jada in that home made Eric extremely uneasy. She had been trying to get him to go for months. At first, he just made excuses, and then he just flat out said he didn't want to go.

"All right." Sometimes her brother could be so pigheaded. "I guess I'll just go then, since it's obvious you don't want to be bothered."

"Yeah, that sounds like a good idea," Eric muttered without looking away from the TV.

Aja leaned over and kissed her brother's head. "You know you can't run me off with that nasty attitude, because I know the real Peanut."

Eric reluctantly smiled. Aja was the only one who still called him Peanut. "Would you stop calling me that? My head has rounded out—it's not shaped like a peanut anymore, okay?"

"Maybe not." Aja opened the door to leave. "But you know you still like your big sister to call you that."

Eric threw a pillow at the closing door.

Aja smiled as she made her way back to her car. It had been a while since she had called her brother Peanut. That had been his nickname when he was little. It reminded Aja of happier times, and happy hadn't visited their doorsteps in a very long time.

Three

Aja glanced at her watch. It was nearing eight o'clock. She was starving and as usual, Roxie was late.

"Excuse me." Aja flagged down her waiter. "I'm going to go ahead and order an appetizer."

The waiter dragged himself over to Aja's table. He acted irritated, like he was mad about having to be at work. "Yes, ma'am. What'll it be?"

"Just a cup of gumbo and a Swamp Thing, please."

"Anything else?"

Aja shook her head. "No thank you—that'll be it."

The waiter gave a look of relief, seeming to be thankful that he didn't have to write anything else down. "You still waiting on somebody?" He pointed toward the empty seat across from Aja.

"Yeah, I guess she's just running late."

The waiter threw an exasperated look. "I'll have your Swamp Thing right out." He picked her menu off the table, then turned and walked off.

Good, I definitely need that Swamp Thing. The icy drink mixture of margarita, hurricane, and tequila was just what Aja needed to calm her nerves after a crazy day at work. Before she could even get out of the bed, her pager had started going off. Aja knew she shouldn't give her pager number to her clients, but she wanted them to know they could call her any time—and they usually did.

This morning it had been Octavia, near tears because her boyfriend, Javier, had walked out on her and she was eight months pregnant. Aja had managed to calm Octavia down and convinced her that Javier would be back, since he'd come back the last twenty times he had walked out. Aja really wanted to tell the fifteen year old she'd be better off if he didn't come back. All he was good for was making babies.

Aja really enjoyed her job as assistant director of The Texas Youth Authority, but she had to admit that sometimes she got too wrapped up in it. The Youth Authority was a social service agency for at-risk teens. Aja was supposed to step back and let her staff deal with the actual clients while she handled the administrative end and made sure things ran smoothly. But she never had been able to step back since she had been promoted from counselor. She had a roster of clients that she dealt with on a regular basis and since the organization was so short-staffed, none of the other counselors seemed to mind.

Octavia, what will it take to get you to see Javier is no good for you? Aja lowered her head and rubbed her temples as she thought of Octavia sitting at home crying her eyes out while Javier ran the streets. Octavia was by herself; her mother had put her out when she'd turned up pregnant. So now the teen was living with a sister who could care less what she did and only let her come live with her because she was counting on the welfare check Octavia would be getting once the baby was born.

Then, on top of everything else, Eric and Elise hadn't made up and it had been a whole week. Aja had called Eric before she left the house today, and her brother had still been in a funk, which put Aja in a bad mood.

"Roxie, why can't you ever be on time?" Aja glanced at her watch again. She was starting to get irritated.

"Speak of the devil and she shall appear."

Aja looked up at Roxie, standing over her, a huge grin plastered across her face.

"Hey, girl. Hope you didn't order without me." Roxie pulled out a chair and plopped down across from Aja. She looked great in a fuchsia shirt that exposed her firm stomach and black bootcut stretch pants that looked like they were especially carved for her size-six figure. Her sandy brown hair was swept up into a ponytail, and she wore a pair of sunglasses on top of her head. Her high arched eyebrows set off her slightly slanted eyes.

Roxie had been Aja's best friend since their days at Texas Southern University in Houston. They'd both dated members of the same fraternity. Roxie had dated a guy named Warren, and Aja had been head over heels for Darwin. When they found out Warren and Darwin were cheating on them, they cursed the guys out, then got together and had a pity party to bond. After that, they became best friends, pledging to the same sorority. Both of them tried out and were rejected from the cheerleading squad. They moved in together their junior year and had been in each other's lives ever since. Aja was the maid of honor in Roxie's wedding three years before to a wonderful man named Brian. And she was also the godmother to Roxie's son, Brendan.

"Just one time. Just one time will you get somewhere on time." Aja tapped her watch and rolled her eyes in frustration.

"So whatcha eating?" Roxie completely ignored the irritation in Aja's voice. Roxie was free spirited and didn't let much get to her.

"Gumbo."

"Ewww! Why'd you order that? You know this restaurant don't use no seasonings."

"I happen to like it like that, okay?" Aja snapped. "And why don't you use correct grammar?"

"Dang. Why you so nasty? I'm sorry I was late okay?" Roxie poked her bottom lip out in a pouty expression. "You forgive me?" Aja shot a disgusted look. The waiter brought her drink and bowl of gumbo and set them down in front of her.

"Are you ready to order?" the waiter asked Roxie. He still had an I-don't-want-to-be-here look. Of course Roxie didn't care. She scanned the menu, taking her time, despite the waiter's obvious huffing and sighing.

"Yeah, I'll take the same thing my mean-ass friend is having." Roxie pointed to Aja's drink. "And bring me a bowl of crawfish bisque. That's just for an appetizer. I'm hungry, so I'll be ordering something else in a minute. I just don't know what I want yet." The waiter nodded—more like grunted—and then took off.

Roxie scanned the menu a little longer, then closed it and set it down. She tore open a pack of crackers, dipped one in Aja's gumbo, and popped it in her mouth. She grimaced at the taste. "Yuck! This is horrible!"

"You don't have to like it. I do."

Roxie cocked her head to the side. "Maybe this was a bad idea. I don't know if you're on your period or just plain irritable. But I didn't come here for you to be constantly snapping at me."

Aja's expression softened. "Look, I'm sorry. I just had a bad day at work."

"Well, don't take it out on me. Nobody told you to take that depressing-ass job in the first place. Everyone has problems, lives constantly falling apart, and everyone is ten seconds from killing themselves or somebody else. As if you need that shit. To this day, I swear I can't understand why you turned down that marketing job with Coca-Cola. That's what your major was in school. Not to mention the fact that you would've made twice as much as what you're making now. But no, you turned it down to work with juvenile delinquents."

"Those kids need me." Aja hated defending her work. It was something she did with great pride. It didn't pay the best of money, but it was her way to help young people out, the way she couldn't help her own family. Everybody had told her how stupid she was to turn down that Coke job, but she knew that it would never have made her happy. What she was doing with those kids made her happy.

"Yeah, yeah, yeah. What about your needs? When's the last time you had your needs fulfilled?" Roxie raised her eyebrows, leaned forward, and lowered her voice. "Come to think of it, when's the last time you had you some?"

"Some what?"

"Don't play dumb with me. Some nooky, some dang-a-lang, some good loving?"

"You sure have a filthy mouth to be a fifth-grade teacher," Aja laughed.

"Hell, I learned half this stuff from them. Now answer the question."

Aja sipped her drink. *When was the last time I had sex? Six months ago? Nah, that was Marcus, he didn't count.* They'd just fooled around. She'd played sick after she'd gone to the bathroom and saw that herpes cream in his medicine cabinet. That was one time Roxie's advice to always check the medicine cabinet paid off. Before that it was Troy, and that was more than a year ago.

"That long, huh?" Roxie said when Aja didn't answer. "You can't even remember, it's been so long. You've probably converted back to a virgin."

"Shut up, Roxie. You have a husband and can have sex every night."

Roxie took Aja's drink from her and slurped it up through the straw. "Honey, the only thing I'm getting every night is Brendan's bottle."

Aja snatched her drink back. "Could you order your own stuff please?"

"I did. That slow-ass waiter is just taking his time getting it to me and I need a drink. Those damn kids got on my nerves today."

"You talk about me? I will never understand why you became a teacher. You act like you can't stand those kids."

Roxie leaned back and rolled her eyes. "I can't. Bad-ass, no-home-training little bastards. But it pays the bills and I like having my summers off. Now, back to what I was saying . . . we're talking about you. I'm married. I don't have to have sex but once a month. Now, that brings me to the point of this dinner. Have I got the perfect man for you." Roxie flashed a huge grin.

There she goes again, trying to fix me up with someone. Roxie had made it her goal in life to find a man for Aja, even though Aja tried to convince her friend she wasn't interested in dating. It was a mission she had taken on since their college days.

"Ummm, if I recall, your track record isn't good when it comes to selecting men for me. Remember Stanley?" Aja said.

"Oh yeah, the Omega. He was too fine and I thought he would be good for you."

"He was good for me, and Leslie and Lisa and Carla and God only knows who else."

Roxie started laughing. "I remember how Leslie threatened to commit suicide when she saw you and Stanley leaving the movies. And then Lisa told you how she had some incurable sexually transmitted disease, but she loved Stanley so much it didn't matter. She was standing outside our window hollering for Stanley to come down. Telling him she could never have children because of him, but she still loved him."

"Then you poured a bucket of ice cold water out the window on her. Told her to take her infected ass home," Aja recalled.

Roxie held her stomach as she doubled over with laughter. "That was too funny and too pathetic." Roxie caught her breath. "But that Carla took the cake. You remember how we dressed in all black to catch her on her way back to her dorm so we could give her a beat down for spreading all those rumors about you?"

Aja laughed at the memory, too. Roxie always had her back. The minute she felt like anybody had wronged Aja, Roxie would shelve that prissy mentality and get ghetto. "Yeah, I only let you talk me into that madness because I didn't think we'd actually go through with it."

"Awww, naw. I was game, all the way."

"I know you were," Aja responded. "You remember jumping out the bushes and grabbing Carla by her ponytail, then throwing her up against that building? You told her if she ever uttered my name again, you'd cut her throat. She was terrified. I was too, because for a minute I thought you were really going to do it."

"I would have," Roxie said, matter-of-factly. "Everybody knew if they messed with you, they messed with me. Hell, I would've cut Stanley's ass for the dog way he treated you but I could never get his big ass alone long enough."

Aja smiled. "But, remember, you were the one who insisted he was the 'perfect man' for me."

"Okay, so sue me. I was wrong on that one. And maybe a couple, twenty others. But this one—I've got a good feeling about this one." Roxie nodded her head, a look of satisfaction across her face.

Aja sighed. "Roxie, if I told you once, I told you a thousand times, I don't want a man."

"Well, what do you want? A woman?" Roxie said with a sly grin.

"Don't be silly. I just have more pressing things to deal with."

"Like what? Saving the world? Newsflash! It can't be done. I know you feel this overwhelming need to look after your family and save every wayward juvenile delinquent this side of the Mississippi, but sometimes you've got to take a little time for yourself."

Aja started eating, hoping her lack of response would change the subject. She looked up at Roxie, who was throwing her a you-know-I'm-right look.

"So, how's your mother doing?" Aja asked. She hoped to get Roxie to talk about something else, but she genuinely wanted to know. Roxie's mother had all but adopted Aja when they were in school. Roxie came from a huge family—six brothers and three sisters. Her family had become Aja's family over the last few years. Aja made a mental note to call Roxie's mother when she got home.

"She's fine. Wondering when you're getting married. Now quit trying to change the subject. As I was saying . . . Look at you. You don't even fix yourself up anymore. You look like crap. No makeup—when's the last time you had a perm? And then you're wearing that Jennifer Beals *Flashdance* outfit. The only thing you're missing are the leg warmers."

Aja knew Roxie was right. She had smooth butterscotch-colored skin and defined features that were enhanced by makeup, yet she seldom bothered to put any on. Her curly brown shoulder-length hair was stuffed beneath an Old Navy baseball cap. She had on a pair of black leggings and an oversize gray sweatshirt, which hung off her shoulder, revealing the strap from her sports bra. Aja had been so concerned with everyone else that she had let herself go. She'd even put on a few pounds, which she was surprised Roxie didn't mention.

"I hope you didn't go to work like that," Roxie said as she surveyed Aja's outfit.

"Of course I didn't. I worked out after I got off, then I went home and changed. I just threw something on."

Roxie narrowed her eyes and turned up her lips in disgust. "You need to throw that mess away. Don't wear that again, please."

"Could you get off of me, please, and tell me why you wanted to meet me in the first place? It's the middle of the week. We never meet for dinner during the week. And you said it was important. I hope it's not about this so-called perfect man."

"Do you watch Channel 13?" Roxie asked out of the blue.

"What does that have to do with anything?"

"If you do, your date next Saturday won't be a blind one, at least for you."

"Date? What date?"

Roxie just smiled mischievously.

"Roxanne Bingham-Daniels, I told you about trying to fix me up. I don't do blind dates."

"Hey, like I said, if you watch 13, it won't be blind."

"And just why is that?"

"Because, drumroll please . . ." Roxie began banging on the table. People were beginning to stare, but Roxie couldn't have cared less. "Your escort for next Saturday evening shall be none other than Channel 13 Eyewitness News sports anchor Charles Clayton. Yes, behind door number one is a luscious, deep chocolate colored, sexy, *working* man, who wants to take you out."

Aja stared in disbelief. "You've got to be kidding me."

"Oh my, are we interested? Could it be?" Roxie chuckled. She leaned back with a look of satisfaction.

"Roxie, don't play, okay.. First of all, Charles Clayton is all that, or at least probably thinks he is. Second of all, what part of 'I don't need a date' are you not understanding?"

"First of all," Roxie stressed, leaning forward and turning serious. "I'm not understanding this celibacy vow of yours. You're twenty-eight with no prospects. I know you want to have a husband and kids and all that. So you need to get started, before your eggs dry up." Roxie leaned back and smiled like she was an expert on the subject.

"You are so nasty," Aja laughed.

"Whatever. Listen, I didn't know this or I would've fixed you up a long time ago, but Charles and Brian went to school together. Brian swears he told me that, but my husband is always claiming he's told me stuff I don't remember."

"You don't," Aja interjected. "You have selective retention."

Roxie rolled her eyes. "Would you shut up and let me finish? Anyway, Charles came by the house this past weekend after playing golf with Brian. I overheard Charles mention to Brian that he had broken up with his girlfriend five months ago and is through mourning and ready to get on with his life."

"And you thought I'd be the perfect one to help him do that?"

"Girl, you know me so well. Hey, where's the waiter? I'm ready to order." Roxie looked around for the waiter, summoned him over, then ordered the fried alligator. After the waiter left, she turned back to Aja. "Anyway, I mentioned you to Charles and showed him your picture. You know, the one of us in Vegas last year? He thought you were cute and asked me more about you."

"And what did you tell him?" Surprisingly, Aja was on the edge of her seat. She was having a hard time believing Roxie, but she was excited nonetheless.

"That you were desperate, hadn't been screwed in a long

time, and would probably give it up on the first date," Roxie joked.

Aja glared at her friend.

Roxie laughed. "What do you think I told him? You are every man's dream and if he is looking for a good woman, you were it. So are you interested?"

"Roxie, I just don't . . ."

"Good," Roxie cut her off. "He's going to pick you up at six-thirty Saturday night. Here's his number in case you want to talk to him before then." Roxie slid Charles's business card toward Aja with his home number written in the corner. "He's taking you to see that play, *Mama, the Rent Is Due and They Fixin' to Turn Off the Lights.*"

Aja took the card and laughed. "It's *Mama, I'm Sorry.*"

"Whatever, they're all the same. A bunch of folks overexaggerating and cracking on each other."

"Then why is it you don't miss one?"

"Cuz, they're still funny as hell. Anyway, don't give me any flack." Roxie turned serious. "Do this one for me, okay? If you don't like him, I'll leave it alone."

"What? Can I get that in writing? If this doesn't work, you won't pressure me about dating again?"

"Girl Scouts' honor." Roxie held up two fingers.

"You were never a Girl Scout and that is not the Girl Scouts' sign," Aja said.

"Whatever. You have my word. I won't pressure you about dating, at least dating Charles." Roxie grinned. "But it'll work, girlfriend, I just know it will. As long as you do something with your hair and don't wear that getup." Roxie pointed to Aja's clothes, then nervously looked around. "I'm embarrassed to be seen with you my damn self," she kidded.

Aja playfully threw her napkin across the table. "You are such a butthole."

"Asshole, Aja, asshole. Nobody says butthole. I've got my work cut out with you. Don't be going and saying no corny stuff like butthole around Charles. He'll think you're a nerd."

"Okay, I'll make sure he knows I'm cool," Aja laughed. As usual, Roxie had made her feel better.

Four

Aja leaned on her desk and looked at the business card again. She had spent all day trying to work up the nerve to call Charles. She didn't want to seem too anxious and had never been very aggressive when it came to men. That was Roxie's forte.

"What am I waiting on?" Aja picked up the phone and dialed the first four numbers, then slammed the phone down. "I can't do this. This man will not be interested in me." Aja didn't have a self-esteem problem. Guys were always telling her how pretty she was. She had light brown eyes, like her mother, accented by extra long eyelashes. Her smooth complexion garnered compliments from men and women. And women paid big money for injections to get pouty lips like hers. While Aja was nowhere near Roxie's size, she was still shapely. It's just that Charles was drop-dead gorgeous. He was probably used to women who looked like they had just stepped off a runway. *He probably will end up regretting ever asking to meet me.* Aja went back to work, determined to forget about Charles. But thirty minutes later, she found herself staring at the card again.

Don't be a wimp. Aja heard Roxie's nagging voice in the back of her head. "Okay!" Aja picked up the phone again. This time she dialed the entire number.

"Eyewitness News Sports. This is Charles."

Aja was silent. She hadn't expected Charles to answer.

"Hello, may I help you?"

"That depends." Aja regained her composure. "Are you the Charles Clayton I'm supposed to call?"

"I'm Charles Clayton. I don't know if I'm the one you're looking for, but I'm the only one by that name who works here, so I guess that would be me," he joked.

"This is Aja James, Roxie's friend. Did I catch you at a bad time?"

"No, not at all. I'm glad you called. I was about to hang up since you wouldn't say anything."

"Sorry, I just didn't expect to get you. I thought I'd get a secretary or something." Aja caught herself nervously twisting the telephone cord around her fingers. She felt like a giddy teenager.

Charles laughed. "Secretary? It's not like I'm Bob Costas or anything. I'm doing good to have the interns give me my messages."

Aja breathed a sigh of relief. He seemed easygoing. She was beginning to calm down. "So how are you doing today?"

"I can't complain. Well actually I can, but I won't," Charles playfully said. "Seriously, I'm doing good. Much better now that you called to make my day."

Aja blushed. It was a good thing he couldn't see her. She wanted to pinch herself to see if this was really happening. Everybody around town talked about Charles Clayton. He was one of the most popular television personalities in town. Mostly because he was so good-looking. If you looked up tall, dark, and handsome in the dictionary, Charles's picture would probably be there. Aja's beautician even had an autographed picture of him hanging up over her station in the beauty shop.

"Well, Roxie told me a little about you," Charles continued, "but I'd like it very much if you could tell me more—over dinner."

Boy, he doesn't waste any time. "That sounds nice," Aja said. "Maybe we can go to dinner before the play Saturday."

"Saturday sounds nice, but I was thinking more like tonight," Charles flirtatiously replied.

"Tonight?" *Is this guy desperate or something?*

"Look, I don't want you to think I'm hard-up or anything," Charles said, as if he were reading her mind. "I'm just a cut-to-the-chase kind of guy. I have to be careful about the women I date, because I come across some crazy women in my line of business. So when I meet someone who interests me, I move full speed ahead. Plus, I'll be in Chicago covering the Bulls' head coach firing tomorrow and Friday, and I wanted to start getting to know you before I left."

"The Bulls are firing their head coach?" Aja didn't follow sports much, but she did occasionally watch basketball, primarily because of Eric. And she used to love the Chicago Bulls, but that was only because of Michael Jordan.

"Yeah, but that's between you, me, and the lamppost. The news is supposed to break tomorrow, but I'm already on top of it. Anyway, my point is, I'll be out of pocket for a few days and I just wanted to enjoy the pleasure of your company prior to that. Roxie and Brian had nothing but good things to say about you."

Charles had a deep, soothing made-for-TV voice. That's probably why he was so good at his job. "Well, then, tonight it is," Aja said.

"Great. Give me your home number and I'll call you for directions to come pick you up. I'd like to take you to this Italian restaurant that's pretty good."

Aja didn't think twice about letting him come to her house. She was usually very careful about stuff like that, but Roxie and

Brian knew Charles and they wouldn't fix her up with a psycho. Plus, he was in the limelight, so she figured he couldn't be too crazy. She rattled off the ten digits.

"So, I'll see you around, say seven?"

"Seven is fine. See you later and have a good day."

"Good-bye."

Aja put the phone down and leaned back in her chair. She felt all warm and tingly inside, like a schoolgirl with her first crush. It had been a long time since anything on her body tingled—in fact, she'd thought her tingle nerves were dead. *Maybe this is just what I needed.* He sounded extremely sexy on the phone. Aja already knew he had the looks to go with that voice. She usually turned off the news by the time they got to the sports part, but she had seen Charles doing special assignments a couple of times on TV. She also saw his picture plastered on a billboard every day on her way to work.

"Knock, knock, can I come in or does that smile on your face mean you don't want to be bothered?" Aja looked up. It was her administrative assistant, Emily, peeking her head through the door.

"Hey, no, come on in." Aja sat up and tried to get back in professional mode. "What can I do for you?"

Emily walked into the little closet Aja called an office and sat down. "Hope you like Chinese. We'll be eating that tonight. Dave wants the Burton report first thing in the morning. The family got an emergency hearing tomorrow afternoon—they're going to try to get the kids back."

"Oh no." This case had been pending for months. The parents were accused of prostituting their twelve-year-old daughter. Why would it come through today of all days?

"I thought the girl was happy in foster care?" Aja asked.

"She is. But her parents got some high-powered attorney.

They probably paid for him with the money they made from prostituting their child. Anyway, they're claiming we can't prove anything. The other sister has recanted her statement, so unless we present a compelling case, they'll probably get her back. Dave wants us to go over her file with our attorneys. It's going to take all night."

I have plans tonight, Aja wanted to say. But Dave was the big boss, the president of the Youth Authority, and what Dave wanted, Dave usually got. "Chinese it is then," Aja bitterly said.

"All right, be back in a little bit." Emily got up. "I'm starving, so I thought we'd eat first if that's okay with you?"

"Yeah, I guess." Aja didn't have much of an appetite. She was so disappointed, and she wasn't concerned about letting that disappointment show.

Emily gave an apologetic smile. "I'll go run out and get the food."

Aja nodded, then glanced at the business card as Emily left. "So much for our perfect date." She picked the phone up to call Charles back and cancel.

Five

Aja struggled to unlock her front door. It had been a long day. They'd been in court since noon, after staying up until two in the morning. The whole process was draining, although it seemed to be worth it. The judge had ruled in their favor and the little girl got to stay in foster care pending a formal hearing. Aja had found it hard to concentrate throughout court, though. Her mind kept racing back to her second conversation with Charles the day before. He'd been so disappointed when she canceled. She was sure any chance they had of hitting it off was out the window.

So much for what could've been.

Between a handful of mail she picked up on her way in, some Mexican food she had ordered, and a bag full of junk she had cleaned out of her car, getting inside was proving to be a hassle. Aja was anxious to get in, eat, light a few candles, and salvage the few hours left in her day.

She had called to check on Eric from her cell phone during a break and, as usual, he was in a bad mood. It's like he was mad at the world and she was forever trying to make him happy again. He had tried to make up with Elise, but she was still pretty upset—rightfully so.

I just hope they work this thing out. Aja finally made it inside her apartment. After setting her food down on the table and dropping the other stuff on the floor, she started sifting through the mail.

"Bill, bill, bill, you may be the next Publisher's Clearing-house winner, yeah right, bill . . ."

Suddenly, Aja stopped. She recognized the scraggly hand-writing immediately. It had been years since she'd seen it, but she still knew it right away. The words "Conner Correctional Facility" scribbled in the corner confirmed it. It was a letter from her father. Aja stared at the letter as her father's face flashed in front of her.

"Daddy, Daddy, Daddy! What did you bring us?" Aja jumped into her father's arms. Jada crawled over and grabbed his legs. Eric was going through his pockets. Their father was a successful insurance agent. He traveled a lot and every time he returned, he had something good for each of his children. They hated to see him leave and were always excited to see him return.

"Gerald, now I told you about spoiling those kids."

"Baby, what good is it to have kids if you can't spoil them?" He kissed his wife and then turned to the children. "Go look out in the front yard, your gift . . ."

The children didn't give him time to finish before they were out the door.

"Oh man! A puppy!"

"A puppy. Oh, Gerald." Their mother followed the kids outside. "You know those kids don't need a puppy."

"Awww, come on honey." Their father walked outside as well. "I was leaving the airport and this woman had them for sale on the corner and this one started barking at me." He picked up the little black and white Labrador and held it close to his face. "It was saying, 'Take me home. I know the lady of the house will let you keep me.' "

"Come on, Ma, can we keep him?" Aja pleaded.

Their mother put her hands on her hips and tried to look stern. Finally, she smiled. "Oh, all right, but you kids are responsible for it."

"Yea!" all three of them yelled.

"Let's call him Cooter," Eric said.

"Welcome home, Cooter." Their father picked up the puppy and walked back inside.

Aja shook her head. *Where had that come from? Why did that pop into my head?* That was back when her family was happy, before her father lost his job and their lives went spiraling downhill. Aja sat emotionless in her living room. All she heard was the humming of the air conditioner.

She glanced at the picture of her family on top of the TV set. It was taken in Florida, on the beach. They looked so happy. Her mother had a warm, refreshing smile. She was one of the most beautiful women Aja had ever seen. She had long, jet-black hair. Her brown, almond-shaped eyes accented her smooth, mocha-colored face. She used to be a teacher, but after Jada was born she became a stay-at-home mom, a decision Aja knew her mother never regretted.

It used to thrill her mother, being able to be there when they got home from school. She cooked dinner for the family, and then every night they would all sit down and eat together. They were a picture-perfect family. Or so Aja thought—she couldn't quite remember when things took a turn. Somewhere around the time they got Cooter. She remembered hearing her father screaming about layoffs and cutbacks. Right after that, her mother went back to work and her father became the stay-at-home person, only he didn't want to be there. All he did all day was drink.

Aja's mother would work, then come home to cook and

clean. Her father wouldn't look for work, nor would he do any work at home.

At first, her mother tried not to say anything. But one day, after her mother had picked her up from school, they came home and her father was sitting on the sofa, drinking and smoking marijuana. As if that weren't bad enough, Jada was asleep on the sofa right next to him. Aja remembered her mother had hit the roof. That was her parents' first physical fight. The first of many.

After things got bad, everyone wondered why Aja's mother stayed with her father. Somebody was always saying, "If it was me, I'd leave him." One relative said her mother deserved to be abused. "If she's stupid enough to stay, then she needs her ass beat." A friend had even remarked, "If it was me, I'd burn him in his sleep, like Farrah did in that movie."

But they weren't in the situation. And they didn't remember the man her mother did, the man who showered his wife with love and affection, who doted on his kids, who worked tirelessly to give his family the best that life had to offer. It was like all their family and friends had forgotten that part of her father. Aja thought that was why her mother hung in there, because she hoped, deep down, that that man would return and things would go back to normal. No, no one remembered that Gerald James. The only Gerald they remembered was abusive and emotionally out of control. The one who made her mother cry and, in the end, took her life. As it turned out, that was the only man Aja could remember now as well.

Aja continued to stare at the letter, debating whether to open it or just toss it away. It had been years since she had heard from her father. She didn't even know that he had her address. *What could he possibly want?*

She considered opening the letter, then decided against it. "I don't want to hear anything you have to say." She tossed the letter in the trash and got up to change out of her clothes.

An hour later, Aja was in a comfortable T-shirt and sweatpants, sitting on the sofa. She had pinned her hair up and was finishing off her now-cold Mexican food. She tried to watch TV, but her mind kept going back to the letter. She had to do something to get her mind off her father. Aja thought of the one person who could make her forget about him—Roxie. Roxie had called six times today alone trying to find out how things went with Charles. Aja had been avoiding her because she didn't want to hear Roxie's mouth about her canceling the date, but maybe talking to her best friend now would be a welcome diversion.

Aja picked up the cordless phone and pressed the speed dial for Roxie's number. The phone barely rang twice.

"It's about time you returned my call."

"I hate Caller ID."

"Whatever. When's the wedding?"

Aja rolled her eyes and smiled. Roxie was not going to rest until she found Aja a husband. Sometimes she acted more like a mother than a best friend.

"Can you let me have one date, please, before you start planning a wedding?"

"What do you mean? Don't tell me you didn't go out with him yet."

Aja inhaled. Maybe she really wasn't up to getting grief from Roxie. She got up and started pacing back and forth, not having realized how much the letter from her father had shaken her up. "Something came up at work."

"Damn, Aja. Something's always coming up with you!"

"Would you stop yelling? I'm not in the mood and I didn't call you for a lecture," Aja snapped.

Roxie paused and her voice immediately softened. That's one

thing Aja loved about her—Roxie could read her like a book. She knew when to play and when to get serious.

"Aja, what's wrong?"

Aja fought back tears. She hated her father for doing this to her. She just wanted to forget him, pretend he never existed. Why did he have to force himself into her life?

"Aja, would you tell me what's going on?" Roxie said after Aja didn't respond.

Aja swallowed, then let out a long sigh. She hadn't even intended to talk about her father when she called Roxie. "He wrote me."

"Who wrote you?"

"My father."

Roxie was silent, as if she were weighing her words carefully. "What did he say?"

"I don't know."

"So you haven't read it?"

"Nope." Aja braced herself for Roxie's speech on how it was time for her to heal and the first step would be to read her father's letter. Every time Aja vented to Roxie about her father, Roxie's response had always been the same—"It's time to heal and move forward," she would say.

Roxie hesitated again before speaking. "Are you holding up okay?"

Aja managed a weak laugh. "What, no 'it's time to heal' lecture?"

"Aja, you know I love you to death. And you also know it's time to let go of that hate for your father. I can't make that happen for you and I can't really judge you because I don't know how I would act in your position. I do think you called me to hear me tell you that you need to move on so then you could get all worked up and remember all the bad things your father did and why you shouldn't forgive him. But I'm not going to go there. You will read that letter when you're ready. You will move on when you're ready. Not when I'm ready."

Damn you, Roxie. As wild and crazy as she was, Roxie could be such a voice of reason.

"I'm not ready," Aja softly said.

"Will you ever be?"

Aja didn't know what to say. Roxie was right. Aja had expected Roxie to fuss. Then she could yell and scream about how worthless her father was and she'd feel better about not reading the letter.

Aja heard Roxie's little boy crying in the background. She remembered that Brendan had a really bad ear infection. Here she was burdening her friend with her problems and her godson was in serious pain.

"Roxie, I'm sorry. I know Brendan isn't feeling well. I'm not going to keep you. I'll call you later, okay?"

"Aja, you know if you need me to come over there and hold your hand while you read that letter I will. If you need me to drive up to Conner and slip somebody a twenty to rough your old man up and get him to leave you alone, I'll do that too."

Aja smiled for the first time that evening. "I know."

"I'm always here for you," Roxie said.

"I know that too. I'll call you later. Bye."

Aja placed the phone back on the cradle and gently smiled. The smile quickly faded when she glanced over at the trash can where she had thrown her father's letter.

"Why are you bothering me?" she mumbled. "Haven't you caused enough damage?"

Aja went into her bedroom and threw herself on the bed. She tried to sleep, and in fact dozed off after a while, but halfway through the night, she found herself up and once again sitting in the kitchen, in front of the trash can. Why couldn't he understand that she didn't want to have anything to do with him? What could he possibly have to say to her? Aja realized she would have no peace until she at least read what her father had to say.

She walked over to the garbage, pulled out the letter, and tore it open. She walked back into the living room and sat down to read:

Hey baby girl,

I sure hope you're reading this, although I honestly don't know if you will. I had to go through hell to get your address. Thank God for your cousin Luther. He's kept me up-to-date on what y'all have been doing over these years. I would've written you sooner, in fact I did. But I tore them all up when I was done. I was just too ashamed, too scared. Finally, I said what the hell and went ahead and decided to mail one.

Aja, I know there's nothing I can say that can erase what I've done. It's hell in here but I deserve every minute of it. I had a problem, a drinking problem. Couple that with me losing my job, my bad temper, and dabbling in dope, and it was disastrous. I wouldn't admit it and it ended up costing me everything. When I lost my job, I lost myself. My daddy was a sorry alcoholic who didn't provide for his family. I vowed to be different. When I saw myself in the same boat, I was devastated. And I turned to drugs and alcohol for comfort.

But the one thing you've gotta know is, I loved your mama. You couldn't even begin to understand how much. My heart aches every day. I still think of her beautiful eyes, her warm smile, and the way she used to laugh at all my jokes, even when they weren't funny. I didn't just take her life. I took mine, and yours, and Eric's, and Jada's. I know that. I've come to terms

with that and God has forgiven me. I've gotten to know Him
well. I pray all the time, especially for you kids. The Bible says
you should forgive and forget. I'm praying now that you can
forgive me. Your mama would want that. . . .

Aja stopped reading. There was still a full page to go, but she
had read enough. *Why is it that everybody in prison always finds Jesus?*
Aja felt the tears rolling down her cheeks and the anger rising inside her.

"How dare you?" she yelled at the letter, then ripped it to
pieces. "How dare you try and talk about my mother and what
she supposedly meant to you! I hate you! I hate you! I hate you!"
Aja threw the pieces of paper across the room and fell to the
floor in tears. As she lay there sobbing, sleep finally captured her
and she drifted off, right on the kitchen floor, dreaming of happier times.

Six

"Come on man, you holding up thangs! The ladies await me!" Bobby Clark was screaming into his cell phone outside Eric's apartment.

Eric had let his friend Bobby talk him into going out tonight. He really wasn't in the mood, but Bobby wouldn't take no for an answer.

"I'm coming. Are you downstairs?"

"With the motor running. Now come on!"

"All right, all right. I'm on my way down." Eric sighed heavily after Bobby hung up. He hadn't felt like doing much of anything since his fight with Elise. He still couldn't believe he had hit her—and all over a stupid argument about money. Elise was mad because he had bought a DVD player. She said things were too tight for him to be going out and spending money on frivolous things like that. He knew his insurance money was thinning out and without him working, Elise was constantly pinching pennies. But Eric felt like she was just nagging. Besides, it was his money and he should be able to spend it however he wanted. He'd even told her that.

"But it's not *just* your money," Elise had reminded him. "We live together, we pay the bills together. And when you don't pay your half of the bills, I have to pick up the slack."

Eric was frustrated. They weren't even married yet, and here she was monitoring his money. But lately she had been picking up more and more of the slack so Eric guessed she had a right. Only he didn't see it that way at the time. At first, their argument was just a small disagreement. Then he blew up, and she blew up, and things just got out of hand. She had gotten smart about something and Eric had hit her. The minute he did it, he wished that he could've taken it back. She grabbed her purse and left. She didn't even take a change of clothes.

That was more than a week ago. He could tell she had been back yesterday. Her small, green duffel bag and some of her clothes were missing. He had hung around the house for most of the week, hoping to catch her. She must've been watching the house or something, because she came as soon as he left to get something to eat—he wasn't gone but twenty minutes. But when he returned, she had come and gone. No note, nothing. He felt a small sense of relief when he realized she had taken only a few clothes and not everything. That meant she at least planned on coming back, at some point.

Eric had called Elise's office, where she worked as a marketing executive for a local rap label, and they kept saying she wasn't in. He called her sister, who lived about fifteen minutes away, but all he ever got there was the answering machine. He had also called two of her friends, but they both claimed they didn't know where she was, either. He wanted to call her parents in Michigan, but he knew they would start asking questions, so he left it alone. Besides, they were preparing to move down to Houston and he didn't want any added problems. He would just have to wait for Elise to decide to call him.

Eric heard Bobby honk again and realized he was still standing with the phone in his hand. He placed the phone back on the receiver, turned out the lights, grabbed his keys and cell phone—just in case Elise called—and headed out.

"Calm down. The club ain't going nowhere," Eric said as he got into Bobby's maroon 300ZX.

"Who am I to deny the women the pleasure of all the time they can get looking at me?" Bobby stroked his chin.

"Silly me, what was I ever thinking?"

"Don't hate me 'cause you ain't me," Bobby smirked.

"Shut up and let's go."

Eric frowned and sat back in the seat. Bobby grinned, turned up the radio, and floored the accelerator, causing the tires to screech as he took off. They went speeding down the toll road toward the Westheimer area, where Club Maxwell's was located. Eric was quiet during most of the ride.

"You still haven't talked to Elise?" Bobby asked.

"What gives you that idea?"

"Oh I don't know, maybe the scowl plastered across your face, or the fact that you're quiet, and you ain't never quiet."

Eric checked himself out in the rearview mirror. He knew he was sporting the look women loved. He had on a colorful Armani shirt. It went well with his brown blazer and black slacks. His bald head was shining and a diamond stud glistened in his ear. He had stubble on his chin, but it wasn't too bad. Eric made a mental note to check the expressions though. The last thing he wanted was the whole world knowing he had broken up with his girlfriend. If they even had broken up. Right now, Eric had no idea what the status of his relationship was.

Eric had told Bobby about the fight—he just left off the part about him hitting her, which wasn't something he wanted to advertise. "Nope, I haven't talked to her." He had a sad look on his face.

"Damn, I hope you ain't goin' be sitting up here pouting all night long."

"I told you I didn't want to come in the first place."

"Well, you're here now, so let's make the best of it." Bobby pulled into the parking lot. "Besides, you are probably goin' to see Elise in here getting her party on."

Eric thought about it. He better not see Elise up in here. He wanted her somewhere pouting, just like him. After Bobby said that, though, he was anxious to get inside. As soon as they pulled into a parking space, Eric jumped out of the car. Despite the grumble of other club patrons waiting in line, he walked straight to the front. Bobby was right behind him. They both paid ten dollars to the club cashier and walked inside. Eric immediately scanned the club looking for Elise. She was nowhere.

"I don't know why I thought she'd be in here. This ain't even her scene," Eric mumbled.

Club Maxwell's tried to cater to the twenty-five and older crowd. It was supposed to be a place for professionals to come and have a good time, but as with most clubs on the Houston scene, riffraff managed to make its way in. This was Eric's first time here, but he had heard plenty about it. Neither he nor Elise were really club people, so they didn't go out much.

"At least we're in. Did you see that line? That's an hour wait. I liked how you just made your way to the front, like you was somebody important." Bobby slapped Eric on the back. "Now come on, let's have a good time." Bobby scanned the room. "There's some honeys already giving us the eye."

Bobby strutted over to a table where three scantily clad women were sipping on what looked like watered-down drinks. All three were attractive, but Eric thought they looked desperate. Eric definitely wasn't trying to pick up any girls, but Bobby was already in the middle of their group, displaying his charm. He

did have a way with women. By the end of the night, he probably would have two of their phone numbers.

Eric took his time getting to the table, stopping to read a flyer
someone handed him. Bobby shot him an "act-right" look when
he finally made his way over, so Eric faked a smile. "Hello ladies.
I'm Eric."

"Have a seat," said a woman with thick black hair that looked
like a wig. "I'm Cheryl. This is Tonya and Marcena." She
pointed to her friends, who smiled and nodded. Cheryl had
thick thighs and was wearing a short leopard-skin dress that
looked like it was two sizes too small. Eric felt his stomach turn
as he looked at the cellulite dents on the girl's legs. *The least she
could've done was wear something to cover that up.*

"I was just asking your friend here what was taking you so
long to come over," she continued. "We saw you guys when you
walked in." Eric noticed a tiny gap in Cheryl's two front teeth,
which wouldn't have been so bad if her teeth weren't so big. You
could see her gums when she talked.

Eric quickly told himself he was just being picky because he
was in a bad mood. He decided to try to have somewhat of a
good time. Eric sat down on an empty seat next to Cheryl.

"Well, he moves a little faster than me," he said.

Bobby was already making the moves on Marcena, the preti-
est of the bunch. She looked half-Asian, with beautiful eyes,
long silky-straight hair, and an extremely pretty smile. She was
also the only one who looked like she had any class. Bobby was
mumbling something about her being the finest woman in the
club. Eric couldn't believe women constantly fell for his lines,
but he had to admit Bobby was what some women considered
handsome. He was tall with fair skin and green eyes. To this day,
he had no idea how he ended up with green eyes. He said his
mom must've been playing off on his dad or something. But

Bobby used those eyes to his advantage. For some reason, women just went gaga over them.

"So, are you having a good time?" Cheryl reached out and gently caressed Eric's arm.

Eric looked at her. He wanted to say, you just saw me walk in, how could I be having a good time already? But he decided against being sarcastic. "It's all right. I haven't been here before."

"It's a pretty cool place. When it first opened, it was too crowded. Then the crowd thinned out. I try to come every Friday night. It's ladies' night and we get in free."

Oh great, a club hopper. And a cheap club hopper at that. Suddenly, Eric felt turned off again.

Cheryl tried to make more conversation, but Eric wasn't interested. He shot Bobby looks to get him to move on, but Bobby was making progress with Marcena, and Tonya was vying for his attention as well. Eric could tell his lack of response was frustrating Cheryl, but he just continued to stare off onto the dance floor.

"What's your problem? Do I bore you?" Cheryl finally asked.

"What?" Eric had tuned her out and only caught that she was talking to him because she had raised her voice. Tonya, Marcena, and Bobby stopped talking and looked at them as well.

"I said, if you so damn bored, you're free to leave." Cheryl lifted her index finger and twisted her neck when she talked. *A definite turn off.*

Eric looked at her, then at Bobby. "Okay." He got up from the table and walked away.

"Motherfucker," Cheryl muttered. "Didn't nobody want him no way."

Eric didn't even look back. He knew Bobby would make up some excuse, get Marcena's number, and catch up with him later. Eric walked to the bar and ordered a drink. Another girl at the bar started eying him flirtatiously. He acted like he didn't see her as he waited for his drink. His mind was on no one but Elise. He knew they'd work this out. Hooking up with some woman would only complicate things.

The girl made her way over to where Eric was standing. She leaned over him seductively and reached for a napkin off the bar. "Excuse me," she said. "I just have to get one of these." She made sure she stuck her butt all the way out. She was actually kinda cute, but her little ploy wasn't working on him tonight. The girl stood next to Eric for a few minutes, slightly bouncing to the hip-hop tunes vibrating throughout the club. She asked Eric his name and whether he was having a good time, but he pretended not to hear. She told him her name and tried to make small talk, but Eric barely responded. Finally, she got frustrated and left.

Eric felt his cell phone vibrating in his jacket pocket as he sipped his drink. He nearly dropped his glass trying to get it out. The only people who ever called him on his cell were his sister, Bobby, and Elise.

"Hello."

"Hi."

"Elise. I'm so glad to hear from you. I've been going crazy."

"Where are you? What's all that noise?"

"Uh, hold on." Eric looked around, then darted into the men's room. "We're at IHOP. Me and Bobby just came to get something to eat."

"At one in the morning?"

"Yeah, he was hungry. How've you been?"

"Better."

"Elise, I miss you. I want . . ." Eric stopped talking when two guys came into the men's room. They looked at Eric and snickered.

"He's begging," one of them said.

"Yeah, that's the only time you talk on the phone in the restroom at a club—when you begging," the other guy laughed.

Eric tried his best to ignore them. "Can I see you?" he whispered.

"Eric, I called because I can't sleep. I don't know what we should do." Elise sounded like she had been crying.

"Let's not do this over the phone. Where are you? Can I come over?"

Elise paused. "Why don't I just meet you at the apartment?"

"For real?" The two guys snickered again as they left the restroom.

"See ya later, Keith Sweat," one of them mumbled.

Eric ignored the comment. At this point his pride had flown out the window and he couldn't care less. "Okay, I'll meet you there in half an hour."

He snapped his phone shut and walked back out into the club. He looked around. Bobby had made his way to another table and was talking to some fat girl sitting by herself. She was dark skinned with blond hair and had splotches all over her face. She looked like she weighed a good 280 pounds. Bobby was an equal opportunity player.

Eric made his way through the crowd and over to the table. "Hey, I gotta go. Elise is on her way to the house."

Bobby looked at him in disbelief. "You've gotta be kidding me. Shante and I are just getting to know each other." Bobby put his arm around the girl's waist—at least as far around as it would go. "I can't leave now."

"Well, you have to leave now. Or give me the keys." Eric held out his hand.

"To my ZX? How am I supposed to get home?"

"I can take you home." Shante looked longingly into Bobby's eyes.

How did he get that girl hooked so fast?

Bobby contemplated the idea. "Are you sure?"

Shante nodded. "It would give us a chance to get to know each other better. I just met you. I can't let you get away that easy."

"Aw'ight, let me walk my boy to the door. Don't go nowhere." Bobby flashed a smile and walked off with Eric.

"You sure can pick 'em," Eric said as Bobby handed him the keys. "That girl is ugly."

"Why? Because she's fat?"

"No, because she's ugly."

Bobby looked back at Shante. She had a huge grin on her face. He waved. She giggled and waved back. "You know I don't discriminate. Besides, big girls are always better in bed. More to work it with. I'm gonna get lucky tonight." Bobby nodded knowingly.

"You better hope that's all you get. Just make sure you wrap it up. And make sure your baby's mama ain't hiding in the parking lot waiting to stalk you." Bobby's ex-girlfriend, Rachel, was as crazy as they come. She had followed them on several occasions trying to get Bobby to take her back, and she used Bobby's son against him every chance she got.

"You don't worry about Rachel. I can handle her."

"Yeah, that's what you say. Just be careful."

"You be careful in my car, man. I'll have Marcena bring me to your crib in the morning."

"Marcena? I thought you said her name was Shante?"

"Ain't that what I just said?"

"No, you said Marcena."

"Damn. I'm terrible with these names. I'm just gonna call everyone 'Baby.' That way I don't mess up nobody's name."

Eric shook his head at his friend. "Have fun."

"I will. I sure will. By the way, that 'I'm leaving' routine worked out pretty good. We're goin' have to use that more often."

"Yeah, okay. I'm out." Eric sprinted out of the club and into the parking lot, where he jumped in Bobby's car and took off.

Seven

Eric made it home with ten minutes to spare. Once he got inside, he tried to straighten up the mess in the living room. Beer cans were still strewn about since he hadn't picked up a single thing all week. After he made a mad dash to get the room looking decent, he stared at himself in the mirror and suddenly didn't think he was so hot anymore. He really needed to shave. He couldn't believe he had even gone out looking like that.

Eric was just wiping the last of the shaving cream from his chin when the doorbell rang.

"Coming!"

Eric took another glance in the mirror. "Come on man, work your stuff." He dashed to the front door and slowed just before opening it to try and gather his composure.

"Hey." Eric opened the door for Elise to walk in. "Why didn't you use your key?"

Elise shrugged and walked in. She sat down but kept her jacket on. She looked beautiful. Her short, curly, cropped hair was freshly cut, a perfect fit for her high cheekbones. The white tank top she was wearing showcased her perfectly shaped arms.

She was wearing a pair of blue Nike sweatpants and matching gym shoes. Eric stared at Elise. *I sure love this woman.*

He had been head over heels ever since they first met at Michigan State University six years before. She was a sophomore and he was a junior, a star basketball player. Women were knocking down his door to get with him. They bought him gifts, did his homework, and let him use their cars. But Elise couldn't have cared less. He first saw her in the school library where she was reading the campus newspaper. His picture was on the front page from a game he had helped win, so—counting on her to recognize him and say something—he arrogantly walked over and sat down. Elise wasn't fazed. She looked up, smiled, and went right back to reading. After realizing that she didn't recognize him, he finally got up the nerve to say something to her. She was friendly, but she had no idea who he was. He found out she didn't follow sports and didn't like athletes or the groupies who followed them. In fact, Eric had a harder time winning Elise's heart because he was an athlete. She didn't want to have anything to do with him.

"Look." Eric shut the door. "I'm going to get straight to the point. I'm sorry. I'm so sorry. You know how much I love you. I'll never put my hands on you again."

Elise reached in her purse, pulled out a brochure, and started reading. "Page two of this domestic abuse pamphlet says, 'The man will always say he's sorry, it'll never happen again.' "

"What?" A shocked look crossed over Eric's face. "Elise, I am not some abusive man who needs brochures. This is bull—"

Elise held up her hand and cut him off. "I don't know what you call slapping the mess out of me, but I call it abuse."

"But, baby, that's the only time that has ever happened." Eric knelt down next to Elise.

"What about the next time, Eric?"

"Elise, we've been together for nearly five years. Have I ever put my hands on you?"

"That's not the point. You did put your hands on me once and I can't have that."

Eric thought back to the one other time he'd almost lost Elise, after they'd been together a year. The basketball team was doing great, so Eric was in the limelight even more. Women were throwing themselves at him, and one time he let one of them talk her way into coming up to his room. Eric really hadn't planned on doing anything with the girl, but before he knew it she was butt-naked on his bed. He was about to give in and have sex when Elise, who was notorious for popping up at his room, knocked on the door. Surprisingly, he had been faithful to Elise and didn't want her to think otherwise, so he panicked when she knocked on the door. He tried to keep quiet so she'd think no one was there, but the girl purposely said something and Elise heard the noise. She refused to leave and just kept banging. Eric made the girl get dressed, then he snuck her out through his suitemate's room. He finally opened the door to reveal a highly pissed-off Elise. It had taken two weeks of begging and apologizing to convince her that nothing happened. He even made the girl call Elise and tell her so.

After Elise took him back he vowed not to let anything like that happen again. He couldn't bear the thought of losing her. Elise was the perfect woman—smart, beautiful, and supportive. He didn't lose her then and couldn't lose her now.

"Look, I said I'm sorry. You know that's not me."

"No, I don't know that. That's what scares me. I've seen you put your hand through the wall." Elise pointed to the patched up spot on the living room wall. "That's when you got mad because my ex called to tell me his brother died."

Then she pointed to an end table that was missing its glass

top. "And that, the glass is in a million little pieces because you got mad over an argument I can't even remember. Last week was just the first time you ever took your anger out on me. But I'm worried that if I stay with you, it won't be the last."

If?

"Elise, I know I get upset sometimes . . ."

"You get too upset. How are we supposed to be together when I'm scared of what you may do?"

Eric felt himself getting frustrated. He thought about throwing out a wedding date to get her back. He knew she wanted that more than anything. He had actually proposed two years ago, but he kept putting off an actual date. Not because he didn't want to marry her, he did. He was just scared right now, especially because he wondered how he would provide for her. In his heart he knew Elise would be happy no matter what he did for a living, but he felt she deserved to be able to live the lavish lifestyle of a professional athlete's wife.

"Maybe you need some anger management classes or something."

"Awww, there you go, sounding like my sister." Eric got up off the floor and sat in a chair across from Elise.

"Well, maybe we both have a point."

"Maybe y'all both need to get off my back," he muttered.

Elise stood up and got her purse. "I can see this is useless."

Eric jumped up after her. "Okay, okay. Whatever you want, baby. Just don't leave me. I'll work on my temper. I'll do whatever it takes to make this work."

Elise stopped and turned around. "Even if that means taking anger management classes?"

Eric hesitated. He didn't know why he had hit Elise. That's how he lost Yolanda and he had vowed it would never happen again. Yolanda didn't play that. And neither did Elise. More than that, he deeply believed a man shouldn't hit a woman, especially after how he grew up.

So why did you do it? It's a question he couldn't answer.

Eric didn't really think he had a problem. It's just that every now and then, the rage took control of him. He knew he had come from an abusive background, but it had only been for a few years. Prior to that, his family had had a happy life. It was when he was about ten years old that things started going bad. That's when his father lost his job and became abusive. That's when Eric started hating his father.

He remembered how, time after time, he had begged his mom to leave. She never would, saying, "Your daddy's not really like that. He's going through a difficult time." Eric had gotten so sick of hearing that. He used to wonder how his father went from being such a good man to a monster who terrorized his own family. Eric finally concluded that it must've been in his father's blood all along—the abusive Gerald James was the real Gerald James. Before, he'd just managed to hide it. Now that Eric thought about it, there was early evidence of just how violent their father could get. Every now and then, he would blow up at the slightest thing. Only he took his anger out on the furniture. A mirror he'd smash. A chair he'd kick over. The worst it ever got was when his father kicked Cooter after the dog chewed up a pair of his father's favorite loafers. Eric had cried for weeks about that. The poor dog had to be put to sleep, his ribs were injured so badly.

Eric glanced at the wall and table Elise had pointed out. *That's just how my father started.* Eric shook his head. *But I'm not him. I'd never get to the extreme he did.*

"So, will you go?" Elise asked after Eric didn't say anything for several minutes.

"Yeah, if you think that'll help. I just want us to make it." Eric pulled Elise to him. "We've got to make it, baby. I can't lose you."

"I don't want to lose you either."

"So, can we kiss and make up?" Eric forced a smile.

"Eric, I'm serious about this." She looked up into his eyes. He looked at her with such intense love.

"I am too, baby." Eric leaned in and hugged Elise. He closed his eyes and inhaled her scent. "I am too."

Eight

Aja had avoided watching television all week. She didn't need to see Charles's gorgeous mug plastered across the screen. It would only make her nervous.

After she canceled their first date, Aja was sure it was over before it had even begun. When he'd turned around and canceled their date for the play, claiming he was hung up in Chicago, Aja figured he was just making excuses because he was no longer interested. She really thought he'd leave her alone. But he didn't. In fact, he'd sent her roses at work on Monday with a note that said, "Sorry about our date. How does this Friday sound?"

Friday sounded great on Monday, but now that it was here, Aja was wondering if she had made the right choice.

She was still having a hard time believing that Charles was interested in her in the first place. He was one of the most handsome men she had ever seen. His deep-chocolate skin was flawless. He had a smooth, small mustache that barely touched the edges of his mouth. His manly physique was evidence of what working out could do for you. And he had beautiful hazel eyes.

Aja was startled out of her thoughts when the phone rang.

"That's nobody but Roxie." Aja glanced at the Caller ID and picked up the phone. "I'm not in. Leave a message at the beep. Beep."

"Girl, stop playing. Whatcha doing?"

"I'm painting the kitchen. What do you think I'm doing?"

"You need to make sure you polish those crusty toes of yours while you're at it. So are you getting ready for your date? You know I had to call and check before you canceled again to go to a 'Save the Whales' rally or something."

"Shut up," Aja laughed. "I'm going, okay? I'm nervous, but I'm going."

"Good. Call me when you get home, unless, of course, he spends the night. In that case call me in the morning."

"You know he's not going to spend the night."

"You know you want him to, though. Tell the truth."

"Good-bye, Roxie."

"Wait, just say it, Aja," Roxie playfully pleaded. "It's been sooo long since you had a man make you feel like a woman. One who got your juices flowing."

There she goes again. Roxie was always thinking about sex.

"Tell the truth, you've thought about how big his equipment is?"

"Now I know it's time to go."

"Okay, okay. You know I'm just playing. But he does have some big hands. Call and let me know if the myth is true about men with big hands."

"You're disgusting. Bye." Aja hung up the phone before Roxie could get any nastier. She was right, it had been a long time. *Damn you, Roxie. Now I'm going to spend all night looking between this man's legs. Just stay in control and everything will be fine.*

Control. Aja was the master at that, but just once she'd like to lose control. Maybe when Charles walked through that door, she'd drop her slinky black dress to the ground. She'd stand before him stark naked, start playing with her own breasts, and ask him if he wanted to play too. Then they'd make mad, passionate love right by the front door. The doorbell jolted Aja out of her fantasy.

"Hellooo, let's get back to reality," she told herself. "You don't even know this man. And besides, as nervous as you are, you'll be doing good to get a kiss."

"Coming," Aja yelled in her sexiest voice. The last thing she wanted was to appear like some dimwit. Roxie had told her that he'd had his share of those.

Aja took one last look in the mirror. "Hair? In place. Makeup? Fine. Dress? Well, it doesn't exactly make my size ten figure look like a six, but it does hide those extra pounds."

Aja brushed her dress down, smiled pleasingly at her reflection, and headed for the door. She stood on her toes and looked through the peephole. *Oh my God! Heaven has opened up its gates and dropped down an angel.* Aja gathered her composure and opened the door.

"Hi," she said, looking Charles up and down. *This man was fine with a capital F.* He looked even better than he did on television, if that was possible. He had on a dark brown sports coat, a cream mock turtleneck, and Tommy Hilfiger khaki pants. The smell of Hugo Boss cologne emanated from his skin. And his shoes . . . Aja had only seen shoes like that in men's magazines. She could tell those had to have set him back a pretty penny.

"Hi." Charles smiled. "Sorry I'm a little early. I just didn't want you to cancel out on me again."

Aja tried to give a sophisticated laugh, but it came out sounding like a hiccup. "Oh, not a chance." She tried to ignore the hiccup-sounding laugh. "Come in."

"I hope you like Italian," Charles said as he walked past her. "I've got reservations at eight at Tony's."

"I love Italian." *How am I ever going to get through this night?*

"Good, since it's seven-fifteen. We'd better head out." Charles turned to her. "Are you ready?"

Ready and willing, Aja wanted to say. "Sure."

Aja grabbed her little black purse and turned off the lamp near the door as they headed out. She smiled to herself. "I am actually going out with Charles Clayton," she mumbled.

"Did you say something?" Charles turned toward her.

"No, I didn't." Aja smiled again and locked her door.

The drive to the restaurant was quiet. Charles asked her if she was okay a couple of times and even tried to make small talk, but Aja's mouth was too dry to utter much more than one-word responses.

"We're here." Charles pulled his black Lexus GS300 up to the valet parking. He handed his keys and a twenty-dollar bill to the attendant as he stepped out. "Hey, Dave, how's it going?"

"Just fine, Mr. Clayton. Just fine."

Aja reached for her door.

"Wait—let me get that." Charles rushed around to the passenger side of the car. "Now, I won't lie and say I do this all the time," Charles joked as he held the door open. "But you'll find that most of the time, I'm pretty much a gentleman."

Charles gently took Aja's hand, helped her out of the car, and led her into the restaurant.

"Hey, it's Charles Clayton," some guy yelled as they walked in. "I watch you all the time!"

"Thanks, man. Are you rooting for the Rockets?"

"You know it!"

Good-looking, fine, and Mr. Personality. Something is wrong with this man. Charles motioned to the hostess, who quickly came over to show them to their seat. *Maybe he is a psycho, or maybe he's gay.*

"Your seat, my lady." Charles pulled out her chair.

"Thank you," Aja managed to mutter.

"Now, are you always this quiet, or is it just me?" Charles sat down.

Aja just giggled, or at least tried to. It sounded like a gurgle this time. She told herself to cut the giggles. "No, I'm . . . just taking in the ambiance."

"The restaurant's ambiance or your date's ambiance?"

Aja looked at Charles's captivating smile. No wonder he was the top sports anchor in town. He had a make-you-wanna-drop-your-drawers, enchanting type of smile. His teeth were so white. *He must have had them bleached. Nobody has teeth that white.* "The date of course," she answered.

After they were seated, a boy who looked like he couldn't be any more than nine or ten walked up to their table. An older woman stood behind him. They both looked nervous. The little boy had a notepad flipped open to a blank page.

"Go on." The woman pushed him toward their table.

"Hi . . ." The youngster nervously took a deep breath. "Mr. Clayton, my name is Byron. May I please have your autograph?"

Charles smiled and took the notepad. "Well of course you may. Byron, what grade are you in?" he asked as he scribbled something on the pad.

"Fourth. I play basketball at my school."

"Do you really? Well, I tell you what." Charles flipped the notepad over to another blank page, then tore it out. "Why don't you give me your autograph, too? Because I bet one day you're gonna be famous and I can say I got your autograph when you were just a little boy."

Byron's eyes lit up. "For real? You think so?"

"I sure do. Especially if you work hard and mind your parents."

The little boy had a huge grin. The woman was smiling just as hard as he was.

"Here. Write 'To Charles,' then sign your name."

Byron eagerly took the paper, signed it, and handed it back.

"Now," Charles lightly folded the paper and placed it in his jacket pocket. "I'm going to keep this in a safe place, because I know one day I'm going to be covering you and all the good things you're doing."

"Oh boy!"

"Come on, Byron. Thank you, Mr. Clayton," the woman stepped in. "We're sorry to have disturbed your dinner."

"You're very welcome. Good luck, Byron."

Byron waved as he walked away, a huge grin still across his face.

Aja was transfixed. That had to be one of the sweetest things she had ever witnessed. "Do you get that often?"

"You'd be surprised. You would think that us sports guys wouldn't get that much attention, but people feel they know you from watching you all the time and they grant you celebrity status. Don't get me wrong—if Puff Daddy walked in here, I think Byron would forget all about me," Charles laughed.

Both of them became silent as their laughter died down. Charles began staring intensely at Aja.

"Do you mind if I order a glass of wine?" Aja was trying to get his gaze off her.

"Why don't we just get the bottle?" Charles summoned the waiter, ordered a bottle of wine, then turned his attention back to Aja. "So tell me, Miss James, why have you been avoiding looking at me all evening?"

Because you're super-fine and I can't understand why in the hell you would want to go out with me. "I haven't been avoiding you." Aja began nervously playing with her bracelet. *Where the hell was that wine?*

"Well, answer this. Are you here tonight because you want to be or because Roxanne made you?"

"Nobody makes me do anything." Aja crossed her legs, letting her thigh peek out of the slit in her dress. Too bad Charles couldn't see it—he sat across from her at the small, secluded table—but it still made her feel sexy. "I'm here because I want to be here."

"That's good to know."

The waiter approached their table with the wine. "Your glass, madam." The waiter motioned for Aja's glass. She picked it up, handed it to him, and he returned it to her filled to the brim with the California vintage. Aja eagerly took a swallow. She let the wine ease down her throat.

"A little thirsty, huh?" Charles joked.

Aja paused, hoping she didn't seem like a lush. "Oh sorry," she smiled. "It's been a long day."

"Well, drink up. I'm here to make you forget all your troubles. Just one more question." Charles leaned forward. "I don't need to watch my back from some jealous man coming in here and seeing us together, do I?"

If only you knew. "No, I'm very much single. Besides, I wouldn't be here with you if I had a man."

"That's just what I wanted to hear." Charles sat back and sipped his wine. For a moment, the two of them just sat in silence, taking in the light sounds of the jazz band. The music was relaxing. Between that and the wine, Aja was beginning to loosen up. By the time they had finished eating, she felt completely at ease.

Over dinner, Aja had learned that Charles had never married either. He'd been engaged once, but it didn't work out. That was the woman he'd just broken up with. He was from Galveston, which was about an hour outside of Houston. He'd played football at Notre Dame, but a broken ankle sidelined his career. He'd been working in the television business for ten years and loved sports. His dad died five years ago and his mom was alone, which was why he chose to stay in Texas, turning down offers from ESPN and FOX Sports. He still did commentary for ABC *Monday Night Football.*

"So Charles, how did you come up with such a TV name like Charles Clayton?" Aja was finishing off her third glass of wine. She wasn't much of a drinker, so the wine had her feeling pretty good.

"Actually, my real name is Eldridge Charles Clayton the third. But, 'Hey Eldridge, how 'bout those Bulls' sounds pretty hokey."

"I'd have to agree with you there," Aja laughed.

"How about you? Where did you get such a beautiful name?"

"Actually, it was my father's idea." Aja's smile slightly faded as she recalled her father's story of how he named her. "My parents were overseas in the military and my mother went into early labor right smack dab in the middle of a fruit market in China. An elderly Asian lady helped deliver me so my father decided to show his gratitude by letting the woman name his firstborn. The woman decided on Aja and my parents loved it."

"Tell me about your father."

Aja hesitated. That was something she never, ever shared with anyone—not even her first love, Troy. In fact, her refusal to open up was one of the main reasons they broke up.

"You know, Charles, I'd rather not get into that."

Charles paused, then grinned. "So, how 'bout those Bulls?"

Aja laughed. Charles leaned back and gently massaged her hand while the jazz band continued playing softly in the background. Aja appreciated his just letting the issue go. *I could learn to like this. I really could.*

Nine

It had been nearly two months since Eric had last worked out. He had done everything he could to forget basketball entirely. The sport had been the center of his life from the time he was old enough to dribble a ball. It was the only thing he ever wanted to do in life; the only reason he went to college. Recently, he had all but given up hope of going pro. It had been three years since he'd left school. He'd tried to play overseas, but that didn't work out. He couldn't take the distance from Elise, plus he still dreamed of the NBA, so he didn't perform like he should have. Now, he just mainly played with friends. But looking at the poster on the wall of the barbershop, the "what ifs" started racing back. The poster touted a three-on-three tournament coming up in two weeks.

"Hey, Phil," Eric yelled to the barber, "you think any NBA scouts will be at that basketball tournament?"

"I don't know, man. I heard Shaquille O'Neal will be in town because one of his friends is getting married, so I'm sure he'll be there. And if he's there, there's bound to be some agents in the house—at least that's what the guy who put that poster up there says." Phil motioned for Eric to take a seat in his chair. "You goin' play?"

"Nah, my hoopin' days are over." Eric continued eying the poster as he sat down in the chair.

"Son, you better get out there and show them boys a thing or two. You know you got game."

Eric thought about what Phil was saying. Maybe there was still hope.

"Hey, I just thought about something," Phil said. "Derrick and Roscoe are looking for another man for their team. Kevin's old lady pulled a knife on him for messing with some chick from the North side. He slapped the shit out her, so now he's up in county."

"Kevin goin' learn to leave them ghetto 'hos' alone," Eric said. A caramel-colored woman with a blond beehive hairdo stopped flipping through her magazine and cut her eyes at Eric.

"My apologies, my sister." Eric nodded his head toward the girl.

"Hmphh!" the blond muttered and went back to her magazine.

Phil laughed. "Don't get cut up in here your damn self. That's Tricia. She comes in here to get her son's hair cut and she will stab you just as soon as look at you." Phil snapped the cape and wrapped it around Eric's neck. "So what's up? You think you'll play?"

Eric seriously considered the possibilities. "Yeah, all right, I'm game." He relaxed and sat back in the chair. "Now shave me clean so I can let the sun shine on my head while I dunk on them fools."

Phil started lathering up Eric's head. "Your wish is my command, my brother. Just don't forget me when you make it pro."

Eric smiled. *Yeah, it would feel good to play again.* He came alive when he was on the court. He loved the feel of the rubber in the palm of his hand. When he was playing he was the king, and the court was his castle.

Eric was terribly out of shape—which was amazing because he used to regard his body as a temple, working out and staying away from drugs and alcohol. But since he had thought his pro dreams were smashed, he'd taken to finishing off every day by sitting on his sofa with a six pack. Now, the prospect of playing again got him refocused.

Eric became so engrossed in getting ready for the game that everything else had to be put on hold, including Elise, who had been bugging the hell out of him about needing to talk. He found out there would indeed be some scouts there and he needed to concentrate fully on getting ready to make a good impression. Elise would have to wait.

The last two weeks were spent gearing up for the game. It started with him pouring the last four beers in his refrigerator down the kitchen sink. He worked out nonstop, hoping that he'd at least get some of his energy back. And it appeared to have worked—now that game day was here, he had never felt more invigorated.

"Hey, you ready?" Roscoe stood in the doorway of the locker room.

Eric laced his shoes and jumped up. "Yeah, let's do this. And don't get mad because I show you up." Eric's adrenaline was pumping. He peeked outside. There had to be six hundred people out there and that just hyped him up even more. He hadn't played in front of a crowd since college.

"Just bring your ass on." Roscoe grabbed a towel and raced outside to the court. Eric was right behind him.

It was a strenuous game, but Eric and his teammates put on

a dazzling performance. He scored fifteen points, thirteen rebounds, and even dunked on Shaquille O'Neal, which sent the crowd into a frenzy and made the scouts sit up and take notice.

Afterward, two scouts came up and expressed interest in talking to him more. Eric was on cloud nine. Maybe he would finally have his chance to do what he did best—play ball.

"Eric, can I talk to you?"

Eric was excitedly talking to some other players when he heard Elise's voice. He turned around. "Hey, baby, I didn't know you'd be here. I thought you had to work." Eric leaned over and kissed Elise ferociously on the lips. "Did you get a load of that game? Did you see how I dunked on Shaq? Of all people, Shaquille O'Neal!"

"Yeah, congratulations. But I really need to talk to you." Elise looked sad.

Eric's excitement waned. *This looks serious.* He didn't want anything messing up his good mood. "Can't this wait?"

"No, Eric! I've been waiting all week, and now I'm going crazy." Elise was near tears now.

"Hey, what's wrong? Chill out." Eric took Elise's hand and pulled her to the side of the court.

"Good game!" Some guy slapped Eric on the back as he and Elise stood off to the side.

"Thanks, man." Eric flashed a look of gratitude, then turned his attention back to Elise. His tone grew serious. "What's wrong?"

"I'm pregnant."

The air around them grew silent. The noise from the people still at the game seemed to no longer exist. It felt as if no one was on the still-crowded court but Eric and Elise.

"Did you hear me?" Elise asked after Eric failed to respond.

He hoped he was hearing her wrong. "Yeah, yeah . . . How did . . . When?"

"I missed my period last month, but I'm irregular so I didn't think anything of it at first." Elise rushed the words out like she had been practicing them all week. "I went to the doctor this morning. I'm ten weeks."

"Damn, Elise, how'd you let this happen?" Eric put his hands over his face and lowered his head.

Tears welled up in Elise's eyes. "How did I let this happen? I told you I had missed some pills! You were the one, 'I'll pull out, don't worry about it!' "

"Hey, lower your voice. People are looking." Eric nervously looked around.

"I don't care about these people!" Elise was in full-fledged crying mode now. "You think I want this? You think I wanted to have a baby out of wedlock? Just forget it! I'm sorry I ruined your day!" Elise started heading back to her car.

Eric paused, then ran up behind her. He grabbed her and turned her around. "Okay, okay. I'm sorry. This is just a shock, that's all."

"Tell me about it." Elise wiped away the tears running down her face. "This isn't how I wanted to bring a baby into the world."

Eric thought about asking Elise if she really wanted to have the baby, but he knew she would explode. She didn't believe in abortion. Besides, he wouldn't be able to live with himself if he forced her to have one. He was one of the few men his age with no children. Luckily, he had never gotten a woman pregnant before, so he never had to deal with the issue.

"I'm sorry, Eric."

Eric pulled Elise toward him and hugged her tightly. "You don't have anything to be sorry about. We'll work this out, baby. We'll work it out together." Eric tried to be strong. He could tell Elise was a wreck. His joy from the game was gone. Now, he was left wondering how in the world he was going to take care of a child. *A baby. That's the last thing I need.*

Ten

Aja was up bright and early Saturday morning. She couldn't wait to tell Jada the news about Elise. She had hoped Eric would come and tell her himself, but as usual, he made up some excuse. Eric and Elise had come straight to her apartment from the game. They looked upset and said they wanted to talk to her, but needed to talk to each other first. Aja gave them a little time alone and went down to Starbucks to grab a Frappuccino. By the time she returned, Elise was smiling and Eric looked nervous.

Then they broke the news. Aja would be an aunt. She was ecstatic—the only thing that would've made her happier was to hear that they had actually set a wedding date. They were one of those couples that spent years being engaged.

"We'll just have to work on that next," Aja told her cat, Simba, after the parents-to-be left. "My little brother's going to be happy, if it's the last thing I do."

The ride to Memorial Greens was a joyous one. Aja sang along with her Lauryn Hill CD and in no time, she was pulling onto the winding road that led to the hospital.

As soon as she stepped in the door, the part-time nurse Barbara came racing toward her.

"Oh, I'm so glad you're here!" Barbara's plump face gleamed with excitement.

"Why, what's wrong?" Aja's heart started to race.

"Good news! No, great news! Fantastic news! Come! Come see for yourself!" Barbara turned and quickly wobbled her large frame toward Jada's room.

"You go on in. I'll wait here." The nurse was smiling.

Aja slowly opened the door and saw Jada sitting in the rocking chair facing the window.

"Jada, are you okay?" Aja walked around to face her sister. Jada looked radiant, a huge smile plastered across her face.

"You're smiling! She's smiling! Barbara! Barbara!"

The nurse peeked in the room.

"What's going on? Why is she smiling?" This was a monumental accomplishment. Jada hadn't smiled in years.

"Jada," Barbara walked into the room. "Show your sister why you're happy."

Jada slowly pulled a letter from her lap. "Dad-dy," Jada struggled to say.

Aja stared in amazement. "Am I hearing things? Did Jada just talk?"

"Your hearing is just fine. Your sister finally got tired of that silent world." Nurse Barbara looked like a proud mother.

Then it dawned on Aja what her sister had said. *Daddy.* Aja snatched the letter. "I know he didn't."

"Noooooooooo!" Jada jumped out of the chair and lunged at her sister. "Mine! Mine!" Jada frantically reached for her letter. The movement caught Aja by surprise and she toppled over backward and landed on the floor.

"Mine! Mine!" Jada continued to scream as she grasped the letter and tore it out of Aja's hands.

Nurse Barbara moved fast. Within seconds, she had Jada back

in the chair, stroking her hair. Jada was smiling again, caressing the letter like it was a gift from God.

"What is wrong with you?" Barbara angrily hissed.

Aja realized she was still sitting on the floor. She pulled herself up and stood, dazed. "I . . . I'm sorry."

"I think Jada has had enough of a visit today. Maybe you should leave." The nurse shot Aja a look to let her know the issue was not open to discussion.

"Jada, I'm sorry." Aja reached for her sister's shoulder, but Jada jerked away. The smile on Jada's face turned into a scowl. Tears trickled from Aja's eyes. She wiped them away, then slipped out the door, trying to take in everything that had just happened.

Aja headed to the front door to leave, but decided to wait. She needed to talk to the nurse. It was almost twenty minutes before Nurse Barbara came out. She noticed Aja and stopped right in front of her. Her excited look was replaced with one of exasperation.

"Good, you're still here. Look, I know your story. I know your father is the reason Jada is in here today. But he's also the only thing that has worked to get her to come out of that shell in the last twelve years. Have you ever seen her smile since she was a child? Heard her talk?" The nurse didn't give Aja time to answer. "Then I suggest you let go of the past and thank God that something has finally helped your sister move toward the future!"

Aja nodded apologetically. "I'm sorry."

"You should be."

"When did she start talking?"

"When the letter came yesterday. Out of the blue, after I told her who it was from and read it to her, her eyes lit up and she said 'Daddy.' The doctors say she can progress quickly from here or that could be the only thing she ever says. We just don't know. It's up to Jada to determine how fast she progresses. What I do know is, I'd be trying to talk about your father all I could if I were you. It's the only thing that's worked." The nurse's look softened. "Let go of that hate and be happy for your sister." She turned and walked off, leaving Aja sitting in the middle of the lobby.

Eleven

Aja was out of breath. She had been on the treadmill for forty-five minutes now and was dripping in sweat. She looked over at Roxie walking briskly on a stair climber. Roxie didn't even have a hair out of place. *How can someone look good working out?* But then Roxie didn't have to work very hard. She ate what she wanted, when she wanted, and still didn't gain an ounce. Let somebody say cheeseburger, and Aja put on two pounds. Aja was desperately trying to get back down to her college size, which meant losing about fifteen pounds. Before, she hadn't really cared, but being with Charles had inspired her. He was so physically fit. In the month that they'd been dating she had already lost five pounds. She'd done so by watching what she ate and exercising vigorously, but she'd had enough exercise for today.

"I'm done." Aja stepped off the treadmill and wiped the sweat from her brow. She walked over to the stair climber, lifted Roxie's headphones, and spoke into her ear. "I said, I'm done."

"What? Already?" Roxie slowed down and removed her headphones. "We've only been working out for twenty minutes."

"I've been working out for forty-five minutes. Remember, I

got here before you. And I'm exhausted." Aja headed toward the dressing room.

"Have it your way." Roxie pushed the buttons on her stair climber to bring it to a complete stop. Stepping off the machine, she grabbed her bottle of water and gulped it down. "Mmmm. I needed that. Speaking of having it your way, let's go get some Burger King." Roxie followed Aja into the locker room.

Aja rolled her eyes. "I didn't just spend forty-five grueling minutes on a treadmill to run right back out and make all my work in vain by eating a Whopper. We can go to Souper Salad, but Burger King's out."

"Souper Salad?" Roxie groaned. "I don't want rabbit food."

Aja opened a locker and took out her gym bag. She eased her sweaty T-shirt over her head, stepped out of her workout shorts, and slipped a white tennis dress on. She noticed Roxie still standing there in her workout clothes. "Aren't you going to change?"

"Nope, I don't feel like it. I'm just going to keep this on. We're just going across the street." Roxie had on a cute little spandex Calvin Klein sports bra and matching shorts. A lot of people wore their workout clothes to the salad bar across the street, so Aja figured Roxie would be fine.

"You should've kept on your workout clothes," Roxie said.

"Everybody doesn't wear a size one. Some of us have to work really hard at it and don't like parading around in skimpy little clothes."

"Oh, come on. You know I don't wear a size one. And why be miserable trying to fit into a certain mold?" Roxie grabbed her bag out of an adjoining locker. She reached inside the bag and pulled out a package of M&M's. She tore the bag open, poured a handful of the candy into her hand, and popped it in her mouth.

"That's easy for you to say. You're married and you're thin."

"Neither of which are anything to write home about. I just don't understand you. I'd give anything to have your body." Roxie looked down at her thighs and turned her nose up. "I've always told you I wished I had more meat on me. Men want meat on their women. Brian is always telling me that."

"Yeah, right. You want my body?" Aja laughed like it was the most absurd thing she'd ever heard.

"Girl, don't front. You know the guys always used to talk about how fine you were in college. They were always trying to buy me some Twinkies or something."

"That was twenty pounds ago. Now, I need to do some serious TaeBo if I want to hang on to Charles," Aja said.

"If you say so, but I ain't mad at you. Lord knows you need to do whatever it takes to keep that man's eye because he is *FIIINNNEEE!*"

"Hold up a minute," Aja said.

"Of course, not as fine as Brian," Roxie quickly retorted.

"You better watch that. I finally like someone you pick out for me, and you trying to move in on him," Aja joked.

"Dang, I just said the man was fine. It ain't like I want him or nothing. Besides, you know the only man in the world for me is my boo."

Aja smiled. Roxie joked about men all the time, but her heart belonged to Brian. They'd met in Cancun at an annual jazz festival that brought in young, urban professionals from across the country and immediately hit it off. Brian would never admit it, but everyone knew Roxie was the reason he'd decided at the last minute to move to Houston and go to law school. Granted, he'd been accepted to the University of Houston law program before they met, but he'd been set to attend Southern Methodist University. That is, until Roxie walked into his life. They had a storybook romance. It only took six months for them to see that they wanted to spend their lives together. They got married on the one-year anniversary of the day they met.

"I'm just teasing you, girl. I know you only have eyes for Brian," Aja said as she gathered up her things.

"I do. But even a blind woman can see that Charles is super-fine."

Aja laughed as they left the locker room and walked across the street to the salad bar.

"So tell me, what's the deal with you and Charles?" Roxie and Aja were making their way through the buffet line. "You told me you two went out last weekend, but I know you didn't fill me in on the whole story."

"That was the whole story."

"Yeah, right. And I'm Princess Diana. Out with it. What's he like? Do you like him?"

Aja smiled as she found a booth and slid into it. "I really like him. You did good."

"I'm glad things are working out. It seems like every time I call you, you're on the phone with him. And you're not even a telephone person." Roxie popped an olive in her mouth.

"I know, but I like talking to him. He makes me laugh."

"Girl, marry him then. Nothing like a man that can make you laugh."

Aja stopped pouring dressing on her salad and narrowed her eyes. "Are you being facetious?"

"Yeah. I don't want to hear about how you were laughing. Tell me the good stuff."

"What good stuff?"

"Have you slept with him?"

"Come on, Roxie. You know me better than that."

"I know you like everybody to think you're a virgin, but I

know the real deal. Now what's up?" Roxie started munching on her salad.

"For your information, I haven't slept with him yet. We're in the 'getting to know each other' stage. But I like him a whole lot."

"Well, he likes you too. At least that's what he's telling Brian."

"What else did he say?" Aja eagerly asked.

"That's it. He said he usually moves fast, but you seem to be moving slow."

"I am. I don't want to rush things."

"You don't have time to take it nice and slow." Roxie turned her nose up. "This salad ain't cutting it. I'm going to get a baked potato."

Aja watched Roxie prance over to the spud bar and load a baked potato with butter, sour cream, bacon, and chives.

Aja looked at the potato when Roxie returned to the table. "You make me sick."

"Ummmm. It's so delicious," Roxie teased as she took a bite. Aja tried to ignore Roxie's taunting as she finished off her bland salad with fat free dressing.

As they ate, Aja filled Roxie in on Charles's failed engagement. "He was madly in love with an attorney he met at a happy hour. Only Charles says she was extremely spoiled and ultimately, that was what ruined their relationship. He's dated off and on since that breakup, but nothing serious."

"Well, at least he's honest. That's the same story Brian told me."

"Honesty is just one of his qualities I like."

"Have you checked out his hands?"

"His hands?"

"Are they big?"

Aja realized what Roxie was talking about and shook her head. "I'm not going there with you."

"I'm goin' ask you again. And this time tell me the truth. Have you screwed him yet?" Roxie said with her mouth full.

"Do you have any table manners?"

"When I want to. Now answer the damn question."

"No, I have not, for your information."

"Quit lying. You have and you just don't want to tell me."

"I have not! We're waiting until the time is right."

"Give me a freaking break! You two are grown, consenting-ass individuals."

Aja looked around nervously. "Would you lower your voice? I know we're grown. And these two consenting individuals decided they wanted to wait."

"Wait for what?"

"The right time."

"Oh, that's a bunch of bull. He's a man, ain't he? So that means if he ain't screwing you, then he's screwing somebody else."

"You know, Roxie, everything isn't always about sex."

"I'm just saying . . . you know I know you like some good lovin' just like the rest of us. But now you trying to act all high and mighty," Roxie snickered.

"See, Roxie, you wouldn't understand because you got married at twenty-two. Those of us in our age bracket who are still single reach a point where priorities change and time for careless, carefree sex has passed. We want meaningful sex with people who mean something."

Roxie narrowed her eyes and saw Aja was serious. "Where'd you learn that shit? On *Oprah*?"

Aja shook her head in frustration. "Like I said, you wouldn't understand."

"Okay. Okay. Damn, don't be so sensitive. I think it's wonderful. Maybe you should wait until after you're married to do anything at all, since you've turned so holy all of a sudden."

"We'll wait until we're ready. Now can we drop it?"

Roxie shrugged her shoulders. "Fine. I won't ask anymore."

"Thank you. Not that I believe you."

"So, when are you seeing him again?" Roxie asked after they finished their meals and were sitting back waiting for the check.

"Tonight. We're going to a dinner party. That's why I'm trying to eat light, so I can get in that little red dress I wore to the Link's dance last year."

"Oooohhh. Hobnobbing with the big dogs."

"Yeah, right," Aja laughed.

Roxie took a ten-dollar bill out of her purse and set it down with the ticket the waitress had just placed on their table. "Let's go. Brian has a meeting this afternoon and he'll have a heart attack if I'm not back to get the baby."

Aja hugged Roxie after they were back at their cars in the gym parking lot. "Thanks for lunch. My treat next time."

"No problem. Oh yeah, you never did tell me if you read your father's letter."

Aja's mood suddenly changed. "Please, I'd rather not get into that."

"Okay, just talk to me about it when you're ready."

Aja looked gratefully at Roxie and nodded.

"By the way, how's your brother? How'd he do at his game?" Roxie asked.

"He did pretty good, and he's fine."

"I know he's fine. That's another good-looking brother. If only I were a little younger and unhappily married, I'd be your sister-in-law," Roxie grinned.

"Well, even if you were younger or unhappy, you wouldn't stand a chance, especially now that he's gonna be a daddy."

"What? Elise is pregnant? Well, I'll be. Your little brother's gonna be a daddy. Is he excited?" Roxie unlocked her car, opened it, and leaned up against the door.

"You know, I really can't tell. I know he wanted a lot of kids, just not right now. But he seems to be doing okay with the idea. They came by and told me after the game last week."

"Well, tell him I wish him and Elise the best. She's a sweetheart. I wouldn't take her man from her anyway," Roxie grinned. She got inside her car and started it up. "And Aja, don't wait until hell freezes over before you give it up."

"Give what up?" Aja stopped when she realized what Roxie was talking about. "Bye, Roxie." Aja started toward her car, parked two rows over.

"Bye, Virgin Mary." Roxie laughed, backed her car up, and sped out of the parking lot.

Twelve

The ominous sculpture towered forward like an eagle about to attack its prey. Aja ignored the "Do not touch" sign and lightly ran her fingers across the ship. The clay models of slaves looked so real, from the anguish across their faces to the tightness of the chains around their legs. She gently touched the eyes of one of the models. Aja felt shivers run up her spine.

Aja read the summary of the slave ship. She was really interested in learning about how her ancestors were dragged from their native land and forced into captivity. She felt she could draw upon their strength when times got tough.

This particular exhibit was a Spanish ship from 1821. It carried more than one hundred slaves from Northern Africa to America. Aja eyed a model of a young woman, clinging desperately to a little child. The woman's eyes were full of fear. Aja's chills grew greater.

Charles rubbed his hands up and down her arms. "You okay?"

"Yeah. It's just . . . I can almost feel them."

"I know, that's what I like about this exhibit." Charles looked at the display. "It's like the slaves' souls are still here."

Aja smiled as Charles hugged her tightly. She couldn't believe how well things were going for them. They didn't get to spend a whole lot of time together because he was always working or traveling, but they did talk on the phone three or four times a day. She had never felt so alive. Charles was everything she ever dreamed of: respectful, handsome, loving, attentive, and ambitious. He was a little arrogant, but nothing she couldn't deal with.

"Look at this one. It's called Whittlin' Willie," Charles said.

Aja looked at the picture of an elderly man sitting on the front porch of an old run-down house in historic Helena, Arkansas. He was whittling something Aja couldn't make out. The caption under the picture read "Willie Sampson, National Whittling Champion, 104 years old."

"Wow, look at the intricacy in his face," Aja said.

"Nice, isn't it? It's stuff like this that makes me love coming here."

Aja and Charles had been so captivated by the paintings, sculptures, displays, and artwork that the last three hours had just flown by. Aja never visited museums, other than on school field trips when she was young. But since she'd been with Charles, she'd been introduced to a lot of things she didn't normally do.

That was another thing Aja liked about Charles. His tastes ranged from classical to hip-hop. Today, they were visiting the African exhibit. Last week it was an exhibit on the Holocaust. Next week, he planned to take her to a Cinco de Mayo celebration.

"Well, what did you think of the exhibit?" They were viewing the last piece of artwork and nearing the exit.

"It was absolutely fantastic."

"Yeah, I think so too. Well, how 'bout some ice cream? I'm in the mood for something sweet." Charles leaned in and kissed Aja lightly on the lips. "Not that you're not sweet enough."

Aja grinned. "Ice cream sounds good. There's a Marble Slab Creamery right around the corner."

"Let's walk."

The air was chilly for a late-April afternoon. Aja wrapped her hands around Charles's arms and leaned her head on his shoulder. It was a little awkward to walk like that, but she didn't care. It felt so good to be close to Charles.

They entered the ice-cream parlor and ordered two waffle cups of strawberries and cream, mixed with fresh strawberries. After Charles paid the cashier, they took a seat by the window. Aja removed her jacket and laid it across the back of the chair. She felt Charles's eyes burrowing into her breasts.

"Umm, hello." Aja waved her hand in his face.

Charles jumped. "I'm sorry. It's just, you're wearing that top."

Aja smiled. She had hoped for that reaction when she chose to squeeze her 36Cs into the gold Donna Karan blouse that dipped in the front.

"Thank you." Aja felt herself getting hot at the seductive way Charles was looking at her.

Charles tried to pull his eyes away from her chest, but they kept darting back down. "Aja, you are so beautiful," he muttered, more to himself than anything else. "And sexy. What I wouldn't give . . ." Charles shook himself like he was trying to snap out of a trance. "I'm sorry." He looked down, a guilty expression across his face. "I'm trying to respect your wish to wait before we're . . . before we make love." He looked down at her breasts again. "But, damn, it's hard. Especially with you looking so good."

Aja felt flattered, but at the same time wondered why she had chosen to wear this form-fitting blouse. Yes, she wanted to turn Charles on, but why? It's not like she was planning to have sex with him tonight. She had told him that she wanted to wait before they took the next step. Surprisingly, Charles had said he respected that and would give Aja all the time she needed.

It's not that she didn't want to be with him. She wanted it badly. But she just had to make sure everything was right between them.

Charles dipped his spoon in his ice cream. "We'd better talk about something else."

"I agree."

They sat in silence for a minute. "So, tell me some more about yourself," Charles finally said.

"What do you want to know?" Aja was grateful the conversation had steered in a different direction.

"Everything. I feel like I do all the talking whenever we're together or talk on the phone. You're a good listener, but now it's my turn."

"Okay, so what do you want to hear?" Aja knew she needed to open up more. It was something she was trying to work on.

"Let's see." Charles leaned his head to the side like he was thinking. "Why don't you tell me about your ex-boyfriend?"

"Troy?"

"Yeah, I think that's what you said his name was."

Aja had told Charles a little bit about Troy. She debated whether to reveal any details about their relationship. All her friends had warned her to never tell a man about another man, but Aja had nothing to hide. Besides, Charles had been so open with her, telling her all about his ex-fiancée and the other women he had dated. So Aja decided to go ahead.

She thought about what to say. "Troy wanted more than I was ready to give. I still care about him. He's a great guy. I just wasn't ready to commit like he wanted me to, so he moved on. We parted on good terms."

"Are you ready now?"

Aja looked at Charles and smiled. They hadn't really talked about the status of their relationship, but she had often thought about them being in a committed relationship. "I think I am."

Charles returned her smile. "Let's see . . . What else do I want to know? . . . What about your family?"

"What about them?"

"You haven't told me much except your parents are dead and you have a brother and sister."

"What else do you want to know?"

"Getting information from you is like pulling teeth," Charles quipped. "How'd your parents die? Where's your brother and sister? Tell me something. Please?"

Aja paused, then started talking as she looked off. "Both my brother and sister live here in the city. Eric, that's my brother, he's trying to play professional basketball. He's actually good enough to play pro, so we're praying that things work out. My sister, Jada . . ." Aja debated whether to continue. "My sister is sick. Mentally sick. She's in a home."

Charles looked confused. Aja was dreading having to explain that. Part of her just wanted to change the subject, but she knew she wouldn't be able to get away with that. Charles wanted some answers.

"Aja! Aja James! Is that you?"

Aja turned toward the voice calling her name. She didn't recognize the man standing at the counter with two small children. He was a tall, muscular man with gray hair and small eyes. The man got his ice cream and walked over to their table. He had a huge smile.

"It's Donald. Donald Patterson. I used to be good friends

with your daddy. I haven't seen you in years, girl, since you were what? Seventeen?"

Donald noticed Aja's perplexed look. "I fixed you all's air conditioner that summer when your brother broke it by hiding his toy cars in there."

Aja nodded, recalling the man her father used to refer to as his running buddy. "Oh yeah. You have a daughter named Tiffany. She was the same age as me?"

"Yeah. These are her two kids." Donald pointed to the two children vigorously licking chocolate ice-cream cones.

"They're adorable." Aja nodded toward Charles. "This is Charles. Charles, this is Donald. He's a friend of the family."

Donald stuck his hand out. "You look familiar. Do I know you?"

Charles grinned like he was used to people asking him that. "I do the sports for Channel 13." He stood up and shook Donald's hand.

"That's where I know you from!" Donald turned toward his grandchildren. "Hey kids, do you recognize him?"

The children, who looked like they couldn't be more than six and eight, cocked their heads in confusion. "Unh-unh," the oldest replied.

"He's the man we watch on TV every night. The one I'm always talking about."

The kids looked like they couldn't have cared less. "Oh," the oldest said. Both kids resumed eating their ice-cream cones.

Donald turned to Charles. "You do a good job."

"Thanks." Charles sat back down.

"Well, I won't keep you guys. Aja, it was so good to see you again."

"It was good to see you too."

"I'm going to visit your dad. We still keep in touch. I'll be up that way next week and told him I'd stop in for a visit. I'll tell him I saw you. Take care." Donald flashed a warm smile and grabbed his grandkid's hands.

Aja looked uneasy. "Uh, okay. Talk to you later."

Charles raised his eyebrows after Donald and his grandkids walked off. "Is he going to visit your father's grave?"

Aja sighed. If she hoped for any relationship with Charles, she knew she needed to tell him the truth. "I'm sorry. I wasn't completely honest. My mother is dead. My father—well that's a whole other story. A long one that I would really rather not get in to."

Their eyes met. "Let's get something clear," Charles said, a serious expression across his face. "My last relationship was full of lies. It's something I can't stand. The quickest way to mess things up with me is by lying."

Aja lowered her eyes and nodded. This was the first time she'd ever heard Charles get even remotely angry. "I'm sorry. It's just a complicated situation."

"I can respect that. But you'll find I do better with honesty. Just say, Charles, I'd really rather not talk about that right now."

Aja kept gazing down.

They sat in awkward silence for a few minutes before Charles finally took Aja's hands. "Maybe you'll feel comfortable enough to tell me one day."

Aja offered up a weak smile and hoped she hadn't damaged their relationship. Maybe she should just go ahead and tell him everything. But what if he thought she had too much drama? What if he decided that being with her was just more trouble than it was worth? Not yet. She couldn't go into her past just yet. He'd have to understand and be patient.

Thirteen

Aja tightened her lips together and struggled not to say anything. She had agreed not to be a backseat driver if Roxie drove her and Elise to the mall. But now that Roxie was passing up yet another parking space because it was "too far away," Aja was getting fed up.

"Roxie, would you park already? This is ridiculous. Just park in the back and we can walk," Aja huffed.

Roxie held up her hand with her palm facing the backseat. "Un-unh. Don't even start. You didn't want to drive, so you just ride. If I want to drive around this parking lot all day, you just sit back, shut up, and ride." Roxie dropped her hand, leaned forward, and peered over into the next aisle of cars.

"But we've been driving around for almost thirty minutes," Aja protested.

Roxie looked over at Elise, who was sitting in the passenger seat trying to muffle a laugh. "What part of 'shut up' does she not understand?"

Elise shook her head, smiling. "I'm not in that. I'm just along for the ride."

"You're the reason we're coming to the mall in the first place. We need to get that little one some baby stuff," Roxie said.

Elise had filled out in the face a little, but other than that, you could barely tell she was pregnant. "Well, this was your idea, Roxie. I'm just three months along. I still think it's too early to be baby shopping." Elise rubbed her stomach, a look of concern on her face.

"Nonsense," Roxie replied. "It's never too early to baby shop." Roxie navigated the Jeep Cherokee down yet another row. She ignored Aja's loud huffing.

"Roxie! There's one right there!" Aja exclaimed, pointing to an empty space on the next row.

"It's too far," Roxie replied without looking back. She just kept driving. "This humidity is a bitch and I am not about to mess up my eighty-five dollar 'do trekking ten miles. I'll just keep driving around until someone who parked up close comes out."

Aja let out a long sigh. "This doesn't make any sense."

"You ever seen the movie called *The Long Walk Home?*" Roxie asked Elise.

Elise nodded. "Yeah, isn't that the one starring Whoopi Goldberg?"

"Yep, that's it. Well, we're about to do a remake. Starring Aja James."

"Ha-ha, very funny," Aja said. "There!" Aja jumped up and pointed again. "There's somebody pulling out at the very front of the aisle."

"Bingo! I told you if we waited long enough we'd find something." Roxie slowed down and put on her blinker. The elderly woman was slowly putting her bags in the trunk.

"Oh, come on, Grandma!" Roxie yelled. After what seemed

like five minutes, the woman backed her GrandAm out of the parking spot. Roxie had to pull back to give the woman more room. "Should be a law against driving once you pass sixty," she mumbled.

As the elderly lady was apparently trying to shift her gear from reverse to drive, a small red Porsche zipped out of nowhere and into the parking spot.

"Awww, hell naw!" Roxie screamed. "That bitch done lost her mind!" Roxie vigorously pressed down on her horn, causing the elderly woman to jump as she took off. Roxie quickly pulled up behind the Porsche, blocked the car in, and jumped out of the truck. Aja shook her head because she knew all hell was about to break loose.

"Didn't you see me waiting on that spot?" Roxie yelled as the petite woman stepped out of the Porsche.

"Excuse me?" the woman responded. She had long blond hair and bright blue eyes. Her entire face was so sunburned it looked like the simple act of speaking was causing great pain.

"Are you deaf?" Roxie spread her legs and placed her hands on her hips like she was preparing for a showdown. "I said, I was waiting on that spot."

Elise, who was obviously nervous, turned to Aja. "Should we get out and do something?"

"No, trust me. Roxie has it all under control. I guarantee you, that woman will end up moving."

"I'm in a hurry. Someone's waiting on me," the woman said, closing her car door.

"Look, Becky," Roxie said, cocking her head to the side. "I don't give a damn if Jesus himself is waiting on you. You need to get your tiny little ass in that car, back it up, and go find another parking space."

The woman flung her hair back. "First of all, my name is

Hillary, not Becky. Second of all, I got here first. So sorry." She hit the car alarm button, dropped her keys in her Kate Spade purse, and started strutting off.

Aja saw the fury forming on her best friend's face and decided it was time to step in. The last thing they needed was for Roxie to get arrested for beating down a white girl in the parking lot of the Galleria Mall. And she knew this confrontation was escalating in that direction.

Sure enough, Roxie grabbed Hillary's arm. "Hillary, Becky, it's all the same. All I have to say is, if you know what's good for you, you will move your car."

Hillary jerked her arm away just as Aja yelled Roxie's name.

"Come on, Roxie, it's not that serious, girl," Aja said, stepping out of the car.

Roxie held her hands up. A sly smile crossed her face as she glared at Hillary. "You know what, Big Lez, you're right. It's not that serious. By the way, do you know how much L. J. over at that chop shop is giving for Porsches these days?" Roxie never took her eyes off Hillary. "Or what about Tyrone? He's out of prison now for raping that white woman, ain't he? Can he still get a person's name, address, where they work . . ." Roxie leaned over and looked at Hillary's license plate, "from someone's license plate number?"

Aja tried to stifle a laugh. It had been a long time since she and Roxie enjoyed one of their escapades. In school, they were always known for getting into something. Roxie should've majored in drama because she was one hell of an actress. Aja decided to play along for old time's sake. She put on her tough look as she walked toward them. "Yeah, dog. That's how Tyrone found that white woman he raped. He had her license plate number. Come to think of it, didn't she cut him off in a parking lot or something?"

Hillary's eyes grew big. She clutched her purse tightly, looking back and forth between Aja and Roxie like she was trying to decide if they were serious. "You know what, forget this," she finally said. "You can have the stupid space." She hit the alarm button again, opened her car door, and jumped back in. Elise scooted over and moved the car so she could back out. Roxie stepped out of the way and let her back out, the sly smile still across her face.

Hillary rolled her window down as she was pulling out. "I wish you people would just stay on your side of town! Can't you find some good deals at Sharpstown Mall?" Then Hillary floored her Porsche and took off.

"What? Bring your little burned ass back here and say that!" Roxie yelled after her.

Aja laughed. "Girl, just let her go. You already put the fear of God in her."

Roxie was still fuming. "What the hell is that supposed to mean: 'Can't you find some good deals at Sharpstown?' "

"Just what she said. You know Sharpstown Mall is straight ghetto. So she was trying to say you're ghetto."

Roxie's anger eased and a smile formed across her perfectly MAC-glossed lips. "I did get a little ghetto on her didn't I?"

Aja laughed. "Yes, you did. It still amazes me how you can go from glamorous to ghetto in a matter of seconds. You don't even know anyone named L. J. or Tyrone. And where did Big Lez come from?"

Roxie made her way back to her car, laughing. "It was just the first thing that popped into my head. Move so I can pull into this spot."

Aja stepped aside, shaking her head. Roxie was too much. She talked a lot of noise, but behind that tough exterior was the heart of a lion.

"Wow, I thought it was about to be some fireworks up in here," Elise said, stepping out of the car.

"It was if that little heifer didn't move her car," Roxie replied as she shut her truck door.

Elise smiled. "You two amaze me. I didn't know you had all that in you."

"Well, now you know," Roxie said. "Now let's go buy up some baby stuff!"

"I am so tired." Roxie plopped down in the chair at La Madeline's Café. "I won't be mad if I never see another store."

Aja set her bags down on the floor next to their table. It seemed like they had hit every store in the mall that carried baby clothes, furniture, or supplies. "We were ready to leave an hour and a half ago. You're the one who had to go in every store in the mall." Aja looked over at Elise. She looked like she was about to pass out. "And look at poor Elise. You know she doesn't need to be doing all that walking."

"Aww, she'll be all right. Pregnant women used to work in the fields up until they went into labor," Roxie responded.

Aja shook her head. "This from the woman who made her doctor put her on bed rest the last two months of her pregnancy so she could have a legitimate excuse to take it easy."

"I'm okay," Elise said. "I just need to rest some. Why don't you two go ahead and order your coffee and croissants. Just get me a small decaf."

"We'll go get the coffee. Come on, Aja," Roxie said.

"Girl, I'm beat," Aja said, taking Roxie's spot as she got up. "Can you bring me a small coffee and biscotti?"

"So, Elise, are you excited about the baby?" Aja asked after Roxie walked off.

Elise proudly rubbed her stomach, a smile crossing her weary face. "I am."

"Do you want a boy or a girl?"

"A healthy baby. That's all I want. But you know Eric. He wants a boy."

"I guess that comes from him growing up with two sisters." Aja laughed, recalling how she would make Eric come to her tea parties. He was never a willing participant—she always had to threaten to expose his latest misdeed to get him to sit through the party.

Roxie reappeared with coffee, setting the cups down in front of Aja and Elise. "No, every man wants a son. It makes him feel like a warrior to be able to plant a seed and carry on his legacy. And Eric—" Roxie abruptly stopped talking, her attention focused across the room. "Aja, look. Isn't that Warren?" Roxie frantically grabbed Aja's arm and pointed to a small table on the other side of the café.

Aja felt a small pang in her heart. It was Warren—he was sitting facing them, laughing at something the woman across from him was saying. She hadn't seen him since college. It was amazing that she still felt pain when she thought about all he had dragged her through. Between having sex with one of her roommates and lying to her every chance he got, Warren had left her heartbroken.

"Who's Warren?" Elise asked.

"Aja's trick-ass boyfriend from college," Roxie said with a scowl. "That bastard put the D in dog. Him and his boy, Darwin."

"Darwin was Roxie's boyfriend," Aja offered.

"And they both were low down. They cheated on us so much it was ridiculous."

Warren's smile widened as he noticed them. He said something to the woman, then got up and began making his way toward them.

"I know that bastard ain't coming over here," Roxie said.

Warren approached their table. He licked his lips before he spoke. "When I woke up this morning I knew it was going to be a good day. My Aja. What's up, baby?"

Aja tried not to let her contempt show. That was too long ago.

"Warren," she said, gently sipping her coffee.

Warren looked over at Roxie. "Roxanne. Still raising hell?"

"Warren. Still being a dog?"

Warren laughed. "Some things never change." He extended his hand toward Elise. "And you are?"

Elise shook his hand. "Elise. I'm Aja's brother's girlfriend."

"Well, Aja's brother's girlfriend, the pleasure's all mine." He turned back toward Aja and took her hand. "Aja, girl, you look good."

"Her man seems to think so," Roxie interjected as she removed Aja's hand from his grip.

Warren ignored Roxie. "It's so funny that I would run in to you. I was just thinking about us the other day."

"Yeah, right," Roxie snorted.

Warren took a deep breath, but kept his attention focused on Aja. "I see your girl still has trouble minding her own business. Maybe if she could, Darwin wouldn't have played her like he did."

"Oh, no you didn't." Roxie started wiggling her neck in full sister-girl mode. "Your boy got played because he's the one that came begging for me to take him back. But he didn't tell you that did he?"

Aja could see Roxie was heated. She had really loved Darwin, so any mention of the pain he caused sent her reeling.

"Come on, guys. That was almost ten years ago. Let it go." Aja turned dismissively away from Warren. "Warren, it was nice to see you, but I'm sure your lady friend is waiting on you."

"She doesn't mean anything."

"Do any of your women mean anything?" Roxie nonchalantly commented.

Warren continued to ignore Roxie, but his irritation was evident. He licked his lips again, his eyes taking in Aja from head to toe. She had on a baby blue velour warm-up with a form-fitting top. The outfit actually complimented her shape. Aja was grateful that today of all days she had curled her hair and put on makeup. While she had no desire to be with Warren, she did want him to see what he had missed out on.

Warren sat down next to Aja. "Damn, girl, you look good. Let me take you out. I know I did some stupid stuff, but I was young. I'm a changed man now."

Roxie leaned in and whispered to Aja. "And if you believe that shit, I have some swampland in California I'd like to sell you."

Aja laughed then turned back to Warren. He looked good with his coal-black skin, enchanting eyes, and the devilish grin that had made her fall for him in the first place. But you couldn't pay her to travel down that road again.

"Warren, Roxie is right. I'm seeing someone."

Warren acted like she hadn't said a thing. "I know it's been a while but you can't tell me you didn't love me."

"I didn't. At the time I thought I did. But I was simply infatuated."

Warren looked crushed. Aja couldn't believe after all this time he would still think she would want him.

"Girl, you know you loved the ground I walked on."

"No, *you* loved the ground you walked on."

By this time, the woman that Warren had been sitting with started shooting him disgruntled looks.

Warren ignored her as well. "Aja, baby, I bet your man can't hold a candle to me."

Roxie held her palm out. "How much you wanna bet? She's dating Charles Clayton. You know, the sportscaster from Channel 13."

Warren raised his eyebrows. "That sports guy?"

Roxie nodded triumphantly. Warren paused before speaking. "And? That don't mean nothing to me."

Aja was tired of dealing with him. "Well, it means something to me. Warren, you gave us up years ago and at the time, I hated you for it. But I now know it was the best thing that ever happened to me."

Warren's date stood up, placing her hands on her hips, obviously angry. "Warren, I'm leaving," she called out.

Warren looked at her and held up one finger before turning his attention back to Aja. "Aja, look boo, take my card." He reached into his jacket pocket and pulled out a business card. Aja took it, turning up her lip as she read it. It had a picture of Warren posing. His name and telephone number were the only things listed on the card. No job, business, nothing. Aja shook her head and tried to keep from laughing.

"I know old dude can't make you feel the way I did," Warren said as he stood up. "Call me if you want to experience some real loving." He kissed Aja's hand, then sprinted off to catch up with his date who had already stormed off.

"I can't believe you dated someone like that," Elise said.

"We were young and stupid," Roxie responded. She noticed Aja looking at the card. "I hope you're not even thinking of calling him."

"Girl, you think I would mess up any chance of something good with Charles for that buster?"

"Good. I taught you well." Roxie held out her hand. "Now allow me the honor."

"Nope," Aja responded. "I want the thrill of this myself." She held up Warren's card, ripped it into tiny shreds, then dropped the pieces in her now cold coffee.

Fourteen

"Hey, babe, did you get a lot of stuff?" Eric was sitting on the sofa playing Sony PlayStation's NBA All-Star game when Elise came back from the mall.

Elise put her purse and bags down and took off her jacket. "Your sister and Roxie went overboard. They are already spoiling this baby."

"Well, my baby deserves to be spoiled. Did you check the mail?"

"Yeah, it was just a bunch of bills and stuff. But this one, I think you'll be particularly interested in." Elise waved a long, white envelope in the air.

"Damn!" Eric screamed at the television set as his team lost the ball. "Oh really? Who's it from?" he said, not turning his attention away from the screen.

"Maybe I'll just wait and tell you when you can find time to tear yourself away from that stupid game." Elise put the other mail on the table and walked over to kiss Eric on top of his head.

"That's fine." Eric pressed the switches on the control, leaning to the side, trying to maneuver as if the PlayStation were a real, live game.

"But if it were me," Elise continued. "I'd want to know right now what the Dallas Mavericks wanted with me."

Eric immediately stopped his game and turned to Elise. "What did you say?"

"Oh, nothing." Elise took the letter, walked into the kitchen, and opened the refrigerator. "What are we eating tonight?"

Eric jumped up and followed her into the kitchen. "Girl, if you don't get back here! Gimme that letter!" Eric grabbed for the letter.

Elise playfully hid it behind her back. "But your PlayStation game is so much more important."

"Elise, stop playing. Give me the letter." Eric was getting nervous now. Elise smiled and slowly handed over the letter. Eric ripped it open and began reading.

" 'Dear Mr. James, This letter is to officially invite you to the Dallas Mavericks basketball camp for free agents on . . .' Oh my God! Oh my God! Baby! Baby! Did you hear that? The Mavericks want me to come try out for them!"

"I heard, baby." Elise was smiling at Eric's excitement.

"Man, I can't believe this! Did you hear that Eric, Junior?" Eric leaned down and kissed Elise's stomach. They had decided to wait to find out what they were having, but Eric was sure it was going to be a boy, so he'd already taken to calling the baby Eric, Junior.

"Do you know they only invite select people to play for these camps? People they're really interested in? All I have to do is impress the coach and I'm in. Yes!" Eric picked Elise up and swung her around.

"Eric! You'll hurt the baby!"

"Oh, sorry." He put Elise down, kissed her on the forehead, then rubbed her stomach. "You hear that, little one? Your daddy's gonna be a Maverick!"

"Uh . . ." Elise interrupted. "Don't you have to make the team first? Anyway, I thought you hated the Mavericks."

"They suck. But that's because they need me." Eric smiled mischievously. "No, seriously, they're not the best team in the league, but at this point I'll take what I can get."

"So, when do you leave?" Elise ran her hands over her stomach.

Eric read on. "In three weeks. The camp runs Monday through Friday." Eric raced to his magazine rack to look for an article on the Mavericks. "I better read up on the team. I really don't watch them much, so I want to be on top of things when I go in."

Elise walked over and kissed Eric again. "I know you'll do good."

Eric pulled out a magazine. "Found it! I knew *Sports Illustrated* had done something on the team." Eric paused and turned to Elise. "I have to do good, baby." He put his hand on Elise's stomach. "For us, I have to."

Eric sat down and started reading through the magazine. Elise went back into the kitchen to take something out for dinner. She found some ground meat, decided to make spaghetti, and placed it in some water to thaw out.

Elise walked back in the living room. She hated to ruin the moment, but she knew she had to bring it up. "Eric?" Elise pulled another letter from the end table. "Sweetie, something else came for you." She placed the letter in front of Eric.

He looked at the envelope, noticed the return address, and the smile escaped his face. "You can just throw that in the trash." He started flipping through the magazine again.

"I think you should read it. You didn't read the last two letters your father sent you."

"Elise, don't go there."

"I don't ever go there," Elise gently said. "Every time I try to bring up your father, you get mad or change the subject. I wouldn't even know what had happened to you if it wasn't for Aja. Do you think it's good to keep all this bottled up?"

"Dang. Are you sure you and my sister aren't related? Why can't I get y'all to understand? I don't have anything to say to that sorry bastard and I don't want to hear anything he has to say to me. Now leave it alone!"

"Shouldn't you at least read it?"

"You read it if you want to know what's in it so damn bad. I don't care."

"But—"

"But nothing! Why you always gotta be messing up the good groove we got going? Damn!" Eric jumped up and stormed out of the room and into the bedroom. Elise heard the music blaring and decided to leave it alone. But she held on to the letter.

"Maybe someday you'll change your mind," she whispered.

Fifteen

"What's up, cuz?"

Aja heard the loud, familiar voice clear across the supermarket. She and Eric were in the meat section of Kroger. They were picking up some ribs and chicken to barbecue for a little get-together celebrating Eric's invitation to camp. He was leaving in two days. Aja had hoped Charles could come to meet her brother for the first time, but he was in Phoenix covering a game and wouldn't be back until the morning.

"Long time no see!"

Aja and Eric turned around to see their cousin Luther, Aunt Shirley's oldest son. It had been nearly four years since they had seen or talked to Luther. He was a troublemaker who ran in different circles than they did and had been in and out of jail on petty charges since he was thirteen.

"What's up witcha?" Luther was standing next to a short girl in stiletto heels and a skintight black catsuit. Her full breasts were protruding from the suit. She had a tattoo across the top of her right breast that said "Luther's." She had long blond and red braids down her back. Luther was dressed in a bright purple Adidas warm-up with matching gym shoes. Three huge gold chains hung around his neck, and a big bulldog emblem was attached to one of them. The chains matched the two gold teeth he had in his front teeth.

"Y'all just don't keep in touch with your kinfolks no more." Luther chewed on a toothpick as he talked.

"Hi Luther, how are you?" Aja responded. Eric nodded his head in a hello gesture, but didn't say anything.

"Trying to make a dollar out of fifteen cents," Luther laughed. "Yo, this is my girl, Mich'el-le." Luther grabbed his girlfriend's hand and held it up. "We engaged. Check out this fat-ass rock."

Mich'el-le blushed as she wiggled her fingers. She had long, curved nails that were painted blue with little intricate designs on them. The ring was huge and screamed dime store. Aja gave a slight smile. "Congratulations. That's a nice ring." Eric had already walked off and was browsing in the meat aisle.

"I know it's nice. That ring set me back some change."

Leave it to Luther's no-class self to talk about how much he paid for his ring. Aja wanted to tell him to go get his money back since it was obvious he got gypped.

"Guess who I talked to yesterday?" Luther continued.

"Who?" She really wasn't interested, but Aunt Shirley had been good to her, so she tried to tolerate Luther. He'd been in jail when she'd gone to live with Aunt Shirley, and she was never around him much.

"Yo daddy," Luther proclaimed with a huge grin. "He called Mama collect and I answered the phone. I started not to accept the charges, but I didn't want to hear her mouth. You know he's up before the parole board in a few months. They may be letting him out on good behavior. He wanted me to come pick him up if he gets out. I said, 'Why would you want me to come get you when you got two big-time kids with fancy cars?' Mama told me y'all rolling deep off that insurance money. Can you hook a brotha up?"

"Anyways," he continued, not giving Aja time to respond. "I told yo daddy he got these two siddity kids, why don't one of them come get him? I don't count Jada 'cause she ain't got it all up top." Luther's girlfriend slapped him on the arm. He looked confused. "What? What I say? She don't. The girl is crazy."

Aja tried not to get upset. She couldn't stand anybody talking about her sister—definitely a sensitive subject with her. "She isn't crazy."

"Call her what you want. I say she's a crazy retard." Luther glared at his girlfriend. "As I was saying before somebody hit me—somebody who goin' get the shit slapped out of them if they hit me again—Mama is gonna have a little welcome home dinner for Uncle Gerald. Y'all goin' be there?"

Aja didn't respond.

"What about you, big man?" Luther asked as Eric placed a packet of meat in the basket.

"Nah, man, I got something to do."

"You don't even know when it is."

"Whenever it is, I'll be busy." Eric shot an angry look at his cousin.

"Aww, come on now," Luther chuckled. "Don't tell me y'all still mad about what happened? Uncle Gerald is good people. He just made a little mistake, that's all."

Eric clenched his teeth. "Killing my mother wasn't a *little* mistake."

"Hey, down boy." Luther held his hands up. "I didn't shoot your mama. Don't be mad at me."

"Luther, I think we need to go." Luther's girlfriend tugged on his sleeve.

"Yeah, aw'ight. I guess we'll be getting on outta here before my beer gets hot." Luther held up a six-pack of Milwaukee's Best. "By the way, Aja, I heard you was going with that guy off the TV, is that true?"

"Yeah, something like that."

"Well, I'll be damned," Luther laughed. "We goin' have us a celebrity in the family. When you goin' bring him over and let me meet him? I want him to send me a shout-out on the news."

"Come on, Luther." Mich'el-le pulled his arm again.

"Aw'ight. Let go of my damn sleeve. You messing up my clothes." Luther jerked his arm away. "Don't get bitch-slapped up in this here grocery store."

Mich'el-le rolled her neck and held one finger up. "Oh no you didn't. I wish to hell you would slap me. 'Cause then it would be a clean-up on aisle three, and it wouldn't be no damn spilt milk."

For a minute Aja thought they were about to go at it, right there in the meat section of Kroger. They were creating a scene and people were starting to stare. Luther frowned, then relaxed and grinned. "That's my baby, don't take no shit from nobody, not even me." He leaned over and wiggled his tongue in Mich'el-le's ear. She stopped frowning, giggled, and whispered something back in his ear. Whatever she said, it was enough to convince him to leave.

"Well, I'll holla at y'all at the freedom celebration." Luther popped his girlfriend on the behind as they walked off. The entire scene made Aja's stomach turn and Eric was looking at the couple with disgust.

"I can't stand him," Eric finally said after they were gone. "Ever since we were little kids, he's been a royal pain in the ass. I don't know why you even entertain him."

"I just don't want any problems. I believe we should just tolerate him for a few minutes and he'll go on his way."

"He's always trying to start some mess, with his fly-girl girl-friend. She know her mama named her Michelle. Mich'el-le, gimme a break."

Aja laughed as they made their way through the checkout line. Luther and her brother never did like each other. Luther was four years older than Eric and had always bullied him around.

"Thirty-three, sixty-two," the cashier said after ringing up all the items.

"He's paying." Aja pointed to her brother.

"No, I ain't. This was your idea." Eric picked up a tabloid paper at the checkout stand. "Besides, this is my celebration. I'm not supposed to pay for anything at my own celebration."

Aja huffed and took out her credit card. "But I bet you'll be the first one with your plate out." Aja handed the clerk her card.

"Sure will." Eric flipped through *The National Enquirer*. "Did you know Oprah has seven illegitimate kids?"

"Boy, shut up," Aja laughed.

"That's what this paper says. She gave birth to quadruplets when she was seven. They all had different daddies."

"Don't believe anything in that trashy paper."

"This stuff is true. Elise knows somebody who used to work there. She says it's basically gossip. You know, people's aunts, uncles, brothers, and sisters, selling them out for a few thousand bucks. So for the most part, all of it's true."

"Not that part. Now put that down and come over here." Aja signed the receipt and headed for the store's exit.

Eric threw down the magazine, grabbed the grocery bags, and followed his sister outside.

"So, you seemed nervous when Luther brought up Charles," Eric said once they were in the car and heading home. Aja just smiled as she maneuvered her SUV through the backed up traffic on the freeway. "Is it serious?"

Aja sighed grandly. "Yeah, I think it is. It's early now, but he seems like a great guy. He makes me wonder if something is wrong with him because he's good-looking, well off, and single."

"Maybe he's gay."

"That was the first thing I thought, but then I said, why do we always do that? Whenever a good-looking, successful man is single, why do we want to label him as being gay?"

"Because they usually are."

"Well, no, I don't think he's gay. He actually just broke up with someone a couple of months ago. I enjoy being with him. At first I couldn't see why he was interested in me."

"What is that supposed to mean?" Eric threw his sister a puzzled look.

She hesitated as she pulled onto the 610 freeway. Ironically, there was a big billboard with Charles and the other anchors from Channel 13 near the freeway entrance. "Charles is a local celebrity. He probably could have his pick of women."

"And what's wrong with him picking you? You're pretty, talented, and smart. You can get on some nerves, but you're still a good catch."

Aja raised her eyebrows in mock disbelief. "What? Is my little brother giving me a compliment? I know it must be true then because it's not often that I get a compliment from you."

"Well, don't get used to it. Hey, this my song." Eric reached over and turned up the radio. The music was thumping in Aja's Ford Explorer. "Let me hear you say, *Unn, nah, nah, nah nah,*" Eric sang.

Aja laughed at how silly her brother looked. Silly and happy. It wasn't often that she saw that side of him. He had a wonderful sense of humor. But somewhere over the years, it had gotten lost in his misery of not making it pro.

Eric bounced to the music, still singing.

"Oh my God. How do you listen to that crap?" Aja frowned. Eric kept singing, or rapping, whatever it was he was doing. "You know, I'm going to make me a record. I'm just going to say *Ahhh* over and over. I'll probably sell millions."

Eric stopped singing and winked at his sister. "Put the right beat to it and you probably will. Let me hear you say *Unhhh,*" he playfully sang.

"You are too funny."

"When am I going to get to meet Charles?" Eric asked after the song ended. "I need to make sure he's suitable enough to court my sister."

"Oh, he's suitable all right. How about tomorrow? He's still out of town, so he won't be able to come by tonight. He'll be back in the morning. Why don't we go out to eat and have a private celebration for your entry into the pro world?"

"Yeah, that's cool." Eric leaned back in the seat and put his hands behind his head. "My entry into the pro world. I like the sound of that."

"You need to make it pro so you can take care of your big sister," Aja joked.

"From your lips to God's ears."

Sixteen

"I'm really excited about you meeting my brother." Aja was looking through her closet for something to wear to dinner. Charles was looking superb as usual in a gray sports coat, black silk shirt, and black slacks. The outfit Aja had planned on wearing seemed like such an understatement compared to what he had on.

"I'm looking forward to it. Eric deserves to celebrate. This is a rare opportunity he has." Charles watched Aja hold up another outfit, then toss it aside. He exhaled in frustration. "I really thought what you were wearing looked fine."

"Yeah, that's because you're a man. How's this?" Aja turned toward Charles and held up an emerald green sarong dress.

"Perfect. Now let's go."

"Okay, okay. Hold your horses. Give me five minutes." Aja walked toward the bathroom.

"You know, I have seen a naked woman before. You can change in front of me," Charles yelled after her.

Aja playfully rolled her eyes. She and Charles had yet to make love, even though she could tell they both wanted it. Aja often wondered if she was making the right decision, but she was adamant about waiting. That was just the point she had reached in life. It was a long way from her college days. While she was never promiscuous, she had had her share of men. After her recent hiatus from sex, though, she'd promised she was going to wait until the time was right. The good thing was Charles said he'd been down that road too and didn't mind waiting. But that didn't stop either of them from kidding around about it.

Aja stepped into the bathroom, then stuck her head back out the door. "You'll take one look at my luscious body and it'll be all over," she said. "And we do want to get to dinner on time, don't we?"

Charles laughed. "I guess you have a point."

Aja quickly changed and in no time they were on their way.

Charles pulled into the restaurant where they were meeting Elise and Eric. After parking, he and Aja walked in and began scanning the room. The maître d' came up. "Table for two?"

"We're meeting someone." Aja noticed Eric frantically waving from the corner. "There they are." Aja nodded to the maître d' and started walking toward the back. "Let's hurry, before he starts calling my name. He has no class."

Charles smiled and followed Aja to a small table in the back of the restaurant.

"Hi guys. Elise, Eric, this is Charles."

Eric stood up and extended his hand. "Good to meet you. I like your work."

Charles shook his hand. "I like yours, too. I'm a big college fan and I used to watch you at Michigan State all the time." Charles turned to Elise. "It's a pleasure to meet you."

Elise stood up and shook Charles's hand as well. "Nice to meet you, too."

Charles pulled out Aja's chair, waited for her to sit down, then sat down himself.

"So, have you been waiting long?" Aja asked.

"Only about five minutes. We thought we'd have you guys waiting," Eric responded.

"We would've been here sooner, if a certain someone didn't have to change their clothes twenty times," Charles laughed.

"Sounds just like my sister."

"Isn't that the pot calling the kettle black, Mr. Fresh-and-so-clean?" Aja said. "Even at six years old, my brother was the only kid on the block who didn't have to be forced to take a bath."

"That's because the little girls were jocking me on the playground and I had to be smooth at all times." Eric dramatically flexed his muscles, making everyone laugh.

After a few more minutes of idle conversation, Charles called for the waiter and ordered a bottle of wine.

"I'd like to propose a toast," Charles said after the waiter returned and filled everyone's glasses. "To Eric James, who—although I just met—I know will take Dallas by storm."

"I will definitely drink to that," Eric said, clinking his glass to Elise's before gulping down the wine. Eric quickly refilled his glass.

Aja fought off the urge to say something to her brother. Granted, it was only wine, but at the rate Eric was going, he'd be drunk in no time.

After watching Eric refill his glass a third time, Aja couldn't hold her tongue.

"Eric . . ."

Aja felt a sharp pain in her calf and jumped. Elise had kicked her under the table and now had a pleading expression across her face. She shook her head, her eyes urging Aja to not say anything.

Eric must have known Aja was about to start in on him. "What?" he said defensively.

Aja looked back and forth between Elise and Eric. She really didn't want to ruin Eric's night, and bitching about his drinking would do just that. Charles looked oblivious to what was going on, but then, why would he think anything was wrong? Aja hadn't told him anything about Eric's drinking.

"Um . . . I was just wondering when you leave?" Aja said.

Eric relaxed and started grinning widely. "Tomorrow. It's all happening so fast."

Elise smiled and mouthed a thank-you.

Aja was grateful when the waiter returned with their food a few minutes later. Eric had ordered a twelve-ounce steak—at least he'd have something heavy on his stomach to absorb the liquor.

"So, Charles," Eric said as he cut into his steak. "What are your intentions with my sister?"

Aja almost choked on the piece of grilled fish she'd just put in her mouth. "Eric!"

Eric held up his hand. "Chill, Sis. I need to check this man out. Just 'cause he's on TV don't mean he's on the up and up."

Aja shot her brother a menacing look before turning to Charles. "You have to excuse my brother, Charles. He can be a little overprotective."

Charles smiled. "It's okay. I like that he's looking out for my baby." Charles gently took Aja's hand. "But Eric," he continued, gazing directly at Aja. "You have nothing to worry about because she's in good hands." Charles lifted Aja's hands and kissed them. "As for my intentions, they are to spend each day making Aja happy."

"Awwww," Elise said.

Eric rolled his eyes. "I think I'm gonna be sick," he joked.

"I love you, Aja James," Charles said, still gazing at Aja. "It's slowly dawning on me just how much I love you."

Aja felt herself tearing up. Was this man actually sitting there saying this to her? What had she done to be blessed with a man like Charles?

"Charles . . ." Aja was at a loss for words.

"Shhh." Charles stroked Aja's face, then leaned in and kissed her. "Just let me make you happy."

"That is so sweet," Elise sighed. She frowned and turned toward Eric. "Why can't you tell me sweet stuff like that?"

"Dog, come on now. You making me look bad," Eric said. "Cut all that shit out. I hate I asked you anything."

Charles let go of Aja's hand and turned his attention back to the table. "Sorry, bruh. When love takes over, you can't hold it in."

Eric looked at Charles like he was crazy. "Are you for real, man?"

Aja laughed and draped her arm through Charles's. "He's for real, all right."

Eric shook his head. "Damn, she got you sprung like that?"

Charles smiled lovingly. "She does."

Elise was grinning from ear to ear. Eric dug into his steak. "You got game, man. I'll give you that."

"It's no game. This is just me."

"Whatever," Eric said, taking another bite of his steak.

Aja was on cloud nine. She didn't even feel like finishing her food she was so happy. Until the beeping from Charles's pager brought her out of her daze.

Charles reached down and pulled his pager off his waist. He glanced at the number. "If you all will excuse me, please. I've been waiting on this call from the station. I'm going to step outside. I'll be right back."

"Well?" Aja said as soon as Charles was gone.

"Well, what?" Eric asked.

Aja could barely contain her excitement. "What do you think about Charles?"

"I think I was right."

"Right about what?"

"When I said he was gay. Who the hell says corny stuff like, 'Let me make you happy?' " Eric mocked.

"Girl, ignore him," Elise interjected. "He definitely gets my vote." Aja's smile dimmed slightly. "So, Eric, you don't like him?"

Eric shrugged. "He's all right, I guess. If he's legit."

"He's legit."

"Well, if you like him, I love him." Eric turned serious. "But if he hurts you, I'm going to have to fuck him up."

Aja's worries eased and she laughed. "I wouldn't expect anything less." She felt better. For some reason, it meant a lot to her that her brother liked Charles. "By the way, I saw Jada today."

"Really, how is she?" Elise said.

Aja looked at her brother. "Maybe Eric could take you to visit her sometime."

"Aja, don't start tonight, please," Eric groaned. "The evening is going good."

Aja left it alone. That was another area in which she had to walk on eggshells with Eric. "She's fine. As a matter of fact, she's better than fine. She spoke."

Eric nearly dropped his fork. "What?"

"I said she spoke."

"Aja, that's great news!" This was the first time Eric had shown any interest in Jada. It was as if dealing with her forced him to face the past. He loved her so much when they were young. And he kept in contact with her when they were split up. But after she was committed, a huge distance started forming between them. Aja knew Eric still loved their little sister, but he got so depressed every time he was around her.

Aja lowered her head. "I guess so."

"You guess so? What does that mean?"

"I'm not too thrilled about what she said when she spoke."

"What did she say?" Eric asked.

"After years of not talking, the first word out of her mouth would be 'Daddy,' " Aja remarked snidely.

"What?"

"I said, she said 'Daddy.' Apparently, she got a letter from him and it made her happy or something."

Eric frowned. Elise, not noticing, grinned. "Wow, what did he say?" She turned to Eric before Aja could answer. "Baby, see—maybe you should read your letter."

"What, you got a letter too? Why didn't you tell me?" Aja said.

"For what? I didn't read it." Eric glared at Elise. "And I'm not going to read it, so drop it."

"I got one too. I didn't read all of mine. The part I did read, he was begging for forgiveness," Aja said.

"Who cares? Can we change the subject, please? This is supposed to be a celebration. I don't want to talk about that sorry-ass father of ours."

Aja was quiet as she played with her remaining vegetables. After a few minutes, she spoke again. "You know Eric, I've been thinking about this. He obviously said something that got through to Jada when nobody else could. Maybe Jada's nurse was right when she said we should just be happy something brought Jada out of her shell. Maybe you should read your letter." Aja was surprised to hear herself saying that.

"You know what . . ." Eric threw his napkin on his plate. "Suddenly I don't feel like celebrating anymore." He threw some money on the table. "Elise, let's go."

"Eric, stop being stubborn." Aja shot her brother an exasperated look.

"Aja, stop trying to force me to talk about that person. Damn, a man can't just have a good time no more. Elise, I said let's go." Eric turned and walked out of the restaurant. Elise shrugged, jumped up, and followed.

Charles returned to the table just as they were leaving. He looked confused. "What's going on?"

So much for not making Eric mad. Aja managed a weak smile. "Welcome to a day in the life of the James family."

Seventeen

"All right, let's go! Move your asses!" The coach's voice bellowed into the dressing room. These three days of camp were pure hell. Of course, that little bomb of a dinner had sent Eric off on his trip with a sour note and he still hadn't talked to Aja. He left town without even saying good-bye.

"I said, let's go!"

Eric thought maybe the coaches were just trying to see which of the free agents would break first. The coaches had been so hard on all of them. Plus, the head coach turned out to be an asshole, and deep down, Eric knew he was racist. The man had no idea how to talk to people. It was taking everything Eric had to keep his temper under control.

He slammed his locker shut, raced out to the court, and began running laps around the court with the rest of the players. When it was time for them to break off into practice teams, Eric felt worn out.

"James, you taking the day off?" the coach asked.

Eric was leaning against a railing. The 5-foot-8-inch coach was standing in front of him. Coach Schutten was a small man with a big attitude. He looked completely out of shape for a basketball coach. He had a huge beer belly that hung over his pants. His skin was the color of a ripe peach. His gray hair protruded from both sides of his head, and the sweat covering his bald spot glistened like raindrops on a sunny day.

"Sorry, coach. I was just a little tired." Eric bent over and rested on his knees.

"Well, you know you can always take your tired ass home. I don't want excuses! I want results!" The coach stormed off and started yelling at another wanna-be player.

Eric gritted his teeth and ran back on to the court. First, the coach had given him a hard time about his playing. He said he had wasted a spot bringing Eric here. Then, the coach got all in his shit because he was ten minutes late to practice this morning. And now, after going two rounds with the team and running three laps, Eric was exhausted. But he had to hang in there. He ran a practice exercise, running up and down the court passing the ball back and forth with another player before trying to make a lay-up.

Being back on the court again reminded Eric of his days at MSU. Back then, it was a given that Eric had a future in the NBA. He was even slated as a first-round draft pick. Twice, he led his team to the Final Four. They had never walked away with the title, but it definitely wasn't because of Eric. Both times he had played his heart out, averaging twenty-eight points and breaking school records.

The agents started taking notice Eric's sophomore year, but the solid offers didn't start coming until his senior year. It was then, just before basketball season began, that things went sour. One of his teammates, who was always giving him a hard time, made a crack about Eric's mother. Eric knew it was stupid, but he snapped. He and the guy started fighting and Eric picked up a chair and slammed it across his teammate's back. When the coaches tried to pull Eric off, he got even more crazed and kicked the boy in the face. The beating left the player with an injured spine and head concussion—and Eric blackballed. The incident made the newspapers, TV, everything. The guy pressed assault charges against Eric. The charges were later dropped with the condition that Eric take anger management classes. But by that time, Eric had been kicked off the basketball team, expelled from school, and nobody wanted to touch him with a ten-foot pole. Eric thought his star status would get him through that, but coach after coach said they couldn't deal with the negative publicity or Eric's bad temper.

"Move it! Move it!" Coach Schutten's voice echoed throughout the gym. "Parker, pass the damn ball! James, my crippled sister runs faster than your slow ass! Stop hogging the ball! This ain't no hood court and you ain't the star!"

The other players laughed. Eric had had enough. He grabbed the ball and stopped.

"What the hell are you stopping for?" Coach Schutten yelled.

Count to ten. Aja had always tried to get him to count to ten when he felt himself getting really angry. Today, Eric thought he might need to count to ten thousand to keep his temper from boiling over. He tried to remember the things his anger management counselor had taught him. The problem was, Eric hadn't paid much attention during those sessions. He didn't think he had a problem and definitely didn't feel counseling was the answer. He went only because he didn't want anything on his record. He never learned anything from the sessions. Now, Eric's mind was coming up blank as to how to keep calm. His mind was filling up with the rage that was bubbling inside him.

"I said, what the hell are you stopping for? Are you deaf?"

Eric grasped the ball tighter and glared at the coach. "Why you all up in my ass?"

Coach Schutten stomped on to the court and really got up in Eric's face. "Because I got a hundred men lining up outside for the chance you have this week and I don't think you're living up to your potential!"

"Yeah, okay." Eric turned to walk away. *One . . . two . . . three . . . four . . .*

"I've been watching you, James. I know your history. I know you could've been a first-round draft pick if it wasn't for that damn temper of yours! You could've been playing pro if you didn't decide to take some chair across a man's back because he talked about your precious little mama. That's the kind of shit seventh graders do! Beat up people because they talked about your mama." The coach was mocking Eric now, talking loud and creating a scene. "So you got a little chip on your shoulder? Well, you're going to have to get that shit under control if you ever hope to play for me!"

Eric bit down on his lower lip so hard he tasted blood. "I said, yeah, okay?" He was turning red with anger now. The other players had backed up out of the coach's path as if they could feel a storm brewing.

Coach Schutten wouldn't let up. "And I know all about your convict daddy. Is that why you're so pissed off? Well get over it! Everybody has problems and you can't bring that shit on the court!"

By this time, everyone in the gym had stopped and was staring at the confrontation on the sideline. Eric glared at the coach again, shook his head, and turned to walk off.

"Where the hell are you going?" The coach reached out and grabbed Eric by the arm.

Eric lost it. "Get your fucking hands off me! I'll kick your ass!" he screamed. Before he knew it, he had pushed the coach down to the floor and thrown the basketball at him. It hit the coach in the side of the head and bounced down the court.

Coach Schutten turned crimson red. One of the assistant coaches raced over and struggled to help him up. "Oh boy, did you just fuck up! Get the fuck out of my gym! I knew we would have problems with you! I told them you were worthless! Get out!" Coach Schutten had a wicked, crazed look. He also had a look of satisfaction, like he had expected Eric to mess up and was happy because he turned out to be right.

"Fuck you and this team!" Eric kicked over a chair and stormed out of the gym.

"Man, you're stupid," some 6-foot-9 lanky guy with braids muttered as Eric passed him. "If anybody was going to make it, you would've. You could've at least waited to sign a contract before you tried to pull a Latrell Sprewell." The guy shook his head.

Eric didn't respond. He just made his way to the locker room where he grabbed his duffel bag, opened his locker, and started stuffing his belongings into it. Five minutes later he was headed back to the hotel to get his stuff, call and change his flight, and take the next plane home.

I don't know who in the hell he thinks he is. Eric was outside the hotel, waiting on a taxi. *I don't need this shit.*

If only he could make himself believe that.

Eighteen

"Come on in." Aja stepped aside to let Charles in. She had been looking forward to this evening and planned to truly let herself go. She was going to give in to that burning desire that was telling her to stop the junior high school petting with Charles and go all the way. They had been dating for three and a half months and her feelings were flourishing fast. She had yet to return his declaration of love, but it was definitely love brewing inside her heart. And now she really wanted to consummate their relationship. The Kenny G CD was playing softly in the background. It was a cool June night, a rarity in Houston, so the windows were open. The breeze sent Aja's curtains gently flapping. The moon reflected straight into her living room. Candles were lit all around. The mood was set.

Aja had bathed in her favorite fragrance, Victoria's Secret Strawberries & Champagne. She let her hair flow freely, with a sort of wild, untamed look. She thought she looked quite sexy in her black halter top and flowing sheer black pants.

"It sure looks nice in here." Charles hung his jacket on the coat rack, then planted a kiss on Aja's cheek. "All this for me?" He flashed that gorgeous smile.

"For you." Aja shut the door, walked to the kitchen, and grabbed a tray of oysters on the half shell and a bottle of wine she had been chilling in the refrigerator. "I thought we'd start the evening with some Zinfandel and an appetizer—oysters." Aja held up the tray. *Thank God for Roxie.* Aja had enlisted Roxie's advice because she was rusty and didn't want to blow anything, and Roxie had given Aja step-by-step instructions on how to make this night special.

"Oysters? Hmmm, you know those are an aphrodisiac?"

Aja put her hand to her chest and faked a surprised look. "Are they really? Well, I'll be."

"You are so cute." Charles kissed her on the forehead and took the tray of oysters.

Cute? A two-hundred-dollar outfit, imported perfume, a seductive attitude . . . and he calls me cute.

Aja cleared her throat. "Alrighty then. I'm cute."

Charles stopped just before sliding an oyster down his throat. "Did I say cute?" He pulled Aja next to him, slowly opened her mouth with his hand, and lovingly slid the oyster in. "I meant beautiful, tantalizing . . ." He dropped the shell on the table with the tray of oysters and kissed Aja on the neck. "Enchanting, sexy . . ." Charles continued to kiss Aja's neck. She struggled to get the oyster to go down and not choke from the excitement that was running through her body. "Exhilarating, amazing . . ." Now he was kissing her exposed back and rubbing his muscular hands over her shoulders.

"Ummm . . ." Aja found herself moaning from his touch.

Charles was kissing her slowly, passionately. Just as Aja tossed her head back and let out a long sigh, he stopped.

"Aja," Charles said, turning Aja to face him. "I want you— bad. I've been trying to respect your decision to hold out—not just for you, but for me too. I wanted to make sure it was right between us, and it is. But if you're not ready, I understand. I have dreamed of this moment. I want to go to the next plateau with you, to feel inside of you, to feel your warmth explode all around me."

Aja took one look in Charles's eyes and knew he meant it. And the thing was, she wanted him inside her.

Aja stroked his face. "I want you too. I'm ready."

Charles leaned in and gave her the fiercest kiss, one that made every inch of her body feel like a volcano on the verge of eruption. His tongue then moved down her neck, across her shoulders, and once again to her back, where he gently untied her halter top. Charles cupped her breasts as he continued to kiss her back. Aja moaned with delight.

"You are so beautiful," Charles whispered. Aja threw her head back as he moved in front of her and began running his tongue over her breasts. Her nipples stood at attention. Her panties were already dripping from the moisture that had been building from the moment Charles walked in. Aja couldn't remember the last time she felt an excitement like this. She was so ready for Charles to make love to her.

Then . . . her phone rang.

Aja paused. *No, just let it ring. This feels too good.* Charles was already ignoring it and continued kissing her breasts, his hands moving inside her panties. The phone rang again just as Charles's two fingers found her wetness.

"I'd better get that."

"No, let it go." Charles nuzzled her neck.

"I can't." Aja broke away. "Just let me see who it is. It might be important." Aja couldn't believe she was doing this, but she hated just letting her phone ring. The night Jada had tried to commit suicide for the first time, Aja was at home but didn't feel like answering the phone. She didn't find out about Jada until the next day. After that, she had never been able to just let the phone ring.

"All right, get it. I'll just stand here and get undressed." Charles smiled, unbuttoned his pants, and started taking them off.

Aja raced to her phone and glanced at the Caller ID. It was Eric. "Hello?"

"Aja!"

"Eric?"

"Aja! Those motherfuckers cut me! Can you believe that?"

"Calm down, Eric. Where are you? What's going on?"

Eric just started screaming and cursing. Aja could barely understand him. She glanced over at Charles. He had stopped undressing and was standing in the middle of the room, half-naked, staring at her.

"I'm back at home. I just got in. Aja, I need you. Can you come over?" Eric was crying now. That meant it was pretty serious. Eric always played so hard and seldom displayed any emotion, let alone cried.

"Eric, where's Elise?"

"She's still out of town! She doesn't even know I'm back. I need you, Aja. Come now!" Eric slammed the phone down. Aja returned the phone to its hook and slowly turned to Charles.

"What's up?" Charles asked.

Aja was extremely shaken up. She'd seen Eric angry numerous times, but this was different. There was a desperation in his voice. "It's my brother," Aja finally said. "He got cut from the camp. He's hysterical. I gotta go." Aja glanced at Charles's rock-hard erection, then picked up her top and slipped it back over her head.

Charles appeared dumbfounded. "Aja, can't somebody else handle this? I mean, is it that serious?"

"Yes, Charles, it's that serious." Aja was flustered. Charles looked so good standing there and she had really looked forward to being with him tonight, but Eric sounded extremely upset and she couldn't stand seeing her brother upset. Aja shook her head as if to ward off any lingering doubt that she was doing the right thing. "Eric needs me. And there's nobody else to handle it." Aja grabbed her keys, slipped on her shoes, and headed to the door. She stopped and turned to face Charles. "I'm sorry. Dinner's in the oven. You can fix yourself something to eat and lock up when you leave."

Charles just stared with an I-don't-believe-she's-goin'-leave-me-standing-with-a-hard-on look.

Aja paused. "Charles, I don't expect you to understand. But that's my brother." The heat that just minutes ago had consumed her body was gone, replaced with worry and concern for Eric. Aja walked over, kissed Charles lightly on the lips, then turned and walked out. Part of her was upset about having to leave Charles, but she thought of Eric and knew she didn't have a choice.

Aja threw her car into park, taking a look at the clock on her dashboard before she shut off her engine. It was almost four in the morning and she was exhausted. As she made her way up the stairs to her condo, her mind replayed the conversation with Eric. He had been so upset. Nothing she said could get through to him. He alternated between near hysteria, deep sadness, and downright anger. Aja knew deep down her brother was upset that this had been his last chance to go pro and he had blown it.

"Eric, what am I going to do with you?" Aja sighed as she unlocked her door and walked inside. As soon as she entered the living room she noticed the melted down candle on the dining table and the two wine glasses sitting next to it. Her mind raced back to what she had left behind. Charles. She remembered how good he was making her feel, how much she wanted to make love to him. *Maybe he's still here.* Aja threw down her purse and raced to the bedroom. It was empty.

Of course you're gone. Probably for good. Aja made her way back into the kitchen and noticed the note sticking to the refrigerator with her "I love Las Vegas" magnet.

She pulled it off and read it. "Hope your brother's okay. Sleep tight. Charles." Aja crumpled the note up. "I'm so sorry. I had to go." She looked at the clock again. *Maybe I should call him.*

"Or maybe you should just let it go," Aja found herself saying. There was just one problem—she didn't want to let it go. These last few months had been wonderful. Charles had been wonderful. She had never been happier and she had never been with a man who made her feel so good. Charles was everything she ever wanted. He was the type of man women prayed for, an absolute dream come true. And as usual, she had blown it. Just like Eric. Maybe it was a family curse.

Oh Eric, why did you have to pick tonight of all nights? Aja changed into her frumpy, torn nightshirt that said "I hate mornings." She pulled the sexy black lingerie she had been planning to wear tonight off the closet hook and threw it on the floor.

"We probably wouldn't have worked anyway, so it's probably best we didn't have sex." With that, Aja crawled into her cold, lonely, queen-size bed, and fell asleep.

The sun snuck its rays through the blinds in Aja's bedroom, waking her out of a deep sleep. She still felt exhausted from Eric. She turned over and thought about going back to sleep, but then decided maybe she'd better call to check on her brother. He had fallen asleep on the sofa after ranting and raving for hours last night.

Aja pulled herself up, reached over, and picked up the phone. She dialed her brother's number. It took four rings before he finally picked up. "Hey."

"Yeah, what's up?" Eric sounded like he was still asleep.

"I just called to check on you."

"What, you wanted to make sure I didn't go back and murder my coach or something? Well I tried, but I missed the last flight back to Dallas," Eric said sarcastically.

"Don't be a smart-ass. I was just seeing how you were doing."

"Well, that's the way you were acting last night, like I was a raving maniac or something."

"That's because you were a raving maniac."

"Like I didn't have reason to be."

"Yeah, I know, li'l brother. I just wish there had been some other way you could've worked this out."

"Well, there wasn't, okay? It's over, any chances of playing pro are over, so fuck it."

"Eric . . ."

He cut her off before she could get her sentence out. "Aja, I'm not in the mood. I'll talk to you later." Eric slammed the phone down.

Aja solemnly looked at the receiver, then placed it in its cradle. *Boy, am I glad Elise is out of town because this is the last thing she needs to be dealing with.* Elise had flown home for her aunt's funeral. Hopefully, Eric would be in a better mood when she got back later today. The phone rang before Aja could finish her thoughts. *Maybe that's Eric calling back.* "Hello."

"So, did you do it?"

"I'm sorry, you must have the wrong number. Good-bye."

"Girl, don't play."

"What do you want, Roxie?" Aja wasn't really in the mood to

deal with Roxie. As much as she loved her friend, sometimes that bubbly persona drove her crazy.

"I want the 411, the lowdown, the nitty-gritty—and don't leave nothing out," Roxie chimed.

"I am not kissing and telling. We're not in college anymore."

"Oh, don't get all high and mighty on me. You know I have to live vicariously through you now that I'm married. So give me the scoop."

"I know you're happily married, so why do you always act like it's a prison sentence?"

"Why do you always try to change the subject? Now spill it!"

"Okay, okay. You ready?" Aja teased. She was trying to remain upbeat about what had happened.

"Yes, girl. It took everything in my power not to call you at five this morning, but I figured he was still there, so I made myself wait."

"Well, he came over and I had the oysters going like you said. The jazz was playing. The ambiance was set. I had the seduction in full operative mode. Then he told me I looked cute."

"Cute?"

"Yeah, that's what I said. But he quickly cleaned it up and things got hot and heavy. He undressed me and started to take off his clothes, too. It felt sooo good." Aja moaned as she thought back to the previous night.

"Ooohhh girl, go on."

Aja's smile faded. "Then Eric called. He got cut from camp and was hysterical, so I had to leave."

"Back up. What did you just say?"

"I left."

"Are you fucking kidding me? You left that fine-ass man standing in your living room half-naked to go see about your crazy-ass brother?"

"Roxie, don't go there. This was serious."

"Damn, Aja, it's always serious with you. You are not going to be happy till you're a sixty-five-year-old lonely old maid getting your thrills from a vibrator."

"Not everyone has to have a man to feel validated." Aja was getting agitated. She knew she had messed things up with Charles. She didn't need Roxie to remind her.

"Oh, tell that bullshit to one of your clients. I'm your best friend and I know better. I know you want love, to be loved. But you'll never find it always playing savior to your brother and sister."

"I don't want to have this conversation with you." Aja fought back the tears.

"You need to have it with somebody! I'm just keeping it real for you—somebody needs to!"

"Look, Roxie, I appreciate your concern, but family comes first, will always come first. And if you can't understand that, then too bad!"

"You want to be alone, Aja? Fine! I'm done! You can't help anyone who doesn't want to help themselves. I'm sorry I introduced you to Charles. I just thought for once, you'd do the right thing. I'll talk to you later." Roxie hung up the phone before Aja could even say good-bye.

What is this with people hanging up in my face? And how dare Roxie? Nobody asked her to play matchmaker in the first place.

Simba came and jumped on the bed. "Hey there, precious." Aja softly stroked her cat. "Nobody understands. I have to be there for my brother. I need to protect him, keep him from becoming my father. I'm all he has. Why can't anybody understand that?"

Simba rubbed up against Aja's stomach and purred as if to say, *I understand, Aja. I understand.*

Nineteen

"Hey, baby, what are you doing here?" Elise pulled her key out of the top lock on the door and dropped her suitcase on the floor. She turned her nose up as she took in the stale, musty odor. It smelled like fresh air hadn't circulated for weeks, even though Elise had only been gone for five days. "And why are you sitting in the dark?" She walked over to the corner and flipped a lamp on. The dark room lit up.

Eric didn't respond. All it took was one look, and Elise knew things hadn't gone well at camp.

"Baby, what's going on?" Elise sat down on the sofa next to her fiancé. He was wearing boxer shorts without a shirt. His eyes were bloodshot and stubble had started to grow on his face.

"Eric, talk to me. Why are you home? I thought the camp ran until next week." Elise leaned closer to Eric. That's when the smell hit her. "Eric, it's one in the afternoon. Are you drunk?"

"And? If I am? Don't come in here starting no shit with me."

Elise took a deep breath. It was obvious Eric was upset. She didn't want to make the situation any worse. "Sweetie, I don't want to argue with you. I just want to know what happened."

"What do you think happened, Elise? I'm home, ain't I? That

must mean I'm not at the camp. That must mean things didn't work out! It don't take a genius to figure that out!"

Elise ignored the sarcasm. "But, Eric, I thought you had a pretty good chance there?"

"Yeah, I thought so too." Eric took another sip of the drink in the glass he was holding. "But of course that was before I knew the Mavericks coach was an asshole."

"What happened?"

Eric looked like he was contemplating a response, then he laughed. "I fucked up, Elise. That's what happened," he said matter-of-factly. "But of course, that's no surprise to you. That's the story of my life, right?" Eric turned the glass up and finished his drink. He went to the bar to pour another one.

"Baby . . ." Elise stopped herself. The last thing she wanted to do was set Eric off by chastising him about drinking.

Eric poured a half-glass of scotch. He turned around and raised the glass midair. "To your man, the fuck-up, who might as well go get a job at the car wash because he'll never make it pro." Eric swallowed most of the drink in one gulp.

Elise got up and walked over to hug him. "It's okay." She wrapped her arms around his neck.

Eric grabbed her arms and flung them away. "Dammit Elise, it's not okay! It's not okay!" He walked toward the balcony, opened the door, and stepped outside. Elise followed him. She stepped up behind him and ran her hands over his smooth head.

"All I'm saying is, we'll make it. All three of us."

"Oh yeah? And how are we goin' do that? Should I go get a job at McDonald's, sell flowers on the street? Or maybe I should just ask your daddy to support us?"

"Eric, I am working." Elise was trying her best to stay calm.

"Oh yeah, my wife the rapper," he said with sarcasm. Elise loved her job, but Eric hated the fact that she worked there. She was always around rappers, wanna-be rappers, and people who had no respect for him. That was just another reason he wanted to go pro. So she could quit that job.

"Eric, you know I don't rap."

"Whatever. I'm just saying, I'm good enough to play pro ball," he snapped.

Elise sighed, then spoke like she was weighing her words carefully. "Then why aren't you playing professionally? I hate to be so callous, Eric, but we have followed your dream for a long time. You said yourself this was your last chance and now it's gone, so it's time to focus on reality."

Eric cut his eyes and frowned. He couldn't believe she had just said that to him. "You act like this is my fault. That racist coach had it out for me."

"Do you really believe that, Eric? Do you not see what part you play in all of this?" Elise put her hands on her hips and readied herself for a confrontation.

"You're treading on thin ice." Eric shook his head, trying not to get even more upset.

Elise was on a roll, though. "I'm sorry if this isn't what you want to hear. But I'm getting tired of your rants about basketball and your failure to see that you are part of the problem."

"What the hell is that supposed to mean? Just because I blew up and got into a fight with the coach, that makes me the problem?"

Elise dropped her hands. A look of astonishment crossed her face. "A fight?"

"Yeah, a fight."

"You mean an argument. You didn't actually get into a physical altercation did you? Not after what you went through at school?"

"Yeah, I did. So now I can forget about playing pro."

Elise sighed and walked back inside. Eric went to the bar to refill his glass, then plopped back down on the sofa. He sat in silence for a few minutes.

"Eric, maybe this is your wake-up call to get help," Elise finally said.

"Damn! There you go again. What are you trying to say? Since when did you get your psychology degree and think you can analyze me? Patient can't control his temper because he's his father's son."

"I didn't say that."

"Yeah, but it's what you're thinking." Eric turned the glass up, quickly swallowing his drink.

"The only thing I'm thinking is how much I'm hurting for you because I know this is what you wanted." Although she was upset, Elise was trying to soothe her fiancé. If she didn't, it would only make the situation worse.

"Well, it's a pipe dream now. And there's nothing else to talk about." Eric went back to the bar to pour himself another drink.

Twenty

After lying around the house most of the day, Aja decided to get up and go running before it got too dark. Maybe it would clear her mind of Eric, Roxie's call, and most of all, Charles. She changed into her running clothes and took off for her three-mile run.

Aja was dripping with sweat an hour later when she returned to her apartment. She had actually pushed herself to run four and a half miles. She loved the feel of the wind slamming against her face. It helped free her mind, and it reminded her of her carefree days running track in high school. As Aja climbed the stairs to her condo, her eyes made their way to an image at the top.

"Charles?"

"In the flesh. And I brought chocolate truffle cheesecake." Charles held up a Cheesecake Factory bag.

Aja walked up the stairs. "I'm surprised to see you." He didn't look mad. In fact, he looked better than ever. He was wearing a black Nike warm-up suit. Underneath the jacket was a white muscle shirt that displayed the outline of his perfectly carved pecs. Aja knew she looked a mess with her hair pulled back in a ponytail and an old top and shorts on. But Charles didn't seem to mind.

"Charles . . ." Aja was standing face-to-face with him now. She could feel the heat from his breath. "About last night . . ."

"Hey," he cut her off, "that's family. I'm not going to lie and say I wasn't disappointed, but I understand. No explanation necessary."

Aja stared at Charles. *This man is not real. God just doesn't make them like this anymore.*

"So, are we going to stand out in your hallway all evening, or are you going to invite me inside?" Charles motioned to the door.

Aja laughed. "Sorry. Let's go in." She pulled the key from the small string tied to her running shoes, unlocked the door, and went inside. "Do you want something to drink with that cheesecake?" Aja walked to the kitchen and opened the refrigerator. "Charles?" She repeated after he didn't answer her. Aja shut the refrigerator door and turned around. Charles was standing right behind her. He was still holding the bag, but he had a serious look in his eyes.

"Uh . . . I said, do you want something to drink?" Aja backed up.

"I want you."

"What?" Aja knew very well what he had said, but something in her wanted to hear it again.

"I want you, Aja James. I want to finish what we started last night." Charles leaned over and softly kissed her on the neck. Aja immediately felt herself getting hot.

She broke away. "Charles, I'm all sweaty and stuff."

He smiled devilishly. "That's okay, you were going to break out in a sweat anyway."

Aja couldn't believe she was getting a second chance. Maybe

he was just horny and needed some. At this point though, it didn't really matter.

"Can I at least take a shower?" Aja slowly backed out of the kitchen. She wanted to take him right there on the kitchen table, but she didn't want to smell tart their first time making love.

"If you must." Charles sat the bag down on the kitchen counter. "I've waited this long. I guess I can wait five more minutes. Just do me one favor?"

"What?"

"Turn off the ringer on the phone."

Aja smiled. *Gladly.* For once, if only for a few minutes, she didn't want to think of anyone or anything but Charles. "You cut it off, while I jump in the shower."

Aja pranced to the bathroom. *Was this really about to happen? Should it happen? What if Charles wasn't the man for her?* Oh, who cares. She heard Roxie's voice in the back of her head. Just screw the man already.

Aja undressed and jumped in the shower. She lathered down with the Strawberries & Champagne shower gel. She was softly humming a Natalie Cole song.

"You need some help?" Charles peeked behind the shower curtain.

"Oh, I think I can manage." Aja modestly covered her breasts and hoped her stomach wasn't poking out too much.

"No, no. I really think you need the assistance of a qualified, certified, back washer." Charles stepped around the curtain. He was completely naked. He stepped into the shower behind her. "Did you know I'm an expert in that field?"

Aja felt on fire now and the man hadn't even touched her. She slowly dropped her hands from in front of her. "Oh, are you really now? Does that mean you wash a lot of backs?"

"Nope, not very many at all. But the ones I have washed, I

wash with total care." Charles took the loofah sponge and gel from Aja. He lathered up the sponge and began slowly running it over Aja's back. She closed her eyes, inhaled the steam, and enjoyed the sensation that had overtaken her body.

Either this man is the ultimate mack daddy or he is the answer to my prayers. Either way, Aja was tired of waiting. She turned to face him. "Back's clean," she said. She kissed Charles firmly and fiercely. Aja felt his manhood rise to full attention. She was surprised at her aggressiveness. She guessed months of celibacy would do that to a person.

Charles reached behind her and cut off the water. She still had soapsuds on her, but that didn't seem to matter to either of them. He led her out of the shower and to the bed. It had been so long since Aja felt so good. Slowly, Charles began kissing her neck, her chest, and then her stomach. That's what she loved about him, he loved to take it nice and slow. Aja moaned with ecstasy.

Finally, after what seemed like an eternity, his tongue moved along her thigh and to her moistness. Aja let out a whimper. Charles's tongue teased the outside of her vagina before darting inside, sending her over the edge. Aja had been fighting it, not letting herself totally go because part of her was still unsure about the timing. But her body decided to take over when her brain didn't react fast enough. After she had one of the best orgasms of her life, Charles pulled his tongue out and eased his way on top of her. She hadn't even noticed when he had managed to slip a condom on, but it was there. So Aja just opened her legs and let her inhibitions float out the window. And as Charles took her to a peak she hadn't visited in months, Aja knew nothing had ever felt so right.

The sound of the garbage truck outside Aja's window woke her up just after eight the next morning. Instead of jumping out of bed as she normally did, she looked over at Charles snoring softly underneath the covers. He was still naked, the comforter stopping just above his waist. He lay on his stomach and his bare back heaved slightly up and down. She and Charles had made love three times during the night. She hadn't gone three times since her college days. But it was absolutely fantastic! As she watched Charles, Aja thought of how deeply in love she was falling. It was time to share her past. She knew a lot about him, but he didn't know much about her because she kept it bottled in. That's the mistake she had made with Troy.

Aja snuggled up to Charles and lightly kissed him on the back of his earlobe. His eyes fluttered open. "Hey. What's up?"

"Nothing much. How'd you sleep?"

"Pretty good." Charles rolled over, smiled, and pulled Aja over on top of him. "That sleeping potion you gave me was right on target," he said with a grin.

Aja laughed, then turned serious. "We need to talk."

"Oh Lord, not the 'we need to talk' talk," Charles joked. "Why is it women feel the urge to talk after sex?"

"This is serious." Aja stood up and walked over to her dresser. She lovingly ran her fingers over an old family portrait. It sat next to another picture of her family at the beach. In this one though, Aja was ten years old. She had long ponytails that touched her shoulders. Yellow ribbons were wrapped around each one. She was grinning widely, even though her two front teeth were missing. Aja smiled at the picture. She noticed that Charles was sitting up, staring at her intently.

"I just wanted to tell you some things about me, let you know what you're dealing with. You may want to turn and run the other way."

"I doubt that very seriously."

"You know I don't like talking about my parents too much. I told you Mom died when I was sixteen."

"Yeah, but you never went into any details." Charles wiped the last little sleep from his eyes so he could focus all his attention on Aja.

"My dad."

"Your dad?"

"He shot her," Aja stoically said.

Charles's eyes widened.

"He says it was an accident and, honestly, I believe him." Aja was determined to get the story out, so she spoke fast. "But that doesn't excuse it. They were fighting. Or shall I say, he was fighting. In the beginning, things were great. I would've sworn I had the best father in the world. Then he lost his job. And I think he lost his manhood with that. My mom had to go back to work and my dad blamed himself. Only he took it out on us. He whipped us pretty bad for little stuff. But it was Mama who bore the brunt of his anger. He started drinking and soon, they were fighting three and four times a week.

"Everybody used to always wonder why she stayed," Aja continued without looking at Charles. "But I don't think they knew the man we did. The man who was loving, caring, and a provider. I think, as bad as things got, Mama hung in there because she always hoped that man would come back. He didn't.

"The night she died, we all knew my father was out of control. We were scared to death. Jada tried to jump in. Eric tried to jump in. And me, I just stood there. I was the oldest. Jada was just a baby. Yet she tried to help and I didn't."

Aja felt her throat getting dry. "I'm sorry. I need some water." She darted out of the room before Charles could say anything. She took her time in the kitchen, grabbing a cup out of the cabinet and filling it with water from her water cooler. She gulped the water down, then slowly made her way back into her bedroom. Charles was still sitting on the bed with a sad look on his face.

"I didn't mean to depress you."

"You didn't. I just feel bad for you, that's all."

"What is it they say?" Aja feigned a smile. "'Don't weep for me.' I've come to terms with it. Those memories of being one big happy family are long gone."

"Where's your father now?"

"At Conner's. He got thirty years in prison. He's done thirteen already and I hear he may be getting out soon for good behavior. Can you believe that? My mother's life was only worth thirteen years of his."

"So that's why you don't like to talk about him."

Aja nodded.

"Have you seen him since that happened?"

"No, and I don't want to," Aja quickly responded. "As far as I'm concerned, my father died the night he killed my mother. There's nothing he can say to make me let him back into my life." She glanced at the picture again. "Absolutely nothing at all."

"Do you keep in touch with him?"

Aja shook her head. "Nope. He tries to write, but as you can tell from that little blow-up with Eric when we went to dinner, nobody's too keen on talking to him."

"I was wondering what that was all about."

"I honestly thought you were going to ask about it."

"I figured when you were ready for me to know, you'd tell me."

Aja sat down on the bed next to Charles. She laid her head on his shoulder. "Well, I'm ready. I just hope you can handle it."

Charles kissed her, stroked her hair, and then eased her onto her back. "I can." He gently held her as they both dozed back off into a blissful sleep.

When Aja woke up, Charles had already slipped out. She remembered his delicate kiss as he told her he had to get to work. Aja recalled how she had finally shared her story. She felt like a burden had been lifted. She still couldn't believe she had actually opened up to Charles. That was something she hadn't been able to do with anybody, except Roxie. Maybe she could finally have real, meaningful love. This sure felt for real.

Aja's heart raced as she thought about last night. It's not like she enjoyed kissing and telling, but she couldn't wait to tell Roxie about her night. Roxie would be as excited as she was. *I'll have to stop by there on my way back from the hospital,* Aja thought. She knew if she went by Roxie's first, she'd never make it to Memorial Greens for her weekly visit with Jada, and they were strict about their visiting hours.

"Roxie, you'll just have to wait for all the details," Aja muttered as she threw back the covers and climbed out of bed.

An hour and a half later, Aja was at Memorial Greens, standing in front of Nurse Overton. But today, Aja was determined not to let that barbarian of a woman spoil her mood.

"You can go in," Nurse Overton bellowed. Aja just smiled and sashayed past the nurse into her sister's room.

"Hi sweetie." She leaned down and kissed her sister on the head.

"A-ja," Jada said. It was a struggle to say the name, but it was more than Jada had done in years. She'd been making extreme progress. Her mental capabilities still seemed to be lacking, but she was talking and expressing emotion. She looked beautiful, in a bright cantaloupe-colored dress. Since she started improving, the light seemed to be coming back into her eyes.

"How are you today?" Aja asked.

"Present?"

Aja grinned. *So all the years of bringing presents were getting through.*

"No, no present today. But I do have something to tell you. I'm in love."

Jada just stared with a smile and a blank look on her face. Aja didn't know if her little sister understood what love was, but she wanted to share her experience anyway. "His name is Charles. He does the sports for Channel 13. And he is absolutely a dream come true."

Jada continued smiling with a perplexed look. Aja laughed and rubbed her sister's hair. "I'm sorry. You have no idea what that love is, do you?"

"Love? I love Daddy. Want to see Daddy," Jada proclaimed.

What? Where had that come from? Aja remembered the incident from last time so she tried to remain calm. She took a deep breath. "Jada, we can't talk to Daddy."

"Daddy! Daddy! Daddy wrote me. Sent me a tape," Jada announced.

"What tape? Why didn't I know anything about any tape?"

Jada jumped up, raced over to her nightstand, and pulled out the small tape recorder Eric had bought her several years ago. She pressed the play button.

Gerald's voice began. "Hi, precious. It's your daddy." Shivers ran up Aja's spine. She hadn't heard that voice in years.

"I'm sending this tape with your letter because I want you to be able to hear my voice. I miss you. Your Aunt Shirley told me you were doing real good up in that hospital. I know one day you'll get to leave there. Maybe by then I'll be out of here and you can come live with me. I may be getting out soon. I'd like that. I have so much to make up for. I'm sorry you have to be there. I love you so much. Maybe you can tell Aja to bring you to visit me sometime. Take care. Sweet dreams."

Jada pushed the stop button and looked up at her sister. "I wanna go!"

"Go where, Jada?" Aja played dumb. She was praying she didn't lose her cool. She didn't want Jada to have a setback.

"I wanna go see Daddy!"

Aja sighed. It was taking everything in her power not to get worked up. Jada probably didn't even remember what happened, which was the only reason she could possibly want to see their father. "Jada, we can't."

"Can! Can! Can! I wanna see Daddy!" Jada started pouncing up and down on her bed. The scenario reminded Aja of the temper tantrums her little sister used to throw back when she was six years old.

Damn you, Gerald. Aja saw there would be no pacifying her sister. "Okay, fine. I'll see what I can do," she lied.

"Yea!" Jada got up and started dancing around the room. "I'm going to see Daddy! I'm going to see Daddy."

Aja fought off the mixed emotions she was feeling. Even though her sister was acting like an eight-year-old, it was a welcome sight. Far more than anything she'd seen in years. Aja's mind started racing as she thought of how in the world she was going to get out of taking Jada to visit their father, because that would be the last thing she would ever do.

Twenty-one

Eric scanned the top shelf. V.S.O.P. Top-of-the-line bourbon. That's what he was looking for. He reached up, grabbed the biggest bottle, and headed for the cashier. He stopped and picked up a small bottle of Crown on his way.

"Can I come to the party?" the short, Hispanic clerk asked. She was grinning seductively. She had beautiful, hollow eyes and long, black hair that touched her waist, a gorgeous shape, and full lips that looked ripe for the picking. For a minute, Eric thought about telling her yeah. He and Elise hadn't made love in almost two months. Part of him wanted to blame it on her being eight months pregnant. But honestly, he hadn't had much interest in sex, working, or hanging out. He hadn't had much interest in anything but getting drunk. And he'd been doing his fair share of that. It helped him escape from his fucked-up life. He drank something—whiskey, bourbon, or beer—every single night. Elise had stopped nagging him about it. She just came home from work and went to their room every day. They very seldom talked and they didn't spend much time together anymore. In fact, Elise had basically decorated the baby's nursery all by herself. He couldn't even get excited about the baby. Yeah, sure, he tried to ask her some questions every now and then, but it was almost as if Elise could sense he was just going through the motions.

"You know, beautiful, I would love to invite you to the party, but this is pretty much a private celebration." Eric knew if he couldn't get excited for Elise, he sure couldn't get excited for another woman.

"That's too bad. I get off from here in an hour and I sure would like to share that bourbon with you." She ran her tongue across her lips as she put the liquor in a paper bag.

"I bet you say that to all the guys," Eric said.

"Only the good-looking ones who look like they could use some cheering up."

"Well, thanks, but I guess I'm going to have to take a rain check." He handed the clerk his money.

She took it, opened the register, and gave Eric his change. "My name's Veronica. I'm here every Friday and Saturday night if you change your mind." She smiled as she handed Eric his bag.

"It was very nice to meet you, Veronica. I'll keep your schedule in mind." Eric flashed a smile and headed out to his car. He had no intention of seeing Veronica, since he was already causing Elise major grief by the way he was acting. He definitely wasn't going to upset her by messing with another woman.

Eric popped his Macy Gray CD into the CD player, rolled his window down, and began his customary Friday night cruise around town. For the past few weeks, it had been the same thing. He'd drive around, alone and drinking. He stayed on back roads, trying to keep away from traffic, since he didn't want to get stopped and get a DUI. He always started making his way home when he felt himself getting drunk.

Tonight, a quarter of the bottle of V.S.O.P. was gone before he started feeling woozy. He didn't realize he had drunk so much. He thought about just pulling to the side and sleeping it off, but he knew Elise would hit the roof if he didn't come home. Besides, he was only about ten minutes away, and he wanted to get home to the comfort of his bed.

Eric eased onto the tollway, being careful to watch his speed. It didn't do any good. As soon as he pulled into traffic, he noticed the flashing red lights behind him.

Damn! Eric pushed the sack with the bottles in it underneath his seat, then pulled his car off to the side of the highway. He desperately, and discreetly, tried to search for a peppermint while he waited for the police officer to approach his car.

"License and registration please, sir."

Eric tried not to look at the officer with his bloodshot eyes. He reached in his glove compartment and pulled out his insurance and registration papers. He handed those and his driver's license to the policeman. "Yeah, Mr. Officer, what'd I do?" Eric was trying to talk slow so his words wouldn't be slurred.

"Well, you zipped right on that tollway without paying."

Eric glanced in his rearview mirror. He hadn't even noticed the tollbooth. He was being stopped over an eighty-cent toll. "I'm sorry, sir, I just didn't see it."

The officer leaned over and flashed his light in Eric's car. "That's a pretty big toll sign for you to miss." He turned the light directly toward Eric's eyes.

Eric squinted and raised his arms up over his eyes. "Hey man! That thing is too bright!"

The officer leaned closer and sniffed. He stood back up. "Sir, would you step out of the car, please."

"Ah, come on now. I'm tired. I just want to get home. If you're goin' write me a ticket, write me a ticket so I can go."

"I said, step out of the car, sir!"

Eric sighed deeply, then opened his car door. He stumbled as he tried to get out. He was a lot drunker than he thought.

"Sir, have you been drinking?" the officer asked.

Eric laughed. "Since I was a baby sipping on my mama's breasts."

The cop didn't find it funny. "Please turn around and place your hands on the car."

"For what? I'm just joking." Eric was swaying back and forth. He had to lean against the car to keep from falling. "Nah. I ain't had nothing—what was your question again?"

The officer pulled his radio to his mouth and muttered something about needing backup. "I'm going to ask you one more time," he told Eric. "Turn around and put your hands on the car."

"Fine. Fine. Don't Rodney King me." Eric turned around and leaned against the car. His head was throbbing. He felt like he was going to be sick.

The officer patted him down, then pulled his arms behind him, placing them in handcuffs. "You have the right to remain silent . . ."

"What the— Am I going to jail?"

"You have the right to an attorney . . ."

"Oh, I don't believe this shit."

"Anything you say can and will be held against you in a court of law."

"Damn, you know you going to make my girl real mad if you take me to jail." The cop ignored Eric, pushed him into the backseat of the cruiser, then walked around and got in the car.

"Hey! What about my car?" Eric shouted as they drove off.

"Another officer is on his way. He'll take care of your car."

Eric leaned back in the seat, contemplating whether he should call Elise or just suck it up and spend the night in jail.

★   ★   ★

Elise sat on the bench in the lobby. She had a look of disgust, frustration, and anger on her face. Eric's eyes met hers as he walked out of the back holding cells. He tried to smile. She didn't return it.

"Thank you for coming to get me." Eric leaned in and tried to kiss Elise.

Elise moved away from him and got up. "Let's go. It's seven in the morning and I'm exhausted." They walked to her car in silence. Eric's head was pounding.

"I'm sorry," Eric said as they drove back to their apartment.

"You know, Eric, I'm getting real sick of hearing how sorry you are. Do you know I had to use the money for the electric bill to pay your bail? Now what, huh? Is this the kind of life you want to bring our child into?" Elise was crying now.

Eric didn't know what to say.

"You need to get it together. I can't take this. If you're not ready to be a father, then I will accept that and raise this child by myself. But I can not, I will not, live like this!"

Eric just gazed out the window. He hated disappointing Elise. He didn't know what was wrong with him. He had just been so depressed since blowing his shot at the pros. He couldn't shake the dark cloud that constantly hung over his head.

"Maybe I should move out."

The words hit Eric like a bucket of ice water on a hot, summer day. "Move out?"

"Yeah, Eric. I can't make you want our baby or me. Maybe I should just give you time to work that stuff out in your head."

Eric shook his head. No, he wasn't about to let her leave. "Elise, I don't want you to go. I'll get it together. I don't know how, but I will."

Elise looked at him skeptically, like she wanted to believe him, but couldn't.

"I know it's a promise I've made before, but I mean it. We're a family now. I know I'm not acting like it, but I will. Just don't leave, okay."

Elise didn't answer. She kept driving in silence. Eric could tell she was on the edge, though. He knew if he didn't straighten up, it was just a matter of time before he lost his fiancée and his baby.

Twenty-two

"Perfect."

Aja wiggled her toes. She couldn't wipe the big cheesy grin off her face, she was so happy. Charles was sitting at the edge of her bed, Aja's legs propped across his lap.

"You are such a sweetheart, polishing my toenails. I didn't know you had it in you," Aja purred.

"Don't let this fool you," Charles said, holding up the bottle of Revlon Ruby Red polish. "I am a straight Mandingo warrior. I'm just doing this to get you. Once we're married, I'm just going to sit in a chair, scratch my balls, and order you around."

Married? Aja didn't want to touch that one. Luckily, the telephone rang and she didn't have to. Aja reached over and answered it, being careful not to move her legs.

"Hello." Aja paused. "Yeah, Mike, he's over here. You will never guess what this sweet man is doing. He's polish—"

Charles threw Aja to the side and dove for the phone, snatching it out of her hand. Aja started giggling as Charles shot her a mean look.

"Mike, what's up, man? Aja . . . naw . . . she said pushing. I'm pushing her sofa out the way. She's rearranging her furniture."

Aja laughed louder. "Tell him the truth."

Charles threw a pillow at Aja, then covered the mouthpiece. "Would you shut up?" he playfully hissed.

Aja smiled and leaned back.

"Naw, man. You know these women. She can't get the sofa moved . . . don't play. You know me better than that. I don't get down like that. If anything, she'd be polishing my nails."

Aja playfully rolled her eyes and smiled. She hadn't intended to tell Mike the truth, she was just messing with Charles. She knew he would just die if anyone knew he was sitting in her bedroom polishing her toenails. He didn't like people knowing how sweet he was. Maybe it was a man thing. She didn't know and didn't care.

Aja patiently waited for Charles to get off the phone, her mood mellowing. She was really feeling this man. But as she surveyed her toenails she couldn't help but wonder if he was just too good to be true.

"You know I would've had to hurt you if Mike found out what I was doing," Charles joked after he hung up the phone.

"Real men aren't afraid to admit they polish their woman's toes," Aja said.

"Don't push your luck, woman. I can't believe you were going to tell Mike that. Do you know I could have my manhood card revoked if something like that got out?"

Aja crawled up under Charles, draping her arms around his waist. "Okay, your sensitivity secret is safe with me."

Charles looked at Aja, then buried his nose in her hair. He inhaled. "I love you, Aja James."

Aja was in love with Charles, too. She knew that without a doubt. But somehow she just couldn't say the words. "So tell me, why are you so sweet?" Aja hoped Charles didn't notice that she always steered the conversation in a different direction whenever he brought up the L word.

"I told you, I haven't always been this way. I've told my share of lies, did my share of dirt," Charles responded.

"I find that hard to believe."

Charles laughed slightly. "Believe me, I'm far from perfect. Yes, I'm handsome, chiseled, and just downright dynamic, but I make mistakes." Charles's mood suddenly changed and he got a faraway look in his eyes as he continued talking. "The first real love of my life was Katrena. I lost her because I cheated on her. She caught me once, forgave me, and I cheated again. I'll never forget the pain on her face when she caught me with another woman."

Aja was intrigued. Charles didn't seem like the cheating type. "So what happened to her?"

A sad look crossed Charles's face. "She died. After she caught me with the other woman—the sad part is I don't even remember who that other woman was. Anyway, after Katrena caught me she went to visit her sister for the weekend just to get away. She was killed in a car accident on the way there."

Aja noticed the pain in Charles's eyes. It seemed like just remembering hurt him. "What a sad story."

"No, the sad part was she had written me a letter. They found it in her purse. Her family didn't know what happened between us, so they gave me the letter at her funeral, thinking it was a love letter. In the letter she had written how much she hated me, how I'd hurt her, and how she'd never forgive me. So that's how she left this earth, hating me. All over some woman who didn't mean anything to me." Charles looked genuinely hurt as he recalled the story. Aja felt her eyes watering.

"I'm sorry," she said.

"Not as sorry as I was. Anyway, that just taught me that the dog lifestyle was not for me. I swore after that, I'd treat women with honor and respect, and that's just what I've been trying to do." Charles gently ran his finger along Aja's face. "So what you see is what you get."

Aja closed her eyes and savored his touch. "I'm so lucky," she whispered.

"No, I'm the lucky one. After what I did to Katrena, I didn't know if I'd get a second chance at love. Then I met you."

Aja kissed Charles's hand. Maybe this was her second chance as well. *I just hope I don't mess it up,* she thought.

Twenty-three

Aja rubbed Eric's back. She still couldn't believe he was actually here. She'd been trying for months to convince him to visit Jada, but he would never come. Then finally, last week, he just up and called and said he wanted to come.

Aja had no doubt Eric loved Jada, but she guessed being around her reminded him of his past, and he'd been trying his best to forget it.

"Is she even going to know who I am?" There was a look of concern on Eric's face.

"I don't know. It just depends on what kind of day she's having. But I do need to warn you—she acts like a child. Even so, the doctors say that's still good."

Eric and Aja walked up to the nurse's station. Nurse Overton was the only one sitting there.

"Hello, we're here to see Jada," Aja said.

The nurse looked at Aja, then peered through her glasses at Eric. "Hello, I don't believe we've met."

"This is my brother, Eric."

"Oh, the one who never visits," the nurse sneered.

Aja wanted to tell the woman to mind her own business and

do her job, but she knew Nurse Overton could make Jada's life miserable, so she kept quiet. "May we see Jada, please?"

The nurse hesitated, then put down the chart she was reading. "One moment. I'll see if she's up to visitors." She walked down the hallway to Jada's room, peeked in, and said something. She nodded then returned to the station. "You can go in."

Aja and Eric headed toward Jada's room, the last one on the left. Eric stopped just outside the door. "Aja, I don't know if I can do this."

Aja gave her brother a reassuring look. "Come on, Jada needs to see you." She eased inside the room. "Hello. It's your sister and I brought someone with me."

Jada was lying across the bed on her stomach with her legs up in the air and crossed. She was coloring something on an oversized pad.

"Look who I have with me." Aja pulled Eric inside the room. He managed a weak smile. "It's Eric. You remember Eric, our brother?"

Jada looked up from the paper and smiled. "Hi, Eric."

"Hi." Eric slowly walked into the room. He stared at Jada for a moment, then gently sat next to her on the bed. Jada went back to drawing on her paper. Eric threw Aja a "what-now" look.

"Jada, do you remember who Eric is?" Aja asked.

Jada nodded and kept coloring. They watched her for a few minutes. She looked peaceful. Her hair was down and swept over her shoulders. Her features were still childlike, but the hollow look in her eyes was gone. She actually looked happy.

"What are you drawing?" Eric asked.

Jada stopped and handed Aja and Eric each a piece of paper.

"Daddy, Mommy, Aja, Eric, and Jada," Jada said. She pointed to two other copies spread out over the bed. "One for Daddy, one for Mommy, one for Aja, one for Eric, and one for Jada." She was proudly grinning.

The picture was a stick figure family, all of them holding hands with huge smiles on their faces. All of the pictures were the same.

Eric threw the paper down and raced out of the room.

Jada didn't seem fazed. "Daddy, Mommy, Aja, Eric, and Jada," she kept repeating.

Aja squeezed her sister's hand. "I'll be right back. I'm going to check on Eric."

"Okay. I have to make Daddy's picture now." Jada tore out a clean sheet of paper and started drawing.

Aja slipped out of the room and scanned the hall for Eric. He was standing at the end of the hallway, looking out the courtyard window. Tears were running down his face. Aja walked up behind Eric and hugged him. "How do you do this every week? How can you stand seeing her like this?" he asked.

"It's not easy, but I have to do it."

"Does she even remember what happened?"

"I know it's hard, but what we're seeing now is more than she's done in years."

"She's acting like she's six years old!"

"At least she's talking."

"But what good is it for her to be talking crazy? Talking about Mommy, Daddy . . . like we're still one big happy family."

"Maybe in her mind we are," Aja said.

"Are you going to let her live in that fantasy land?"

"Eric, of course it bothers me that she seems to have forgotten what our father did. But, she is making progress. Should I go tell her about Mom and risk a setback? I don't think so."

Eric walked over to a nearby bench and plopped down. He rested his head in his hands.

"Jada's doctor thinks it would be good for her if we just forgave him," Aja said. "They said it would help her heal."

"How am I supposed to forgive that bastard when he's the reason she's like that? Do you think she'd be in this godforsaken place if it wasn't for him?"

"There's no love lost from me as far as our father is concerned, but what are we supposed to do?"

Eric took a deep breath, wiped his face on his sleeve, then stood up. "I don't know. But, I tell you what I'm about to do. I'm about to go sit in the car. I can't deal with this shit. Seeing her like this makes me want to drive up to Conner's and strangle that motherfucker to death. She may be able to forgive and forget, but I damn sure can't!" Eric turned and stormed down the hall and out the front doors.

Twenty-four

Aja was so nervous. She was going to meet Charles's mother for the first time and she had the strangest feeling it was going to be a disaster. Charles was an only child, born when his mother was forty-six years old and after doctors told her she couldn't have any children. He was very close to his mother, so that probably meant that Mrs. Clayton thought no one was good enough for her son.

"I really need to go shopping," Aja remarked out loud as she ransacked her closet in search of something to wear. "Maybe this will work." Aja pulled out a red-and-white checkered dress from the back of the closet. It was a very conservative ankle-length dress with puffy arms. Aja had never worn it before; it was a gift last Christmas from Aunt Shirley. It was nothing she'd ever wear, but she had held on to it because it was just like Aunt Shirley to ask about it. Aja took off her bathrobe and pulled the dress over her head. She surveyed herself in the mirror. "Oh my God. This dress is horrible." Charles had told her what a classy lady his mother was and that she was still in her late seventies, so for some reason, Aja felt she should dress extremely conservatively.

"Hey, open the door!" Aja heard Charles's voice through the front door. She had been so engrossed in trying to figure out what to wear, she hadn't heard the doorbell ring. She raced to answer it.

"What took you so . . ." Charles stopped in the middle of his sentence. He cocked his head to one side as he studied the outfit. "Why are you wearing a picnic tablecloth?"

Aja looked down at her dress. "You don't like it?"

"You do?"

Aja glanced at the two poufs from which her arms extended. She looked like she was ready to take off in flight at any minute. "I guess not," she laughed. "Come on in. I was just trying to find something to impress your mother—something that wouldn't attract too much attention."

"About the only thing you'll attract in that getup is an army of ants."

Aja giggled and raced back into her room to try to find something else to wear.

"And hurry up, we're already late."

Aja stepped back in her walk-in closet, scanned the rack, and quickly settled on a black ankle-length skirt and a burgundy and black cashmere sweater set. This would just have to do. She slipped the outfit on, threw on her Dolce & Gabbana sandals, grabbed her purse, and raced out of her bedroom.

"Much better," Charles said when she stepped out. "Now let's go."

"Do you think she'll like me?" They were in the car and starting the forty-five minute drive to Galveston, where Charles's mother lived.

"And why wouldn't she?"

"Did she like your last girlfriend?"

Charles smiled without answering.

"Umm huh. What about the one before that?"

Charles chuckled, but still didn't answer.

"See, I knew it!" Aja huffed. She crossed her arms and glared out the window. "Has she ever liked any of your girlfriends?"

Charles paused. "Well, there was this girl once when I was in high school. But then, her dad was the mayor."

"Oh great. Wonderful. You know, maybe it's too soon, maybe we shouldn't do this."

"Maybe you should stop worrying. You'll be fine. My mother is a little overbearing, but nothing you can't handle."

Aja leaned her head back and pouted. She thought about playing sick and making Charles take her back home, but she decided against it. She and Charles were getting closer. She knew she was going to have to meet his mother sooner or later. Aja began mentally preparing herself for what lay ahead. For some reason, she was extremely nervous. She had never met the parents of a boyfriend before. Troy was from Trinidad. In their year together, they never made it over there for a visit.

In no time, it seemed like they were passing the "Welcome to Galveston" sign and turning in to Charles's mother's neighborhood. They parked in front of a medium-size blue and white two-story house. It looked kind of modest for someone who supposedly came from a lot of money. Charles had shared stories of how his family was well-off and came from a long line of successful businessmen. His dad was the first black congressman from Texas and owned a hotel on the beach. They had sent Charles to private school. He went to Notre Dame on a football scholarship, but they could've easily paid his way through there as well.

Charles put the car in park and gave Aja a reassuring look. "We're here."

They barely made it up the sidewalk before the front door swung open.

"Charles!" Mrs. Clayton was wearing an elegant blue lounging dress, with matching fancy blue slippers. She had a strand of pearls around her neck, pearl earrings in her ears, rings on nearly every finger, and several bracelets on each arm. Her hair was completely white and neatly combed back into a French twist. She had a few wrinkles across her face, but looking at her, you'd never know she was nearing eighty.

"Hello, Mother." Once they got to the door, Charles hugged his mother and kissed her on the cheek. "This is the woman I told you about, Aja."

"Hello, Mrs. Clayton." Aja stuck out her hand. She was trying not to let her nervousness show. "It's so nice to finally meet you."

Charles's mother carefully studied Aja before finally extending her hand. "Just call me Mother Clayton, that's what all Charles's other girlfriends did, including that pretty lawyer he was engaged to." She turned to her son. "Charles, whatever happened to her? She was such a beautiful girl."

Charles rolled his eyes in irritation. "Mother, please, don't start. You didn't even like Candace."

"She was still pretty. Well, don't just stand out there letting all my air-conditioning out. Bring your friend on in." Mrs. Clayton used a walking cane to help her get around. She wobbled on the cane back to her rocking chair in the family room. Charles and Aja followed—Aja could already tell her fears were justified.

Aja surveyed the family room. It was immaculate, filled with antique-looking furniture. There was a beige sofa and matching love seat with cherry wood trim. An armoire sat next to a small piano on the back wall. There were pictures of Charles everywhere.

His baby pictures, little league football pictures, graduation, pictures of him in his Notre Dame uniform. Two walls were covered with five-by-seven and eight-by-ten portraits and four eleven-by-fourteen photos.

"Charles, sweetheart, I've been having some trouble with that ceiling fan in my back bedroom. It keeps shaking and rattling something terrible," Mrs. Clayton said before Charles could sit down. "Can you go take a look at it?"

Aja tensed—she didn't want to be alone with this woman and she hoped Charles could sense that.

"Oh come on, Mother. I didn't come over here to do any manual labor," Charles replied.

His mom shot a disapproving look. "Okay, okay, I'm going." Charles looked at Aja, then his mother. "Be nice, please."

Mrs. Clayton nodded her head with a smirk. "Always dear." She flashed a smile. It was far from genuine.

Charles leaned over, kissed Aja, and whispered in her ear. "Be strong." He smiled and left the room.

"So, Charles tells me you're a soror?"

"Yes, ma'am." Charles had informed Aja that she and his mother pledged the same sorority, albeit decades apart.

Mrs. Clayton's eyes made their way up and down Aja. "Back in my day, sorors were selective about whom they let in. Not anymore," she snidely remarked. "Seems like they'll take anybody now."

Aja paused. *Was that an insult or was she just being paranoid?*

Mrs. Clayton didn't give her time to think about it. "And I understand you're a social worker?"

"Something like that," Aja responded. "I'm the assistant director for a program that helps troubled youth."

"Hmmm, how noble," Mrs. Clayton sneered. "I don't imagine it pays much, though?"

Aja looked taken aback. She hesitated, not knowing how to respond. "No, it doesn't. But I'm not in it for the money."

"Isn't that sweet? I guess you know Charles makes a lot of money. Not that he needs it. His father left us pretty well off, but I guess you know that too."

"No, I didn't know that. But I don't really care either." Aja was trying to keep her cool as she wondered where Mrs. Clayton was going with this conversation.

"Yeah, my baby's on TV. I watch him every day. So do a lot of other women. They see him and they think, 'oh, he'd make a good catch.' So he attracts *all types*."

"Granted, I had seen him on television before, but I didn't express interest in him first. He expressed interest in me," Aja said defensively.

"If you say so. So, darling, where are you from?"

Aja noted how Charles's mother was able to go from one conversation to another without taking a breath. "Born and raised in Houston."

"Oh? Are your parents there? What do they do?"

Aja hesitated before answering. "My mother is dead. She died when I was sixteen."

"Well, my goodness. I'm sorry to hear that. So I guess your father raised you?"

Aja was so ready to go. She felt like she was being interviewed for a job. And to make matters worse, she didn't know how much Charles had already told his mother. "My father . . . is dead too."

A sad look flickered across Mrs. Clayton's face. "You poor, poor thing." The look lasted only a minute and was quickly replaced with a proud smile. "Did Charles tell you his father was a respected congressman?"

"Yes, Mother, she knows that." Charles appeared in the doorway. "You're all fixed up. The fan is working fine. I just tightened some screws. Now could you stop asking so many questions?"

"I was just trying to get to know her better, that's all. She doesn't mind. Do you, Aria?"

"Mother, it's Aja," Charles admonished.

"Oh, I'm sorry. You know I'm getting up there in my years. Aja. I got it. What a strange name, though. You know black folks can come up with the craziest sounding names." Mrs. Clayton shot another one of her fake smiles. Aja was about to say something, but decided to be quiet. She looked at Charles to let him know she was ready to go. He didn't catch on. He sat in the recliner next to Aja.

"Mother, do you have some of your pecan pie in there?"

"Of course, baby. You know I made your favorite pie." She turned to Aja. "Did you know that is his favorite pie? Do you know how to make it? Probably not." Mrs. Clayton didn't give Aja time to answer. She kept rattling on. "You don't look like you spend too much time in the kitchen." Mother Clayton's eyes made their way down to Aja's hips. "Cooking, that is." She turned to Charles. "I'm going to go get you and your little friend a piece of pie." She pulled her walking cane to her side, heaved herself up, and wobbled into the kitchen.

"That woman is too much!" Aja hissed when she was sure Mrs. Clayton was out of earshot.

Charles laughed. "Oh come on, it's not that bad."

"Yes it is," Aja snapped. "I'm getting the fifth degree from her. She's drilling me about my background *and* she is one of the rudest people I've ever met. She is just straight-up insulting me!"

"She's very protective of me. She's just scared I'll find a beautiful woman, get married, and leave her all alone."

Aja angrily crossed her arms and leaned back. "Hmmph. She

deserves to be alone. I don't mean to be disrespectful, but she . . ." Aja stopped talking when Mrs. Clayton reappeared in the doorway.

"Here's your pie, dear." She handed Charles a huge quarter of a pie piece on a saucer. "Here's yours, dear." Mother Clayton then handed Aja what looked like a tiny corner of the pie. It didn't even fill up the little circle decoration on the saucer. "I didn't give you much because I figured you wouldn't want those thighs to spread any more than they already have."

"Okay. That's it . . ." Aja stood up ready to give the woman a piece of her mind and tell her what she could do with her funky pecan pie. Aja was usually pretty laid back, but Charles's mother was pushing her over the edge.

"Honey," Charles quickly interjected. "Did I show you the Emmy I won for best sportscaster?"

Aja glared at Charles, saw the pleading in his eyes, and slowly sat back down. "I've suddenly lost my appetite. Thanks, but no thanks for the pie."

"It's probably for the best anyway." Mrs. Clayton set the pie down on the coffee table.

Aja bit her tongue. If they didn't leave soon, she was sure to borrow some words from Roxie's vocabulary and go clean off on this woman.

"So, dear," Mother Clayton looked at Aja. "How did your parents die?"

"Mother, you've asked enough questions for one day."

"Nonsense. Ajay doesn't mind."

"Aja. My name is Aja," Aja said through gritted teeth.

"I'm sorry, dear," Mother Clayton chuckled. "I'm just having a hard time with that I guess. What was I asking again?"

"You wanted to know how my parents died?"

Charles threw Aja a "please don't" look. Aja ignored it and

calmly continued talking. "My daddy was an alcoholic. One night he was drunk and mad, and he blew my mother's brains out. That's the story of my life. Any more questions?"

Mrs. Clayton sat in her rocking chair with a shocked look across her face. Charles looked shocked, too.

"Thank you, Mrs. Clayton for the pie, and for inviting me into your home. I must say it's been an experience. Unfortunately, it's time to go." Aja reached for the keys on the coffee table, picked them up, then stood and turned to Charles. "Either you can leave with me, or I can just take your car back home and come get you when you're ready."

Charles looked dumbfounded. "No need," he managed to say. "Mother, we really must be going." He stood up as well.

Mother Clayton was still sitting, clutching her pearls, like she couldn't believe someone had finally stood up to her. Or maybe she was just shocked about Aja's revelation. At this point, Aja didn't care. She picked up her purse and headed to the door. Charles kissed his mom on the cheek. "We'll see ourselves out. I'll call you, okay, Mother?"

Mother Clayton just slowly nodded.

Charles raced out the door after Aja. She was already sitting in the passenger side of the car.

"Why would you talk to my mother that way?"

"Why would you let your mother talk to *me* that way? Not only am I no good for you and only after your money, but I'm fat as well."

Charles giggled.

"What's so funny?"

"You. I don't think I've ever seen that side of you."

Aja stared out the window. "Me neither."

"I'm sorry. I guess I should've warned you."

"Yeah, I guess you should've."

"Well, believe it or not, I think she likes you."

"I think you need your head examined."

"Okay, you're right. She doesn't like you. But so what? I do." Charles flashed his pearly whites at Aja and she couldn't help but return his smile with one of her own.

Twenty-five

"Eric!" Elise screamed at the top of her lungs as the water came gushing down her legs. "It's time! Your daughter is ready to make her entry!" Elise felt no pain. She looked down at the pool of water sitting on her bathroom floor. She had gotten up to go to the restroom, but before she could make it to the toilet, her water had broken.

Eric jumped out of the bed and raced to the bathroom. He was still groggy, but Elise's scream had jolted him up. "Did you say what I think you . . . ?" Eric stopped mid-sentence and looked at the soaked floor. "Wh-what's that?"

"Pee," Elise sarcastically said. "What do you think it is? It's my water. Now are you going to get me to the hospital or stand there gawking?" Elise knew this would happen. Eric tried to play it so cool throughout this pregnancy, but Elise knew once the real thing came he'd freak out, and he was definitely freaking out.

"It's too early, ain't it? We still got three weeks!"

"Well I guess little Madison doesn't have a calendar." Elise rubbed her stomach, recalling her excitement when they found out it was a girl. They had initially planned to wait, but Elise couldn't take the suspense. She thought about how disappointed Eric was at first when they found out it wouldn't be a boy, despite the fact that he tried to act like he was fine with it. She hoped that when he saw the little girl he'd be just as happy as she was. "I'll call the doctor. You get my stuff." She slipped out of her underwear, dropped a towel on the wet floor, then wobbled out of the bathroom.

"Oh my God! Oh my God! I hope nothing's wrong!" Eric raced around the room in a daze. He completely forgot the disappointment he had been feeling since returning from Dallas. He had been in a funk for the last four months and he and Elise argued constantly. He still hadn't found a job, but actually hadn't been looking too hard. He applied to a couple of places, but for the most part, he just sat at home depressed. "Are you okay?"

"I'm okay. The baby's okay. But I really think we should be going."

"All right . . . Where are my keys? Where's your night kit? Should we call the hospital?" Eric frantically paced back and forth.

"First, *we* should calm down. I think my contractions are far enough apart that we don't have to break every speed limit getting to the hospital. I just think we should go." Elise made her way into the front room and leaned against a wall.

Eric followed her out of the bedroom. "Contractions? When did you start having contractions?"

"Yesterday morning. I didn't say anything because of your mood. Plus, I just thought they were false labor pains."

Eric shot his fiancée a chastising look. "Okay, baby. Okay." He swung open the closet door, grabbed Elise's suitcase, picked his keys up off the dresser, and slipped on a pair of shoes. "Let's go." Eric darted out the front door and let it slam with Elise still standing in the living room.

"Hel-lo! Aren't you forgetting something?" Elise called out.

Eric opened the door again. "Sorry. Come on."

Elise laughed. "Leave it to me to have a made-for-the-movies delivery. Do you think you're calm enough to dri— *Ahhhhh!*" Elise kneeled over and screamed.

"Oh shit! What?"

"Owww," Elise moaned. "That one hurt. Come on!"

It took all of eleven minutes to get to the hospital. Elise screamed only one other time, but Eric wasn't taking any chances. He raced into the emergency room. They had already filled out the paperwork, so they were able to go straight upstairs to a labor and birthing room.

While the doctors prepped Elise, Eric ran to a phone and called Aja at home.

"Aja!" he screamed when his sister picked up. "We're at St. Anthony hospital. Elise is about to have the baby!" He slammed the phone down and raced back to be by his girlfriend's side.

"Isn't she adorable?" Aja and Charles stared at the tiny little girl swaddled tightly in a hospital blanket. Even though Elise had a private room, the baby was in the nursery with five other new-borns. "She's gotta be the cutest one in here," Aja swooned.

"She is, even though I think you're a little biased," Charles said.

Elise's labor had gone so fast, there was no time for any drugs. She had come through like a trooper and little Madison Simone James made her debut at 3:37 A.M. Eric was the one who had the hard time. You'd think he was giving birth. He huffed, puffed, screamed, and shouted with Elise and nearly fainted when the baby came out.

"Hey, y'all checking out my little girl?"

Aja and Charles turned around. Eric looked relaxed and happy, and he now stood looking like a proud papa.

"Yeah, and she is absolutely beautiful." Aja glanced back at her niece. "She reminds me of Jada."

"I think so too," Eric said. The nurse picked up Madison and held her to the window. The infant's eyes were tightly closed; the corners of her mouth were slightly turned upward, forming a smile.

"Look, she's smiling at me already."

"That's called hiving, silly. She's just hiving, not smiling," Aja responded.

Eric cut his eyes at his sister, throwing her a mean look.

"Okay, okay, she's smiling because she knows her daddy is standing right here," Aja laughed.

"That's right." Eric tapped the window. The infant opened her eyes wide, stretched out, then curled back up and went to sleep. The nurse placed her back in the bassinet.

Eric continued staring at his daughter. "Yeah, she's smiling because she knows just how much her daddy loves her and wouldn't trade her for all the boys in the world."

Part Two

Twenty-six

"Grab her bottle out of the refrigerator. You can heat it in the bottle warmer. I'll go change her," Aja yelled to Charles as she carried a wailing Madison into the bedroom.

This was Aja's first time keeping the baby. Madison was only six weeks old, but the baby had been wearing Eric and Elise out. Aja had offered to baby-sit at her place while they went out for some time to themselves.

Aja changed the baby's soaked diaper. She struggled with the tabs, which kept getting stuck to Madison's skin. Finally, she got the diaper on the baby. "There you go . . . nice and dry." Aja picked the baby up, patted her bottom, and sat on the edge of the bed. Madison kept crying.

"Here. Here's her bottle." Charles handed Aja the four-ounce bottle of formula. Aja popped it in Madison's mouth and the crying ceased.

Aja and Charles looked at each other and sighed. "No wonder Eric and Elise are going crazy," Aja joked.

Madison sucked ferociously on the bottle as Charles caressed her head. "I don't know. I think it's kind of cute."

"That's because you only have her for one night. You know

you can give her back." Aja rocked the baby back and forth. It wasn't long before the infant was off to sleep.

"Let me lay her down," Aja said. "She's out like a light and I don't want to chance waking her up." Aja eased the bottle out of Madison's mouth, pulled back the covers on her bed, moved the pillows, and lay the baby down on her back. She leaned over and kissed her on the forehead. "There, maybe she'll sleep for a while."

Charles grabbed Aja's hand and pulled her to him. "Maybe she'll sleep long enough for us to go in the other room and make one of our own."

Aja playfully jerked her hand away. "Yeah right. Come on, let's go finish the movie." They were watching one of her favorite movies of all times, *Imitation of Life*.

Charles gently pulled her toward him again. "I'm serious, Aja."

Aja stopped and looked at him. They were officially a couple now. After the visit to his mother, they had agreed to date each other exclusively. They had been doing this anyway, but they just made it official by putting a title on it. "You are crazy, Charles, that's what you are."

"Okay, maybe I'm not serious about the baby—yet, anyway. But I am serious about us. Aja, I want a family, a wife, two point three kids, a dog named Rover—the works. I'm thirty-four and tired of coming home to an empty bed."

"Buy a dog," Aja joked.

"I'm serious, Aja. I'm ready for happily ever after. I want all that with you."

Aja pulled herself away again and walked downstairs to the living room. She sat down on the sofa, grabbed the remote, and turned the TV off.

"Whew, Charles. I don't know what to say."

Charles sat down next to Aja and took her hands. "You can't say you didn't know I felt this way. We both love each other and we're both not getting any younger. I know we've only been together a short time, but I'm old enough to know that when something feels right, it's right."

Aja looked away. "Charles, being around the baby . . . it's just got you in a family mood."

"Come on, Aja, you know me better than that. I'm talking about us, our future. I think I'm a pretty good catch, too." Charles stroked his chin.

"Your modesty kills me," Aja laughed.

"Seriously, I'm just saying I'm good for you and you're good for me. This isn't an official proposal or anything, I just want to know where your head is."

Aja got up and walked to the window. The wind was slamming against the building, creating a hollow sound. It reminded Aja of summers in Chicago. Her father used to take the whole family there to visit his parents. How she loved those times. But those memories were quickly fading.

"Why'd you get quiet?" Charles slipped up behind Aja and wrapped his arms around her waist. Aja was silent. *What is wrong with me?* Most women would kill for a man like Charles. So why wasn't she jumping at the prospect of marriage?

Aja thought of her mom and the stories she used to tell about how perfect her father was. They'd met when she was a student at Howard University. Her father was in the army and stationed near the university. He was, as Aja's mother often said, "every girl's dream." So how did he turn into her mother's worst nightmare? And what if the same thing happened with Charles? He could be a little cocky at times, but other than that, he was almost perfect. Too perfect. What if he turned out to be like her father? It was a possibility Aja couldn't bear to even consider.

"Charles, I can't do this. I'm not ready." Aja wriggled out of his grasp and walked away. "There's no such thing as happily ever after."

Charles lowered his head in frustration. "So, Aja, what are you ready for?"

"I don't know." Aja didn't want to tell Charles about her fear of having her own marriage turn out to be like her parents'. "I got too much going on. There's Jada . . . and Eric."

"What about you?"

"Look, don't push it!" Aja raised her voice. "I'm just not ready, okay!"

"So what am I, Aja? Just somebody for you to fuck?" Charles was always a master at staying calm, but he was starting to get really angry.

"Now you sound like the woman."

"What the hell is that supposed to mean?"

Aja paused. "Just forget it, Charles. Let's just not even go there. We got a good thing going. Why can't we just keep it like it is? I can't leave my sister and Eric to run off and play house. Besides, Eric and Elise are having major problems."

"Nobody is asking you to leave your sister! And Eric and Elise are grown."

Aja didn't know how to handle this conversation. She loved Charles so much and would've loved to share a future with him. But something inside her kept telling her it wouldn't work. "I said leave it alone! Why can't we just kick it for now? Forget about the future, okay? At least until I get things straight with my brother. Until then, I can't focus my attention anywhere else!"

Charles backed up and raised his hands midair. "You don't have to beat me over the head. I'll be damned if I beg somebody to be with me. But see, I'm through 'kicking it.' That's not what

I'm trying to do. So, since I'm sounding so much like the woman, let me add this—maybe we are going in the wrong direction." Charles walked over to the sofa and picked up his shoes, which were sitting on the floor.

"Why does it have to be like that, Charles?"

Charles shot Aja an exasperated look as he slid his feet into his loafers. "You make it like that, Aja. I don't understand you. I have been patient, understanding, everything. I'm starting to feel like I'm wasting my time with you."

"Well, if that's the way you feel, then maybe you are wasting your time."

Charles glared at Aja. "I am so tempted to say forget this . . . this . . . whatever the hell we got going. There are plenty of women out there who would love to have a good man. Women who aren't in a dysfunctional situation."

"Oh, so now I'm dysfunctional? Fine! Maybe we're both wasting our time! So why don't we just forget about it?" Aja took a deep breath and rubbed her head. She couldn't stand fighting. "I can't deal with this." Aja turned to walk away.

Charles grabbed her by the arm and pulled her back. "Don't walk away from me!" he shouted.

Aja felt Charles's grip tighten around her arm as he jerked her back toward him. She flashed back to the fights her parents used to have. Her mother never fought back, but Aja had always vowed if she were ever in that predicament, she'd fight to the finish. And here she was, being manhandled by someone who claimed he loved her. Charles shook Aja's arm. "We need to finish this!"

Aja saw his lips moving, but she couldn't make out anything he was saying. All she felt was his grip on her arm. "GET YOUR HANDS OFF OF ME!" she suddenly screamed. Before she knew it, Aja started swinging. Her arms frantically swung from side to side like an eleven-year-old caught in a fifth grade fight. "DON'T YOU EVER PUT YOUR HANDS ON ME! EVER! EVER!" Aja was out of control. She clawed at Charles, barely missing his face and leaving scratches across his neck. Charles was caught off guard. He jumped back and tried to reach out to restrain Aja, but each movement made her even more hysterical. It's like she had become possessed.

"What the hell is wrong with you?" Charles yelled as loud as he could. He finally grabbed Aja just as she reached out to scratch his face. He put her in a fierce front hug. "Aja! Aja! Calm down! You know I would never hurt you!"

Aja continued to go ballistic. She broke free. "GET OUT! GET OUT!" She backed up to the living room window, grabbed a vase full of fresh flowers that was sitting on a table underneath the window. Aja threw the vase—still full of flowers and water—full force at Charles's head. "GO! GET OUT! DON'T EVER PUT YOUR HANDS ON ME!" The vase crashed into the wall just beside Charles's head. It shattered into little pieces, sending broken ceramic flying across the room. Charles stared in disbelief. He saw there was no getting through to Aja in this state.

Aja slid to the floor, sobbing and muttering. "Get out, get out, get out. Don't ever touch me. Don't put your hands on me!"

Charles was in a daze himself. It's like Aja wasn't even talking to him. Yet there was no mistaking that was his head she had just tried to smash. The whole thing caught him by surprise. He had never so much as gotten angry with her before, let alone put his hands on her. So why would she go so crazy? One thing was for sure, now wasn't the time to figure out the answer to that question. Charles grabbed his jacket and keys and headed to the door. Before he opened it, he stopped and turned to Aja. "Your brother isn't the only one who's crazy. You need some help." Charles let the door slam behind him.

Aja was still sitting on the floor crying when Roxie showed up at her door an hour later. "Knock, knock." Roxie softly eased the front door open. She walked in the living room and looked around. "Aja?"

"Yeah?" Aja whimpered. She tried to ease herself up off the floor. Her eyes were red and puffy. The clamp that had been holding her ponytail in place dangled loosely from a couple strands of hair.

"Damn, girl. Charles called me. What's going on? Tell me he was exaggerating and you did not freak out on him?"

Aja's mind raced back and played out the scenario that had just unfolded in her living room. Her eyes went to the shattered vase laying on the floor near the front wall. Then she remembered the baby. "Madison . . . I need to check on Madison." Aja raced up the stairs to her bedroom and peeked in, on Madison who was still sound asleep. Aja couldn't believe the baby had slept through that entire ruckus. "Maybe it wasn't as bad as I thought," Aja said out loud.

"Yeah, it really was." Roxie had followed Aja upstairs. She stood in the hallway with her arms crossed, a scowl across her face. "You are forever fucking some shit up."

"Don't start, Roxie, okay?" Aja brushed past her friend and went back downstairs. Her head was pounding and she didn't feel like going at it with Roxie.

"Oh no, I'm just getting started." Roxie followed closely behind. "I go out and get you the best catch in town and you act a fool. Do you know how many women would die to have a fine, educated, loving man like that wanting to be with them?"

Aja ignored her friend, walked into the kitchen, and looked in the refrigerator for something to drink. Her silence didn't matter to Roxie. "That man really and truly liked you. No, let me correct that, he loved you. Notice I use past tense because who the hell knows what he feels right now!"

Aja pulled out a container of yogurt, popped the top, grabbed a spoon, and started digging in. She shot Roxie an "I-wish-you-would-shut-up" look.

"He called me, upset. Not just because you freaked out. But because he was actually worried about your crazy ass."

Aja stopped eating and stared at Roxie. "He grabbed me."

"Grabbed you how? Violently by the hair? Did he bust you in your eye? Smack you upside your head? Did he call you a bitch? He said he just grabbed your arm to keep you from running out!"

Aja sat down at the kitchen table and continued eating her yogurt. She didn't want to argue with Roxie. She couldn't explain what had come over her. She hadn't had a physical altercation with anyone since junior high school, let alone somebody she supposedly loved.

"You know what I think?"

"No, but I'm sure you're going to tell me."

"I think your daddy flashed before your eyes. That's what I think. That's why you need to do like Charles said—like I've *been* saying—and get some help. You are always bitching at your brother, but you have got issues your damn self."

"Roxie, I'm tired and I need to go feed Madison. So if you don't mind."

"Actually, I do mind. But I have to go pick up Brendan anyway. I left him with my sister and her bad-ass kids liable to have my son strung up by his ears.

"You think about what I said, okay?" Roxie continued. "Can you salvage this relationship with Charles? I don't know. But before you even think about trying to work things out with him, you need to work that shit out in your head." Roxie leaned over and hugged her friend. "Just remember, though, I'm always here for you, crazy ass and all. Now get some rest."

Twenty-seven

Fourteen-year-old Renee Davenport rattled on about how nobody liked her and how she didn't have any friends. She blamed it on being overweight, the fat kid in school, as she said. Aja looked like she was listening intently, but in actuality her mind wasn't there. She was still thinking about how she had acted with Charles. It had been a week now and she hadn't talked to him. She was devastated. And she was still trying to figure out where that rage had come from.

At first she had tried to justify the situation by saying he was about to hit her. But Aja knew Charles wasn't going to hit her.

"Sometimes I think if I put a bullet in all of their heads, they'll stop teasing me."

Aja was jolted out of her thoughts. "What? What did you say?"

"I said, maybe if I shoot them, they'd leave me alone."

"Whoa. Hold on." *Snap out of it.* Aja knew she had to give Renee her complete attention. She couldn't—she had too much on her mind. "Renee, maybe I should let you talk with another counselor. We have a wonderful woman who is trained in cases like this." Aja picked up her phone and dialed Emily's extension.

"Hi, Em. Is Sandy busy right now? . . . Great. I have someone here who really needs to talk to her. Aja smiled at Renee. "I'll send her down." Aja placed the phone back on the receiver. "You know where Mrs. Logan's office is, down the hall?"

Renee nodded.

"Good, Sandy's just the person you need to talk to. She's waiting on you now."

Renee pushed her chair back, got up, and headed to the door. She stopped and turned back to Aja. "But I like talking to you."

Aja smiled reassuringly. "When you're done with her, you can come on back and see me if you still need to talk. Deal?"

Renee nodded reluctantly and left the office. Aja took a deep breath. She never pushed her clients off on anyone else, but today her heart just wasn't in it. She wasn't in the right state of mind to be dealing with somebody else's problems, especially problems of the magnitude Renee had.

Aja thought about picking up the phone and calling Charles. She really wanted to apologize, but she didn't know what to say. *I'm sorry I'm a lunatic?* That didn't sound right. Then part of her was also still mad that he called her crazy. *Maybe you are, though.*

It was three o'clock. Three hours before Charles went on the air. Aja considered going to the television station and asking to see him. *But what if he refuses to come up?* She decided to take that chance. Aja scooted her chair back from her desk, grabbed her car keys, and let the secretary know she'd be back shortly.

Aja made record time getting to Channel 13. She was anxious to see Charles. She parked in front of the station and walked into the beautifully decorated lobby. Charles's eight-by-ten picture hung on the wall, next to the other on-air personalities. He looked so handsome. The receptionist looked up just as Aja walked in.

"Hi, may I help you?"

"Yes, I'm . . . I'm . . . here to see Charles Clayton."

"Do you have an appointment?"

Aja clutched her purse tightly. *Maybe I should just go. I haven't given her my name, so Charles would never have to know I was even here. No, I'm going to go through with this.* "No, I don't."

"May I ask what this is in regard to?" The receptionist eyed Aja suspiciously.

Aja felt herself getting a little irritated at the barrage of questions, but Charles had told her how protective the front office people were. They had to be because all kinds of wackos tried to come see the television personalities.

"Can you just let him know Aja James is here to see him?"

The receptionist looked at Aja like she was a psycho fan trying to worm her way into the station. "Fine. I'll see if he's available." She picked up the phone and called Charles's line. Aja heard the receptionist whisper that he had a visitor, then she gave him her name. When she paused, Aja was worried that Charles wasn't going to come up.

The receptionist hung up the phone. "He'll be right here." Aja nodded, then went and sat down.

Charles took his time coming up front. Aja didn't know if it was on purpose or if he actually was busy. He smiled at the receptionist as he walked through the glass doors and into the lobby.

"Hi," he said dryly when he approached Aja.

"Hello. I'm sorry to just drop by, but I had to see you. Can I talk to you for just a minute?"

Charles looked like he was considering it. "This really isn't a good time, Aja. I don't want to do this here at my job."

"Please? Maybe we can step outside. It'll only take a minute."

Charles sighed. "All right." He followed Aja outside. They walked over and stood by her truck. "I'm listening."

"I just wanted to say I'm sorry."

"Okay, apology noted," Charles coldly responded.

"Look, I don't know why I lost it. I don't know what happened. All I know is I'm sorry. I don't know if I flashed back, saw my dad, or what."

"You know, Aja, I can believe that. And I actually think that was the case. But I'm tired of you using what happened to you and your family as a crutch. That's what I'm talking about when I talk about getting over the past. If every little argument makes you think I'm going to turn into a woman beater, then we've got a problem."

"Charles, I know you wouldn't hurt me," Aja softly said.

"I can't tell. Not by the way you threw a vase and tried to smash my head in."

"I'm sorry about that."

"Yeah, you're sorry. Again, apology noted." Charles looked off. Aja could tell he was still angry, but she could also see he was softening a little.

"What about apology accepted?" She wanted his forgiveness more than anything.

Charles was silent.

"What can I do to get you to forgive me?"

"The same thing you're always telling your brother to do: Get some help, see a counselor or psychiatrist."

"Okay, I will." Aja had never thought about getting professional help, even though she was always pushing her brother to do it. But after that episode with Charles, she was beginning to think maybe they both needed help facing their demons. She promised herself she would make some calls as soon as she got back to the office. Maybe she could make appointments for her and Eric.

"Look, I have to get back to work."

Aja reached out and touched his arm. "So am I forgiven?"

She got nervous as she noticed Charles was about to protest. "Yes," he sighed. "But if you ever try to kill me again, I'm leaving for good."

"I didn't try to kill you."

"Well, that's what I call it." Charles stroked his face. "This is my livelihood, you can't mess with that."

Aja leaned forward and kissed Charles's chin. "You don't ever have to worry about that happening again. I promise."

She felt like a giant weight had been lifted from her shoulders.

Twenty-eight

This shit is for the birds. Eric angrily stacked the videos back on the shelf. He stopped when he came across a movie called *Love and Basketball,* staring Omar Epps and Sanaa Lathan. He hadn't seen the movie, but looking at Omar on the box cover reminded him of where he could've been, versus where he actually was.

Eric threw the video on the shelf and walked back up to the front. The line was getting long, but he definitely wasn't trying to get Employee of the Month, so he took his time getting to his register. He still couldn't believe he was working at Blockbuster. All he could think of was how he was only making seven dollars and fifty cents an hour. He had thought that by this point in his life, he'd be making at least six figures playing professional basketball, but instead he was stuck in a video store, on a Friday night at that. The fact that they had placed "Assistant Manager" under his name did nothing to make him feel better.

"I can help the next person in line."

"Well, I'll be damned. If it isn't Mr. 'I'm-So-Bored' himself."

Eric looked at the woman standing in front of his counter. He was trying to figure out who she was.

"Oh, so now you don't remember me? Well, I'm sure you got

too many videos logged up in that head of yours to remember. I'm Cheryl, from Club Maxwell's."

Oh damn!

"So how's life been treating you?" Cheryl continued. "I understand your friend Bobby has been keeping in touch with Marcena." Cheryl smiled broadly. Eric knew it was definitely Cheryl then; the gap between her two front teeth confirmed it.

Bobby had actually told Eric about his dates with Marcena. He said he couldn't stand the girl because she was as dumb as a "tick," but he was determined to have sex with her, so he was hanging in there. Surprisingly, Bobby was actually seeing more and more of Shante, the girl who took him home that night.

"Yeah, I remember you." Eric wasn't interested in conversation. "Do you have your rental card?"

Cheryl reached in her purse and pulled out her card. "The way y'all were high-profiling in the club, I would've thought you were a big baller, not a block buster." Cheryl laughed as she handed him her card.

Eric was just about to say something mean when a tall, muscular man walked up next to her.

"Hey, baby. They're out of *The Hurricane.*" The man wrapped his arm around Cheryl's waist. "So I just got this one." He held up a copy of *Frequency.*

Cheryl took the movie and placed it on the counter. "That's fine, baby. We're gonna get this one too." She pushed the videos toward Eric with a big smile on her face. "Oh, by the way, Eric, this is Bruce. Bruce, Eric." She turned toward Bruce. "Eric is a friend of the guy Marcena's going out with."

Eric was so ready to get them rung up and out of the store. "Your total is nine dollars and thirty-two cents."

"Bruce, sweetie, are you gonna pay for the movies with your gold or platinum card?" Cheryl threw her long ponytail back and smiled at Eric. Eric silently wished her hair would fall off as she swished the fake thing all over the place.

"I guess I'll just pay cash." Bruce pulled his wallet out.

Cheryl leaned in, "I hope you can change a hundred."

Eric eyed her with disgust. He couldn't believe this guy couldn't see straight through her.

"I think I have a twenty," Bruce said.

Cheryl giggled. "He never carries anything less than a hundred. We're always having trouble getting stuff cashed." She leaned over and kissed him viciously on the lips, then turned back to Eric. "By the way, if you're ever in need of legal counsel, Bruce is a top-notch attorney."

Eric changed the twenty-dollar bill. "Anything else?"

"No, that'll be all. You know, I don't know how you work here. This job would bore me to death." Cheryl smirked and then grabbed Bruce's keys out of his pocket. She held them up, making sure she let the Mercedes emblem show. "We'll be seeing you. Don't work too hard." Cheryl laughed and sashayed out the door with her arm still entwined with Bruce.

"I don't believe this shit," Eric muttered once they got out the door. He couldn't believe his luck. Out of all the people in the world, why would she have to come to his register?

Another customer stepped to the counter. "I'm closed." Eric put up the closed sign and walked away, leaving the customer standing at his counter with a confused look. The other cashier gave Eric an angry look, but he couldn't have cared less. It was bad enough that he had to work at this dead-end job, but then he had to be humiliated by that two-bit gold digger. Eric went to the back, clocked out, and walked toward the front of the store.

"Where are you going?" the other cashier asked.

"I'm outta here. Have them mail my last check." Eric didn't look back as he walked outside to his car.

He took the long way home, contemplating how he was going to tell Elise he had just quit this job. He only took it in the first place because he needed to do something now that they had a child. But tonight was too much.

Eric pulled his truck into a Conoco gas station. He ran in, bought a six-pack of Lowenbrau, and continued his drive around the city.

By his fifth beer, Eric figured it was about time for him to head home. He didn't feel drunk, but the last thing he needed was to get another DUI. He'd yet to go to court for that first one, and Elise would totally lose it if she had to come bail him out of jail again. Besides, it was just after midnight, the time he'd normally be getting home anyway. He prayed that Elise was already asleep. He wasn't in the mood to talk to her.

Eric gently pushed the door open and peeked inside. Elise was asleep on the sofa. He tried to slip past her without waking her up, but the door squeaked as he closed it.

Elise sleepily sat up. "Hey . . . how was work?"

"Fine," Eric grunted as he made his way up the stairs.

"What's wrong?" Elise threw back the afghan and followed him up. "You look like something's wrong."

"Nothing's wrong, aw'ight."

"Eric, I know you well enough to know when something's bothering you."

"Where's the baby?"

"In her room, asleep. Now answer my question."

"Damn, Elise. Why are you always nagging?"

"I just want to know what's wrong, that's all. I can tell something's wrong."

"I quit, okay. I quit that funky-ass job."

Elise was silent.

"What? What do you have to say?"

"Nothing, Eric." Elise shook her head. "I'm going to check on Madison, then I'm going to bed." She turned and walked out of the bedroom.

She was only gone for a few minutes, but when she returned she didn't say anything, just quietly began changing into her nightgown.

"So, you worried now?" Eric asked. "Don't worry, I'm goin' to find something else, okay?"

"I'm not worried. About the job anyway." Elise walked to the bathroom and threw her sweatpants and T-shirt in the dirty clothes hamper. She had a solemn look as she walked back into the bedroom.

"So what are you worried about then?"

"You. What will it take to make you happy again?" Elise climbed under the covers. Eric didn't answer immediately. He thought about her question while he undressed. After he had taken off his clothes, Eric climbed in the bed next to her.

"What will it take, Eric?" Elise asked again and snuggled up close to him. Having her next to him like that made his anger ease up some. He had expected her to throw a fit, but it was just like Elise to be more concerned about his well-being.

"I wish I knew the answer to that question, Elise. I'm trying to find it though, I really am."

Twenty-nine

Aja was getting pissed.

Why would he schedule a date with me, then take his sweet time getting here? Although he was still a little upset with her, Aja thought Charles had forgiven her. He'd even had his secretary call to ask her to meet him for a drink after work. It had been four days since she apologized and Aja thought he was truly over it. But they hadn't really talked much or even seen each other since that day at his job. Maybe this was his way to show her he was still mad.

The flamboyant, openly gay bartender walked over to Aja. "Hey honey-pie, can I get you anything? You look like you could use a sex-on-the-beach." The bartender put his hand to his chest and chuckled.

"No thanks."

"Well, just whistle if you want me." The bartender strutted back to the other end of the counter.

Aja looked at the large clock that sat over the bar. It was five after eight. The sports secretary from Charles's station called her this morning and said Charles wanted to meet her at seven. Now he was more than an hour late.

"I'll give him ten more minutes."

"That won't be necessary."

Aja turned around to face one of the most beautiful women she had ever seen. The woman looked like a model. She was about 5 foot 10 with a thin build and jet-black hair that hung past her shoulders. Her light-brown complexion was smooth and her makeup looked like it had been applied professionally. It looked like she had just stepped off the cover of a magazine.

Aja caught herself from giving the woman the once-over. "Excuse me, were you talking to me?" *Why does this woman look familiar?*

"As a matter of fact I was." The woman sat down on a stool next to Aja. "I said that won't be necessary. Charles isn't coming."

Aja stared at the woman, trying to figure out where she knew her from.

"I'm Candace Hamilton." She held out her hand.

Then it hit Aja. Candace Hamilton, Charles's super-successful ex-fiancée. She was an entertainment lawyer whose clients ranged from Brian McKnight to Warren Moon. *Why was she here?* Panic started to set in as Aja could feel something was wrong.

Candace pulled her hand back after Aja failed to shake it. "First, let me apologize for the little 'sports secretary setting up a date' thing. But I didn't know how else to get you to meet me." Candace didn't give her time to speak. "I feel really awful about this, but I don't know what else to do. I know you and Charles had been seeing each other for some time now, but . . ."

Had? Aja cut her off. "Wait. I don't think I like where this is heading. Maybe you need to take this up with Charles." Aja got up to leave.

"Don't go, please." Candace touched her arm. "Just hear me out."

Aja stood there for a minute. Of course she wanted to know what the hell this woman was talking about. At least she thought she did, anyway. Curiosity won out. Aja sat back down.

"Thank you." Candace paused to flag down the bartender. "You want anything?" she asked Aja.

"No thanks. I just want you to get to the point."

"Can I get a martini?" Candace asked the bartender. She turned to Aja. "And a rum and Coke for her. I think you may need a drink."

Okay, this definitely is not good.

"I'll get straight to the point." Candace swung around on her bar stool and crossed her long, sultry legs. "As you know, Charles and I were engaged . . ."

"And? That was almost two years ago."

"And," Candace continued, "we were inseparable until I got too wrapped up in my work and started neglecting him. To make a long story short, as much as we loved each other, we went our separate ways."

"Could you tell me something I don't know, please?" Aja was getting agitated. "You didn't lie to get me here to rehash your history with Charles."

"Okay, okay." Candace took a sip of the drink the bartender had set next to her. She handed Aja the other drink. Aja reluctantly took a swallow.

"As I said, Charles and I were very much in love. I handled all his contract negotiations for his station. Well, when it was time four months ago to renew his contract, he kept me on, knowing I'm good at what I do. I renegotiated his contract, then renegotiated my way back into his life. I didn't know he was involved with someone until it was too late." Candace smiled innocently.

Aja just stared blankly. *This woman can't possibly be saying what I think she is saying.*

"Anyway, we have been involved since then. I've tried to give Charles ample time to break it off with you but he says you're fragile and he wants to break it to you easy. He told me he tried to tell you last week but you went crazy, tried to throw a vase at him and stuff, so he couldn't get it out. I've tried to be patient, but now that I'm expecting, my patience has worn thin."

"Expecting what?" Aja was dumbfounded. She knew what Candace was talking about, but there were so many things racing through her mind that she had to hear the words.

Candace laughed and gently ran her hands across her stomach. "Charles Clayton, Junior, of course. Or Candace Junior. It's too soon to know."

Candace grabbed one of the olives from her drink, seductively ran her tongue around it, then popped it into her mouth. She picked the drink back up, then stopped just before drinking. "Oh, what am I thinking? I shouldn't be drinking this. In my condition and all." Candace smiled, set the drink down, and pushed it away.

Aja was speechless. She tried to take it all in. Every moment that she was apart from Charles started to race through her mind. Was he with Candace those nights he claimed to be on special assignment? What was all that bullshit about them spending their life together? And how his dog days were over? He'd even given her that sob story about Katrena and how he vowed to treat women with honor and respect. Here she was feeling bad about blowing up at him. When was he going to tell her? Was that why he hadn't called these last couple of days? How could he do her like this, knowing how hard it was for her to love? *I knew he was too good to be true.*

"I've got to get out of here." Aja grabbed her purse and raced toward the door.

"Wait," Candace called after her. But Aja was gone. Where, she didn't know.

Thirty

Aja looked at the Houston Ship Channel sign. It seemed like she had just passed that. She glanced out the window and realized she had been driving in circles for more than an hour. She was in a daze—too numb to cry, too mad to blow it off. She exited the highway and started heading back toward the city.

Thirty minutes later Aja found herself in front of Troy's house. Troy Walton was the only man she had come close to loving before Charles. He was an all-or-nothing kind of guy and when Aja couldn't give him her all, he gave her her walking papers. But they had remained good friends. She sat in the car pondering her next move.

"Aja? Is that you?" Troy peered into Aja's tinted windows. He had come out to take in the garbage can. "Girl, what are you doing?" He leaned over, opened Aja's car door, and noticed her tears.

"Why are you crying? What's wrong?" Troy pulled Aja out of the car. His touch took her back. She always felt so safe with him. Why couldn't she have been the woman he wanted?

"I'm sorry. I don't know how I ended up here." Aja tried to smile, but before she knew it, she was in Troy's arms crying hysterically.

"Shhh. It can't be that bad. Stop crying. Come on inside." Troy wiped Aja's face then took her by the hand and led her inside. Aja was so distraught that it took nearly twenty minutes to explain to him what happened.

". . . and that's it. The love of my life got his ex-girlfriend pregnant." Aja sniffed, sat up, and tried to pull herself together.

Troy had listened intently the whole time, rubbing her arm when needed, wiping away her tears, and never letting go of her hand. "Hey, I thought I was the love of your life," he joked.

Aja smiled through her tears. "You were. The current love of my life then." She looked at the handsome, intelligent man whom she had once cared about so dearly. He was a stockbroker who wanted to give her the world. If only she could have let go of the past. But she couldn't, and he got tired of trying.

"Troy, I am so sorry to lay all this on you. I just needed someone to talk to I guess." Aja started weeping again. Troy reached over and hugged her.

"Hey Li, don't cry."

Aja sighed heavily as he called her Li. That was his pet name for her when they were together. It stood for happi-ly ever after. Yeah, it was pretty corny, but it's what they both thought they would be.

"You know I've never been able to stand seeing you cry. It'll be all right."

Aja tried to muffle her crying. She took a deep breath and looked Troy directly in his eyes. As she gazed at him, she longed to go back to where they used to be, to forget she even knew Charles. At least Troy had never cheated on her, to her knowledge anyway. "Make it all right Troy. Make love to me."

A surprised look crossed Troy's face. He saw Aja was serious and pulled away. "Come on, Aja. You know I love making love to you. And it's been a hell of a long time, but not like this."

"Yes, like this. I need you. I need the pain to go away." Aja pulled Troy to her and began kissing him ferociously. She knew once she nibbled his neck that it was over. She slowly moved her tongue down his neck while beginning to unfasten his pants.

"Aja, don't. You're upset." Troy grasped her hands, trying to stop her.

"Well, then make me feel better," Aja whispered in his ear. *Fuck Charles. He wants to hurt me? Well, two can play at that game.* She backed away and slowly began unbuttoning her blouse. She let it fall to the floor, then slipped out of her bra and skirt. She stood before him clad only in her panties.

"So you don't want me?" Aja seductively asked. Her eyes were swollen and she was still reeling from the pain of finding out about Charles. She thought making love to Troy would help her forget.

Troy's eyes scanned Aja's partially naked body. "You know I do."

"Then make love to me." Aja leaned in and kissed Troy again. He sighed as he took her into his arms and carried her upstairs.

Their lovemaking was intense. At first, Aja was simply trying to block out thoughts of Charles and what he had done to her. But soon, all of her thoughts were on Troy and for a moment, it seemed like old times. Although their session was good, Aja still felt an ache in her heart after it was over.

"So what did the snake have to say for himself?" Troy asked as he ran his fingers along Aja's chest.

Aja stared up at the ceiling. "I . . . I . . . didn't talk to him about it. I just left Candace and came straight here."

Troy sat up in bed, astonished. "You mean you didn't even give him a chance to explain?"

"What's to explain? How could he resist this woman? She's drop-dead gorgeous."

Troy sat on the edge of the bed. "Damn, Aja."

"What?" Aja sat up also.

Troy looked at Aja, then reached back and tenderly touched her face. "You know I will always love you, but you're wrong. I'm not trying to send you into some other man's arms, but he needs a chance to explain."

"Explain what, Troy?"

"I don't know. You don't even know this woman and you're just going to take her word without giving your man a chance to explain?" Troy scooted up near Aja, lifted her chin, and looked her in the eye. "You know, I think you don't want him to explain. Because it gives you a reason to run away just like you did me. Only you think you can do this guilt-free, because you think you can say he wasn't nothing but a dog."

Aja teared up again. Troy could always read her. She had such issues with trust, and she felt it all went back to her father. She had trusted him and he let her down. Now she had a hard time trusting any man.

"Aja, this was great, but you got some things you need to handle," Troy said. Aja laid her head on his lap. He lovingly stroked her hair. "Tonight, you rest. Tomorrow, you talk."

Thirty-one

Tomorrow came quickly. Aja dressed and left Troy's before he woke up. She hadn't decided if she was going to talk to Charles or not. She had tossed and turned all night trying to figure out what to do.

When she finally walked into her apartment, she looked at the message light on her answering machine. Four calls. Aja pressed the play button.

"Hey, it's me. Call me when you get in." It was Charles, acting like nothing was wrong. The other two messages were hang-ups, then Charles again. "Hey, me again. Where are you?"

Aja threw her purse down. "I'm sure he knows I know!" she shouted to herself. No, she wouldn't wait. She picked up the phone and dialed. Charles answered on the first ring.

"Where have you been? I've been worried sick about you."

"Oh, have you? I thought maybe you'd be too busy with your attorney to worry about me."

"What? What are you talking about?" Charles asked.

"Oh, now you think I'm dumb? What kind of fool do you take me for?" She couldn't believe he was going to try and play her like that.

"First of all, you need to lower your voice," Charles calmly said. "Now, what in the hell is wrong with you?"

"Ask Candace!" Aja slammed down the phone. She half expected it to ring right back, but it didn't. She sat down on the sofa and cried. Why did it seem like she was always crying about something lately?

Fifteen minutes later the doorbell rang. Aja looked out of the peephole and saw it was Charles. She thought about just ignoring him, but changed her mind. *Good, let's get this over with.* She opened the door.

Charles barged right in. "Since you want to play this juvenile, hang-the-phone-up-in-my-face bullshit, I thought maybe our conversation would be more productive if we talked in person." He turned to Aja. "*Now* what is your problem?"

Aja glared at Charles with a hateful look. "How could you do this to me?"

"Do what? What are you talking about?"

"I saw your ex yesterday."

"My ex? . . . Candace? So?"

"*So,* she informed me about your little reconciliation. When were you going to tell me?" Aja was furious.

Charles looked at her and then burst out laughing.

"What the hell is so funny?" Aja was boiling now. Not only was Charles cheating on her, he thought it was funny too.

Charles held his side and eased up his laughing. "Aja, baby, I am not back with Candace. Candace is a spoiled brat who is used to getting what she wants. She wants me back, yes. But I want you, and that's exactly what I told her."

Aja stared in disbelief. "Don't lie to me, Charles, if you want her . . ."

"I'm not lying to you. Candace is the liar. She probably

wanted to make you leave me so she could have me. She told me she could get me if she really wanted me, but I had no idea she'd go this far."

Aja eyed Charles suspiciously. "What about the . . . the baby?"

"Baby? As in pregnant with a baby? Come on. I haven't even held Candace's hand, so there's no way in hell she could be pregnant from me." Charles was still fighting back laughter. "How did you end up seeing her anyway?"

Aja shook her head. She was so confused. "Your secretary called me and said you wanted to meet me. Only, I guess it was Candace who called."

"You should've known it was something fishy from the start. I told you the first time we talked that I don't have a secretary."

Aja didn't know what to believe. "Well . . . how did she know about our fight?"

"Okay, if I'm guilty of anything, that's it. I did tell her about our fight, but only after we were through going over some legal work and she kept asking me what was wrong."

"Don't lie to me!" Aja snapped.

Charles stopped laughing and turned serious. He glared at Aja. "You need to watch your tone. I don't know what kind of men you're used to dealing with, but you're not going to talk to me like I'm crazy."

"Don't tell me what to do!"

Charles saw that Aja was serious. He stared at her for a moment before speaking. "Get your shoes, we're going to Candace's." Charles grabbed Aja's purse and headed to the door. She stubbornly stood there for a minute, then finally followed him out to his car.

Aja sat in the passenger side in a funk. She didn't know who to believe. Candace had been so convincing. And besides, what man could resist her? Maybe that's why Aja couldn't give her heart to Charles, because deep down she knew he was a dog. Or was he?

"This is some real childish mess."

"We don't have to do this," Aja sarcastically replied.

"Yeah, we do. Since it's obvious you don't trust me, we need to. Besides, I don't appreciate Candace trying to play me."

Aja crossed her arms and continued to be mad. Part of her wondered if this was an act, if Charles was putting on a show because he knew she'd stop him before they actually got over to Candace's. That's the main reason she didn't stop him. Plus she wanted to see the look in Charles's eyes when they confronted Candace. Then and only then would she know the truth.

They had just exited the freeway and were turning into Sugarland Community, where Candace lived. All the houses were massive. They passed home after home, all beautiful, the picture of tranquillity. When they finally pulled in front of Candace's house, Aja had to bite her lip to keep her jaw from dropping. The two-story maroon house was huge. Candace had to be making big money. "So this is her house."

"Yeah, come on." Charles ignored the smirk on Aja's face, threw the car in park, and jumped out.

Is he really going to go all the way with this? Aja was hesitant but knew it was the only way she'd get some peace of mind. She opened the car door and followed Charles, who was already stomping up the walkway.

Charles fiercely pressed the doorbell. "Candace, open the door!" He pounded on the door several times.

The door swung open. Candace smiled. She was wearing a long leopard-skin silk robe. Her hair was pinned up with several strands hanging loosely around her face.

"Sweetheart, that is so incredibly rude," she purred.

"Don't sweetheart me." Charles pushed his way past Candace and walked inside. Candace shot him an irritated look, which quickly turned to an innocent smirk when she saw Aja.

"Come in. Since Charles already did." Candace stood back and let Aja pass. "Well, would my unannounced guests care for a drink?" Candace asked after she'd closed her front door and walked into the den where Charles was standing with a pissed-off look on his face.

"Cut the crap Candace."

Candace smiled. "What are you talking about, dumpling?"

"I want to know what type of game you're playing."

Candace seductively walked over to the bar. She purposely let her robe fall open to reveal her matching sheer negligé. Charles didn't seem fazed. "Well since you two aren't drinking, I hope you don't mind if I pour myself a little something." She took her time opening the cabinet, finding a glass, then pouring herself a drink. She looked at Aja and stopped just before putting the glass to her mouth. "I just keep forgetting that I'm not supposed to be drinking." She smiled and then turned and leaned against the bar. "Now, Charles, what were you saying? Oh yeah, a game. Just what game is it you think I'm playing?"

"Why the hell would you tell Aja all that stuff?"

"Oh, so it's like that now, huh Charles?"

"Don't play with me."

"Who's playing?"

Aja stood off to the side taking it all in. She still didn't know what to believe. The stuff Candace told her did seem so out of character for Charles. What if Charles wasn't lying—then she had let that little skank send her into a frenzy for nothing. *Oh my God! Troy. If this isn't true . . .* Aja's thoughts trailed off and she tensed up.

"Candace, you know I am beyond this."

Candace reached back, picked up the glass, and went ahead and took a drink. She flashed a smile again before sighing, then playfully sticking out her bottom lip. "Dang, it was just a joke. You're no fun, Charles."

"Why would you—first of all—call Aja, then tell her some bullshit like that?"

"No, I think the question is, why would she believe it?" Candace responded matter-of-factly, without looking at Aja.

Aja wanted to reach across the room and smack Candace across the head. But she wanted to have some class about herself. It was bad enough she had Charles here in the first place.

"Charles," Candace continued as she walked past him and into the den. "You know me. I'm a sore loser. I like to get what I want by any means necessary. But you know, you really should be thanking me." She tossed her head back, shaking the strands of hair from in front of her eyes. "I tested her love for you. And you know what? She failed. If I were you Charles, I wouldn't want to be with anyone who didn't trust me. Someone who would take the word of a stranger over the man she claims to love."

Charles pinched his eyebrows in anger. "I better leave before I do something I regret." He turned and stormed toward the door.

Aja looked at Candace and muttered, "Bitch!" She then turned and followed Charles out.

"You know Charles," Candace called out after them, "nobody could've ever made me doubt your love for me. That's what true love is. What we had. This shit you have ain't real! Sooner or later you'll see that, and you'll come running back to me!"

Charles raced to his car without looking back. He barely gave

Aja time to get in the car before he sped off. "Are you satisfied now?"

Aja sat without saying a word. Of course she was happy that it turned out Candace was lying. But she was disgusted that she had believed her in the first place. And she was even more disgusted about what had happened with Troy. Maybe Candace was right. Maybe she didn't deserve Charles.

Thirty-two

Aja looked at her planner. The bright red X on last Monday's date seemed to scream at her. Aja counted the days out loud again. "One, two, three, four, five, six, seven, eight, nine, ten, eleven. Eleven."

Aja slammed the planner closed. She had always been like clockwork, so eleven days late was not a good sign. It had been three weeks since the Candace incident. She was still kicking herself for letting Candace dupe her into believing that crap about Charles.

Troy had been calling for the last few weeks, but Aja was too ashamed to talk with him. Charles knew something was wrong, but her indiscretion was something Aja could never admit. The whole guilt thing was killing her. She had to talk to someone. *Roxie.* If she left now she could be at Roxie's school by three and catch her before she left campus. Aja grabbed her keys and headed out the door.

Aja caught Roxie just as she was stuffing papers in her briefcase, preparing to go home. Roxie was sitting behind her desk, which was covered with knickknacks. All of them looked like children had handcrafted them.

Roxie noticed Aja standing in the doorway. "Hey, what are you doing here?"

"Do you have a minute? I need to talk." Aja had that "don't-play-Roxie-this-is-serious" look, so Roxie just nodded for her to come in the classroom. Roxie got up from her desk, walked over, locked the classroom door, then turned around. "What's wrong?"

Aja buried her face in her hands. "Oh Roxie, I did something terrible."

Roxie sat back down and took a deep breath. "Just spit it out. What did you do?"

"You know how I told you about the whole situation with Candace and all?" Aja got up and started pacing nervously back and forth.

"Yeah, that spoiled bitch almost made you mess up a good thing."

Aja starting bawling. "She did! She did make me mess up a good thing! And I have nobody to blame but myself!"

Roxie let out an exasperated sigh. "Aja calm down. You know you are always crying. Now, what in the world are you talking about? I thought you and Charles had worked that out?"

Aja grabbed a tissue off Roxie's desk and blew her nose. "I . . . I didn't tell you the whole story."

Roxie licked her lips, like she was afraid of what was coming next. She leaned back and folded her arms. "I'm listening."

"After I left Candace . . . I didn't go home. I went to Troy's."

Roxie's eyebrows flared up. "Troy? As in your ex, Troy?"

Aja rolled her tear-filled eyes at her friend. "Yeah, how many other Troys do you know?"

"Why'd you go there? Better yet, what happened when you went there to get you so upset?"

Aja shifted nervously. Roxie had a way of making her feel like such a little girl sometimes. "I don't know. I guess I wanted to pay Charles back for hurting me. I wanted to just kick myself for getting so wrapped up in a man. I was mad, angry, hurt."

"Aja, what does that mean?"

Aja looked down in disgust.

Roxie hit the desk. "Tell me you did not sleep with Troy!"

Aja didn't answer.

"You did! You slept with him!" Roxie threw up her hands in frustration. "Damn, girl!"

"I know! I know!" The tears started back up.

Roxie snatched more tissues from the box on her desk and handed them to Aja. "Okay." She took a deep breath. "It's not the end of the world. What Charles doesn't know won't hurt him. You just have to act like it never happened."

"I can't."

"What do you mean, you can't?" Roxie looked confused. Then she watched as Aja's hands made their way toward her stomach.

"Shit, Aja, please don't tell me it's that. Please don't tell me you're pregnant." Roxie shook her head like she was trying to shake away the possibility that Aja could've put herself in such a dilemma.

"I don't know. I'm eleven days late. I haven't taken a test or anything. I'm . . . well, you know I'm never late."

"Damn!" Roxie got up and walked to the window. She stood in thought for a few minutes. "Okay," she said, turning back to Aja. "First of all, calm down. We'll get through this. Secondly, the baby could be Charles's, right? You only slept with Troy one time?"

Aja glared at her friend. They both knew it only took one time to turn up pregnant. One of their friends in college had gotten pregnant by a guy she slept with only one time. And they had had sex for only about two minutes because his girlfriend caught them.

"Okay, so that was a long shot. But I tell you what, if you are pregnant, you best make that baby Charles's."

"Roxie, I can't do that. I feel like such a slut. A tramp. What if I am pregnant? How could I have possibly put myself in the predicament where I wouldn't know who the father is?"

"I'm not going to talk about you now, but you know later, I'm going to have to tell you about yourself."

"You don't need to chastise me, I feel horrible enough as it is. In fact, I need to break it off with Charles. I don't deserve him." Aja slumped into a desk.

"Girl, quit talking that nonsense. You got a fucked-up history, so you made some fucked-up choices. Look, we are not going to stress out about this. We are going to wait. Don't go breaking nothing off. Just play it cool with Charles. You're too damn old to be having an abortion. So we just have to figure this out. We'll take a test and see. If you are really pregnant, we are going to go, you and me, and have the best ultrasound we can to pinpoint exactly how far along you are. Then we are going to count those days to the penny and try to figure this shit out."

Aja could only look at her friend. Her tears were drying up. Aja thought it was because she was just all cried out. "I wish it were that easy."

"It is. Before you slept with Troy, when was the last time you had sex with Charles?"

Aja thought about it. "Right before our big fight. About two weeks."

"Good. Two weeks is good. Sperm can only last inside you for two or three days, something like that. So we can figure this out. We can!"

Roxie smiled like she had just solved the problem. Aja could only hope it would be as easy as Roxie made it seem.

Thirty-three

Aja stared at the little stick.

"Well?" Roxie was just as anxious as Aja. "Come on, girl, what does it say?"

Roxie and Aja had left the school and gone straight to the drugstore to buy a home pregnancy test. They ignored the "this test works best in the morning" label and raced to Roxie's house to take it.

"Gimme that!" Roxie grabbed the stick when Aja didn't move. "Praise Jesus!" She grasped the stick tightly. "A minus sign! You're not pregnant!"

Aja slumped to the floor. Pure relief ran through her body. She had never been so scared.

"See, it was probably all this stress that made your period late. Now what if you had broken up with Charles? It's a good thing you got your girl around to help keep you in check." Roxie patted herself on the back.

Aja started crying.

Roxie stared at her with a confused look. "What are you bawling for? The test was negative."

"I know, but I don't deserve him. I don't deserve Charles."

"Oh, would you cut that shit out? If anybody deserves happiness, it's your ass."

"No, I don't. The fact that I even had to go through this proves that." Aja pulled herself up off the floor and ran to the door.

"Aja!" Roxie screamed. It was too late. Aja was out the door and on her way to do what she should've done after she slept with Troy—break up with Charles.

Aja pulled out her cell phone and dialed Charles's number as she sped along the 610 Loop. "Hey," she said when he picked up. "It's me. Where are you?"

"I just got through working out at the gym and I'm getting ready to make something to eat."

"Good. I'm near your place. Can I meet you there in a few minutes?"

"Sure, what's up? You don't sound like yourself."

"I'll tell you when I see you." Aja hung up the phone and started practicing how she would break the news.

"Come on in." Charles stood in the doorway. He was still in his workout clothes. "What's going on? You got me a little nervous."

Aja walked in but didn't sit down. "Charles, we need to talk."

Charles closed the door and walked to his recliner to sit down. "Okay, what's wrong now?" He kicked back in the chair. "Did Candace piss you off again?"

"No, nothing like that." Aja sat down on the sofa across from Charles and started fumbling with her purse strap. "Look, I've been thinking about us."

"Good things, I hope." Charles leaned forward and flashed a smile.

"Please, Charles, you're not making this easy."

Charles stopped smiling. "Aja, what's going on? Not making what easy?"

"As I said, I've been doing a lot of thinking. And I just think . . . well . . . I just believe . . . I don't think things are working out between us." Aja fought back tears. She was determined not to cry.

"What? Where did this come from?"

"It's just not working."

"Aja, this is crazy. You come to me out of the blue with this crap. Does this have anything to do with Candace?"

"No, it doesn't. It has to do with us. You and me." *Actually me,* she wanted to say. *I'm a slut who doesn't deserve you.* "It's just I don't think I should be focusing on a relationship right now. My sister's getting better and she needs my attention. Then there's Eric."

"What?" Charles rubbed his temples. "You've got to be kidding me! Where did this come from?"

"I'm sorry, Charles. I knew I should've never gotten involved in the first place. I knew I wasn't ready," Aja softly said.

"Wasn't ready?" Charles was still having a hard time understanding what was going on. "*You* came to me after our last breakup. *You* wanted to work this out. I don't understand you, Aja. One minute things are great between us and the next you come at me with this bullshit."

"It's not bullshit. You never have understood my relationship with my brother and sister, how important they are to me." Aja knew she was grasping at straws, but she didn't know what else to tell him.

Charles stood up and started pacing. "I don't believe this shit. I have been there for you and your family, put up with your histrionics, your lack of trust in me. Here I am talking about a future and you're telling me you don't think things are working?"

"I'm sorry."

Charles spun around, his face fiery with anger. "You're sorry? Is that the best you can do? You're sorry?! No, you know what Aja, I'm sorry! I'm sorry I got involved with *you!* I'm tired of dealing with this shit. You women are always hollering about finding a good man and you get one and don't know what the fuck to do with him!"

You are so right. This was breaking her heart. But she couldn't live with the guilt of what she had done.

"I put up with you trying to smash my fucking head in! I put up with you constantly putting me second! And for what?!" Charles stomped into the kitchen, opened the pantry, grabbed a plastic garbage bag, and went into his bedroom. He started stuffing Aja's things into the bag as he continued ranting. "You know what? Fuck this! Here's your shit," Charles came back into the living room. He held out the bag. "If I find anything else, I'll send it to you in the mail! You are free and clear to go. You don't have to worry about me bothering you ever again!"

"Charles . . ."

"Don't Charles me." He lowered his voice. "I'm tired of this indecisive bullshit. You got issues, Aja. And I can't deal with 'em. Maybe you're right. Maybe we weren't meant to be."

"I was hoping we could handle this like adults and stay friends."

"Friends? No thanks, I got enough friends."

"Charles, please."

"Aja, go. Just go." Charles turned his back.

Aja could no longer hold back her tears. She reached in her purse and pulled out a tissue.

"What are you crying for? This is what you wanted," Charles said, without turning around.

"You don't have to be so mean."

"Mean?" Charles laughed, then turned to face Aja. "You're the one who came over here with this shit. Mean? No, Aja, I'm not mean. I'm tired, tired of trying to make you love me, of always coming second and pretending like it doesn't bother me, tired of watching you make your life miserable over your damn brother, tired of you blaming yourself for something that happened fifteen years ago. I'm just tired." Charles walked over and opened the front door. "So I'm through. You got your wish, I'm through." Charles held the door open.

Aja slowly stood up. Her face felt full and swollen. "Charles, can we talk about this some more?"

"Good-bye, Aja."

Aja wanted so badly to tell him the real reason that she was breaking up with him. She did make some screwed up choices in life. But she felt she was doing the right thing now. She wanted to explain things to him, maybe he would forgive her and things could get back to normal. But she didn't know what to say, so she didn't say anything. She just looked at Charles, then walked outside.

She stopped and turned to face him. "I do love you."

"You have a hell of a way of showing it." Charles slammed the door.

Thirty-four

"Would you hurry up? We're going to be late!" Elise yelled to her fiancé, who was in the bathroom.

"So? Maybe then we'll miss it," Eric mumbled. He was in no mood to party with a bunch of Elise's coworkers.

"Now, Eric, don't be like that. We won't stay long." The Geto Boys rap group was back together and they were throwing an album release party.

Eric grumbled some more before walking to the door. Just because her colleagues worked at Rap-A-Lot Records and the company was becoming one of the hottest in the country, they thought they were above everybody else. Eric intentionally slammed the door behind him. He wanted to make sure Elise knew he was mad. It didn't seem to bother her, though.

It only took a few minutes to get to the party. That was with Eric driving ten miles below the speed limit the entire way. Eric swung his car into an open parking space. He took his time getting out of the car, despite the impatient looks Elise was throwing him. They walked into the hotel, but the minute they stepped in the ballroom, Eric knew he should've stayed at home.

"Yo ba-by, what is yo' fine, sexy self up to?" some gold-toothed guy said as he stepped toward Elise, completely ignoring Eric.

"Move, T-Lee. I'm here with my boyfriend." Elise pushed T-Lee to the side.

T-Lee turned his nose up at Eric, then smirked. "Hey sweet thang, my bad."

"I'ma sweet thang you . . ." Eric clenched his fists and moved toward the wanna-be rapper. He was liable to get straight-up stabbed in here, but he wasn't about to be disrespected by some thug.

T-Lee just flashed those gold teeth, tilted his fur-lined hat, and strutted off.

"See that's the kinda shit I'm talking about." Eric turned to Elise. "This is exactly why I didn't want to come. It's bad enough you have to work around these fools with made up names, but now you want me to come socialize with them."

"Awww, come on, sweetie." Elise snuggled up to Eric. "This can be fun. And you know I'm in charge of marketing for this album, so I have to be here."

"Yeah, whatever. I'm going to get a drink. Maybe some Crown and Coke will calm my nerves." Eric stormed to the cash bar, leaving Elise standing by herself.

Elise gritted her teeth, determined not to let Eric spoil her mood. She was a new mommy and had a great job. If only Eric would actually set a wedding date and marry her, life would truly be good. But she had promised herself that she wouldn't pressure him. It had to be a decision he made on his own.

Elise made her way through the ballroom, mixing and mingling with her coworkers. A few times she tried to go over and make small talk with Eric, but she could see he was determined to stay in a bad mood. She didn't want his temper tantrums putting a damper on her evening. After her last attempt had gone nowhere, she just shrugged it off and walked back to the bar.

Elise had just received her amaretto sour when she heard the most distinctive voice.

"Hi there, Elise. Great job on those posters."

She turned around to face a tall, dark-skinned, clean-shaven man. He had light gray eyes, naturally wavy hair, and a smile that seemed to permeate kindness. He looked dazzling in a camel-hair jacket, a beige mock turtleneck, and FUBU jeans.

"I'm sorry, I don't believe we've met," Elise said.

"I'm Dr. David Josephs, Lorna's brother. We met at the office once before."

Oh yeah. Elise remembered him. Lorna worked in the pro-motions department at Rap-A-Lot. Her brother had come to take her out to lunch last month. All the women in the office swooned over how gorgeous the 6-foot-3-inch "hunk of steel"—as the receptionist had called him—was. Immediately after Lorna had returned from lunch, everybody was begging to be hooked up with him, but Lorna was protective of her brother and blew all the women off. She did tell everyone he was single, which sent them into even more of a frenzy.

"Oh, Dr. Josephs, nice to meet you—again." Elise extended her hand.

David gently shook it. "Please, just call me David. Lorna told me you're responsible for the cover." He pointed to the enlarged cover blowup that was propped up by the entry. "It's fantastic."

"Thank you." Elise smiled. She had worked hard trying to come up with a design for the cover. It was her first graphic art project and she had received rave reviews. "I am pretty proud of it." David's smile was actually making her blush. "So are you en-joying yourself?"

"Not particularly," he chuckled. "This really isn't my cup of tea."

Elise laughed. The two of them made small talk for a while. David told Elise that his sister had dragged him to the party. She was afraid she'd run into a guy she had just broken up with, and she needed David to help her be strong and not leave with him.

Elise glanced over and noticed Eric leaning against a wall glaring at her. She then realized how long she'd been talking.

"Well, David, it's been nice chatting with you, but I'd better go check on my fiancé. He doesn't look too happy. He didn't really want to come here either."

"Tell him I know what he's feeling." David laughed as he walked off.

"Take care." Elise smiled, then turned back and walked over to Eric, who had a pure look of funk on his face.

"So, you still got an attitude?" she playfully poked Eric in the stomach.

"Let's go!"

Elise crossed her arms. "Eric, why are you acting like this?"

"I said, I'm ready to go!"

Elise didn't feel like arguing. "Fine!" She turned and stormed out of the party with Eric close on her heels.

Eric was silent on the ride home. Elise, however, refused to give in to his tantrum. She turned up the radio and sang along with the songs all the way home. At the apartment, Eric stormed inside before Elise could even get out of the car.

"Are you going to pay the baby-sitter?" Elise asked when she got inside. Eric was already in the bedroom and didn't answer.

Elise rolled her eyes and walked into the den where the sitter was watching a movie on HBO. "Hey, Tasha. Was Madison any trouble?"

"Not at all. She's sound asleep now."

"Okay, here's your money." Elise handed the sitter a twenty-dollar bill. "Thanks a lot, and we'll call you when we need you."

"Thank you, Elise." Tasha said as she gathered her things.

Elise put the chain on the door after Tasha left. She checked in on Madison and saw that she was indeed sound asleep before heading to the bedroom. Eric had changed his clothes and was checking his hair in the mirror.

"Where are you going?"

"Out."

"Out where?"

"Just out."

Elise shot Eric an angry look. "Fine." She strolled into the bathroom and began running some steaming hot water in the tub. Just what she needed. She poured in some bath oil, undressed, and got in the water. Minutes later, she heard the front door slam and instead of getting mad, Elise relished the peace and quiet.

Thirty-five

After her bath, Elise tried to sleep, but she kept tossing and turning. This thing with Eric was getting to her. They hadn't been happy since the camp fiasco with the Mavericks. Granted, he had temporarily gotten better once the baby was born, but even that had worn off and Eric was back to his usual grumpy self. He hadn't found a job since he quit Blockbuster. Elise was trying her best not to nag him about it.

Elise grabbed her blanket, went into the den, and turned on the television. She grabbed the remote and lay down on the sofa. She was hoping some late-night *I Love Lucy* reruns would help her sleep, but it didn't work. Her mind kept racing back to Eric. She knew he was upset about being cut from the team, upset about the whole pro thing. But at what point would he ever get over it? Elise pondered that until she dozed off on the living room sofa. The sound of the key in the door jolted her out of her sleep. She glanced at the clock. Five A.M.

Elise jumped to her feet when Eric stumbled in. "Where have you been?"

Eric ignored her and kicked off his shoes.

"I said, where have you been?"

"Why don't you ask your doctor friend where I've been?" Eric threw down his keys and fell on the sofa. He was obviously drunk.

"Doctor? What doctor?" Elise looked confused.

"The doctor you spent all night talking to."

"David? What does David have to do with anything?"

"David," Eric mimicked. "Doctor David, whatever his last name is. I saw the way the two of you were talking tonight. You didn't think I'd notice? You think I'm some kind of fool?"

"Eric, what are you talking about?" Eric tried to stand up, but stumbled. "Oh, forget it. You're drunk, we'll continue this discussion tomorrow." Elise snatched her blanket off the sofa and marched to the bedroom.

Eric grabbed her arm and jerked her back. "Bitch, don't you ever walk away from me." His eyes were a deep red.

Elise glared angrily at her fiancé. "Don't you ever call me a bitch!" She jerked her arm out of his grasp, turned, and walked away.

"I'm talking to you, dammit! I want to know what's going on with you and this David!"

Elise spun back around. "Keep your voice down before you wake up the baby," she hissed.

"I will talk as loud as I want! Don't nobody tell me how loud I can talk in my own fucking house!" He lowered his voice and leaned in to Elise. His breath stank from the liquor. "So tell me, how long have you been fucking him?"

"You're being ridiculous now. You're drunk and unreasonable and this discussion will not happen," Elise calmly said.

"I ain't drunk! I just got a little buzz. Don't a man have a right to get a little buzz when he finds out his woman is cheating on him?" Eric held on to the counter to steady himself.

"You *are* drunk and I'm *not* cheating. I am, however, going to bed." Elise tried to step around Eric and go toward the bedroom.

"It's because he's a doctor, right? I heard somebody call him doctor. That's it, isn't it? And your man had to get a job as a fucking Blockbuster clerk? You want him 'cause your man can't get a decent job. Tell the truth, that's what it is, isn't it?"

Elise was fed up. If Eric wanted a fight, he'd get a fight! "My man *can* get a decent job, he just *won't* because he's so damn sure the NBA is going to come calling. Mind you, they haven't all this time, but hey, what the hell, let's wait our whole lives on the damn NBA!"

"Oh, so that's it—now I'm a washed-up has-been."

Elise sighed in frustration. "Eric, you're a *never*-been, when are you going to get that through your head? You haven't even bothered to go to the anger management classes, even though you promised you would. You sit around here in a foul mood, making life miserable for everybody. You talk about how much you hate your father, and you're turning out just like him!"

Elise spun around and continued walking to the bedroom. She knew she shouldn't have gone there, but she was getting tired of dealing with the same old stuff with Eric. She had been so patient with him, but now she was fed up. They couldn't get married until he went pro. They couldn't be happy until he went pro. She just wanted a nice, simple life, even if it meant Eric would be working at a car wash.

Eric felt his temper flaring. "Come back here!"

Elise ignored him and went into the bedroom and closed the door.

Eric quickly followed, throwing open the bedroom door. "I'm talking to you, dammit! What the hell do you mean I'm turning into my daddy?"

Elise was putting the blanket back on the bed. She ignored Eric's ranting. Suddenly, Eric came up behind her, grabbed her, and viciously flung her around. "DON'T FUCKING IG-NORE ME!"

Elise tried to jerk herself free. She lost her balance and fell down, hitting her head on the corner of their king-size metal sleigh bed. Eric paused and looked down at Elise. "Get the fuck up! You're not goin' turn this around! I wanna know how long you been cheating on me!"

Elise didn't move. Eric knelt down beside her. That's when he saw the blood. He touched it lightly to see if it was real. He froze after he looked closer at the blood and saw that it was indeed the real thing. "Elise? Elise? Oh my God . . . Elise, baby, wake up." Eric gently shook her. She didn't respond. "Oh no, what have I done?" Eric mumbled as he picked up Elise's head and laid it in his lap. "Baby, wake up, wake up. I'm sorry. I'm sorry," Eric moaned. Elise still didn't move. "You're right. I had too much to drink. I was just so scared of losing you." He felt for her pulse. He wasn't quite sure where it was, but he couldn't feel anything anywhere. Eric started crying and continued begging Elise to wake up.

The memories came rushing back.

"You pull a gun on me and then tell me you don't want to use it?" Eric's father and mother were face-to-face. "Go ahead, shoot me," he laughed as he placed his chest to the gun's barrel. "Your little weak ass doesn't have the nerve."

Eric could hear his mother's trembling voice, but for some reason he couldn't move. "Just go," she said.

His father laughed again and then, Eric heard Aja scream. His mother's cries got louder. But he still couldn't move. The blow his father had just given him left him in a world of darkness.

"Okay, Superwoman, who's bad now?" his father laughed.

"I'm just like him. I'm just like him." Eric rocked back and forth. Elise's head was still in his lap.

Eric had been sitting with Elise for half an hour. Sometime during those thirty minutes the baby had started crying. He eased Elise's head off his lap, then got up and went to get Madison. She was on the verge of hyperventilating because she had been wailing so long. Eric was in a daze. He propped the baby on his hip and went back to the bedroom. He stared at Elise's still body lying on the floor. Eric ignored the screeching cries of his daughter and sat her down on the bed. He then walked over to his dresser and opened the bottom drawer. He pulled out the small black box pushed way in the back, opened it, and removed the small thirty-eight pistol that he had bought the last time someone broke in to the condo. He walked back to the bed and sat on the edge of it. He then picked up the phone and dialed his sister's number.

"Hello." Aja answered on the third ring.

"Aja."

"Eric, is that you? It's six in the morning. What's going on?" Aja was still half asleep.

"Aja."

Eric was crying. The baby was wailing in the background.

Aja sat up. "Eric? Eric? Talk to me. What is going on?"

"Aja, Aja, Aja."

Aja's heart started racing. "I'm here, Peanut, talk to me."

"She's dead. I killed her . . . I'm just like him. He's in my blood. I'm him, he's me. I couldn't stop him, but I can stop me."

"Eric, what are you talking about? Who's dead? Elise? Oh my God! Where are you? Are you at home?" Aja quickly turned on the lamp near her bed and looked at her Caller ID box. "You are at home. Just hang on, baby brother, I'm on my way." Aja flung back the covers. She frantically tried to pull a pair of sweatpants out of her dresser drawer while keeping the phone to her ear.

"I loved her, Aja. I loved her with all my heart. It was an accident. Don't let Madison hate me like we hate him. Please. I love you."

"Eric, wait . . . wait."

It was too late. A single shot. Aja heard it like she was in the same room.

"Eric, NOOOOOO!"

Thirty-six

Aja quickly hung up the phone and dialed the emergency number. She gave them Eric's address, then raced over as well. Aja had never driven so fast in her whole life. Thankfully, there was very little traffic.

The police stopped her before she could get to the front door. "I'm sorry, ma'am. This area is off limits," a tall police officer said.

"My brother! My brother is in there!"

"Excuse us." The paramedics raced by, rolling Elise on a cart. Her eyes were closed. There was blood all over the side of her head. Aja followed the paramedics to the ambulance.

"Elise! Is she dead?"

"No, she'll be okay. Just a bad head injury," one of the paramedics responded.

"What about my brother?"

"You should let the officer talk to you about that." The paramedic nodded toward the tall police officer, then loaded Elise in the ambulance and shut the door. Aja stared at the officer, whose eyes told her the prognosis wasn't good. She pushed past him and ran inside the apartment. As soon as she entered the bedroom, she stopped in her tracks.

Aja felt her mouth open. She felt the scream build from deep inside. But all she could hear was silence as she stared at her little brother lying on his bedroom floor. Some man in plain clothes was about to cover him with a yellow sheet. Another plain-clothed man wearing gloves was picking up a gun and stuffing it into a plastic bag.

"Excuse me, ma'am, I'm going to have to ask you to step out-side." Aja heard the voice but she didn't know where it was com-ing from. In fact, she didn't remember much after that. Her whole world had gone black.

The smell of ammonia caused Aja's eyes to pop open.

"Wha . . . what's?" Aja tried to focus her vision on all the ac-tivity going on around her. A different paramedic was standing over her.

"Can you hear me?"

Aja started trying to piece together what was going on. She remembered a call from Eric. "My brother." Aja tried to push herself up off the ground, but she stumbled and fell back down. The paramedic caught her.

"Ma'am, is there someone we can call for you?" a policeman standing nearby asked. "I'm sure this is quite a shock for you. You shouldn't be alone."

"My brother. Is he . . . is he dead? It was a dream, right?" Aja was praying for confirmation that this was all a really bad dream. She grabbed the paramedic's jacket. "Please tell me."

The paramedic eased her hands off his jacket. "I'm sorry."

Aja felt her body go limp again. She slumped back down to the ground.

"Let me call somebody," the policeman repeated.

Charles was Aja's first thought, but they hadn't talked since that day at his house—almost two weeks ago. "Roxie. My friend, Roxanne."

"What's her number?"

Aja was still in shock. She couldn't remember Roxie's number and it had been the same for seven years. "Umm, it's, umm, five, three, five . . . six, three, seven, seven. I think that's it."

"I'll go call her right now," the officer said. He walked back to his patrol car, grabbed his cell phone, and dialed the number. Aja couldn't hear what he was saying, but a few minutes later he hung the phone up and walked back over. "Your friend is on her way. Just hang tight, okay?"

"I need to see my brother."

"I'm sorry, ma'am, we can't let you do that," the officer said.

"You're going to be fine. Just rest until your friend gets here," the paramedic said. He got up and gathered together his medical equipment, which he loaded back into his truck. "We're going to head out," he told the police officer.

"Thanks, Jack. See you around," the officer responded.

"Hopefully not tonight. I'm tired and my shift is almost over."

"Hope you make it home before they have any more shootings," the officer laughed.

Aja looked at the nonchalant way they were interacting. Her brother had just died and they were joking and playing around. She glanced at the officer's badge. "H. Rodriguez." Aja made a mental note to call and complain when things settled down. But right now, she was just in a daze.

She was still sitting on the curb in a state of shock when Roxie arrived.

"Aja!" Roxie cried as she jumped out of her car. "I'm so sorry." Roxie ran up to Aja and hugged her tightly. "What happened?"

Aja couldn't bring herself to say anything. She just clung to Roxie for dear life.

Thirty-seven

It seemed like the people just kept coming. Aja's living room was packed with people paying their last respects. Aunt Shirley's pipe had burst, so they were forced to hold the post-funeral activities at Aja's place. And she was none too happy about it. She didn't want to be bothered with all of these people. She wished she could just close her eyes and make them all disappear.

"I'm so sorry, baby," some woman in a big brim hat said.

"Oh, he was such a good boy," another hat lady said.

Aja was sick of hearing it. She knew the people meant well, but they did little to make her feel better.

Aja got up from the sofa where she'd been sitting since coming home from the funeral. She walked upstairs to the guest bedroom, opened the door, and peeked inside. Jada was asleep across the bed. She still had on the black dress and shoes she had worn to the funeral. Aja had been hesitant about letting Jada come to the funeral because she didn't want her to have any setbacks. But Jada had done fine. She sat stoically through the service. She had even reached up and softly rubbed Eric's cheek, saying, "Bye-bye" as they passed for the final viewing of the body. That in itself made Aja start hurting all over again.

Aja closed the bedroom door, walked back downstairs into the living room, and made her way over to the fireplace mantel where she picked up a picture of her, Eric, and Jada. It was from Christmas 1982. Aja could remember that day well. She and Jada were posing with their new dolls. Eric had his new G.I. Joe. Aja had tried to pretend she was too old for dolls, but it thrilled her heart to get that Barbie doll and matching pink Corvette. And when Eric snapped the doll's arms off, saying she was in combat with G.I. Joe, she had gone berserk. Aja smiled at that memory. Then her thoughts turned to that horrible night and the smile faded.

"I'm so sorry, little brother. I wasn't there for you then either." Aja couldn't help the tears that seemed to overtake her. She held the picture and cried.

All of a sudden she felt arms wrap around her waist. She turned around. "Charles!" Aja stared into Charles's eyes. "What are you doing here?"

"I was at the service today, sitting in the back the whole time. I wanted to be there for you. It hurt like hell not being able to come up and comfort you."

Aja didn't say anything. She would've loved to have Charles by her side. She had needed Charles by her side. Maybe he would've been able to help her stay strong because Lord knows she had broken down something terrible.

"Aja," Charles continued. "There are a lot of things I don't understand. I have been over and over it in my head trying to figure out why you threw us away. And eventually, I'd like some answers. But right now, I just want to be here for you. Please let me be here for you."

Aja looked lovingly at Charles and felt any ounce of fight drain from her body. She laid her head against Charles's chest and began sobbing. "He's gone. Eric's gone."

"Just let it go, baby." Charles squeezed Aja tight, rocking side to side.

Aja did just like he said and let it go. She cried for the loss she felt in her heart, for the time she would never have back, and for a brother she wasn't able to save.

Charles stood there silently holding Aja while she alternated between heavy sobs and silent whimpers. Finally, he led her to her bedroom, laid her down, and climbed in next to her. Aja continued crying, only this time she felt safer. She drifted off into a much-needed sleep with Charles lying right next to her.

The next morning Aja woke up on her own. She hadn't set her alarm and knew she had overslept. She looked down. She was still fully dressed in the black dress she had worn to the funeral, but someone had taken off her shoes and covered her with a blanket.

"Charles?" Aja remembered how good it had felt to have him there. She sat up and looked around. Surely he wouldn't have left without saying good-bye.

Aja threw back the blanket, got out of bed, and walked to the kitchen. Charles was standing over the stove flipping an omelet.

"Good morning." Charles walked over and kissed her on the forehead. "I figured you might be hungry. How'd you sleep?" he asked.

"Okay. I am hungry." Aja looked at the clock on the microwave. "It's nine-fifteen. Why didn't you wake me up? I'm going to be late for work and I have to get Jada back."

"I know you're not thinking about going to work today. You just buried your brother. You need some time," Charles replied. "Plus, your Aunt Shirley took Jada back."

"Oh. Well, I probably should've still gone to work. It's therapeutic for me."

"Not today. Your boss called to check on you and I told him you wouldn't be in. You're just going to have to be mad."

Aja looked at Charles, about to protest, but she was too worn out to argue. "What time did everybody leave?" she asked.

"Just after you went to sleep. I assured your family I would be here to stay with you, so they went on home."

"Thank you. I couldn't really deal with them anyway. Especially Luther. I could tell he was on the verge of being drunk as it was."

"Was he the one with the purple suit on?"

"Don't forget the matching purple shoes. He matches up everything he wears. Yeah, that's good ol' cousin Luther, Aunt Shirley's son. He's the black sheep of the family." Aja looked over at her briefcase sitting on the kitchen table. "You know, I really should've gone to work today." She didn't want to sit around the house thinking about Eric. It would only make her sad.

"Don't even think about fighting me on this," Charles said. "I also called in today. That new guy has been itching to get a seat in my anchor chair anyway, so today's his chance. I'm staying here with you."

Charles checked to make sure the omelet was done, then slid it onto a plate. He walked over and placed the plate in front of Aja. "Now eat."

Aja eased onto the bar stool at the counter. She smiled at Charles and began nibbling. "Why are you really here?" she finally asked.

"Would you prefer I leave?" Charles turned, serious.

"No, of course not. It's just . . . well, we haven't talked since that night at your apartment."

"Roxanne called and broke the news," Charles said as he poured Aja some coffee. "I can't believe you didn't call me."

"And say what? 'I know you said it was over, but I really need you?' "

"That would have been a start. Anyway, I tried calling you but never got an answer. Two sugars, no cream?" Aja nodded and Charles pulled out the sugar cubes from the cabinet. He picked up her cup, dropped them in her coffee, and set the cup back down. Aja carefully took a sip.

"The phone was ringing off the hook and I've been in a daze. I was staying with Elise at her mom's. She's taking it really hard."

Charles eased onto the bar stool next to Aja's. "I can imagine. How's the baby?"

"Madison is with Elise's sister. They didn't want the baby at the funeral. Elise was released from the hospital the day before the funeral. She's doing okay. She said she needs to clear her head and decide what she's going to do, whether she's going to stay in the condo or move in with her parents."

Charles reached out and rubbed Aja's hand. "Aja, I know this is hard—"

"Charles, you don't have to . . . it is hard, but I'll deal with it."

"Well, I'm here to help you deal with it. Even if it is just as your friend."

Aja smiled. It had been just three weeks since they had broken up, but it seemed like forever. She found herself wondering how she let him get away. She thought back to her indiscretion with Troy and reminded herself that Charles deserved better.

"By the way, you got a phone call this morning," Charles said.

"From who?"

Charles hesitated.

"From who?" Aja repeated.

"Your father."

Aja looked harshly at Charles. "I hope you hung up on him."

Charles looked down at the table and started toying with a napkin.

Aja leaped up from the table, knocking over her coffee in the process. "Eldridge Charles Clayton, what did you say to my father?"

Charles got a towel and started wiping the coffee up. "Aja, it's time. He called. He was sick about not being able to come to Eric's funeral, but the prison was on some sort of lockdown. You have got to go see him. He's supposed to get out next month and he desperately wants to talk to you."

"You have lost your mind. I don't care what he wants!"

"Maybe it's time you did start caring. Don't do this. This . . . this anger, it's why we broke up in the first place. It's what killed Eric."

"I don't believe you!" Aja's butterscotch complexion was turning red with rage. "You want to know what killed my little brother? Huh? The fear that he would turn out like my no-good, sorry-ass daddy! That's why he's dead right now. That's why his baby is fatherless! BECAUSE HE WOULD RATHER BE DEAD THAN TURN OUT LIKE HIS DADDY!"

Aja stormed out of the kitchen and into the bedroom, making sure Charles could hear the bedroom door slam.

"This fight is far from over!" Charles yelled out. "If we're ever going to have a future, it can't be."

Charles and Aja spent most of the day not speaking. She was very upset that he talked to her father, let alone even suggested that she go visit.

"I've got half a mind to call him myself and tell him to stop bothering me and my family," Aja muttered out loud. But the wounds from Eric's death were so fresh and the last thing she felt like doing was dealing with her father.

Aja heard all her relatives' voices. "He's changed." "He's so sorry." "It was an accident." "Let it go." Everybody wanted to tell her to let it go, but nobody was in her shoes. How could she ever let it go, especially now that Eric was dead because of him?

"So are you still mad at me?" Charles poked his head in the bedroom. Aja was sitting on the bed, lost in thought.

She didn't answer.

"That's okay." Charles walked in and sat next to Aja on the bed. "Be mad. But if I'm supposed to be your man, I have to do what I think is best for us. And I think what's best for our future is you facing your past."

Your man? Aja paused. "Charles, don't," she softly said. "Don't come back to me because you think I need you right now."

"Oh, so you don't?"

"That's not what I'm saying. It's just . . . well, I can make it through this. You made it quite clear you didn't even want to be my friend."

"Aja, I don't want to be just your friend. You broke up with me. I just told you I can't play back-and-forth games. And I don't want to be with anyone who doesn't want to be with me."

"I know, I'm sorry. I do want to be with you. It's just . . ." Aja's voice trailed off.

Charles rubbed her hands forgivingly. "That's okay," he said, trying to lighten the mood. "But I have to be honest and say I was mad. Besides, you were the one who wanted to break up for no reason."

"I didn't *want* to break up. I *had* to break up," Aja said.

"Had to? Why? Aja, tell me the real reason you broke up with me," Charles continued. "You owe me that much."

Don't do it. Aja heard Roxie's voice whisper in the back of her head. *Don't spill your guts.* "I just didn't feel I deserved you, that's all."

"That's the craziest thing I ever heard. If anybody deserves happiness, it's you."

"That's the same thing Roxie said." Aja managed a weak smile.

"Well, she was right." Charles took Aja's hand again. "Aja, I don't want it to be over. I love you with all my heart. I just want you to love me back."

"I do, but—"

Charles put his index finger to her lips. "See, it's that 'but' part that I have a problem with. But—you can't give me all your heart."

"I—"

"No, let me finish," Charles interrupted. "You can't give me all your heart because it's too filled with hate. You can't love me because you can't love yourself. You can't forgive yourself or your father. Aja, you were sixteen. What could you have done?"

Aja felt the tears welling up. She stood and moved away from Charles. "You just don't understand."

Charles reached up and took Aja's hand to pull her back down on the bed. "I do, Aja. That's what *you* don't understand, I do. Eric fought for your mother, Jada fought for your mother. And you have had a lifetime of guilt because you didn't. But if you had, it wouldn't have made a difference. I don't ever want you to let Jada or the memory of Eric go, but I want—no I need—for you to let the past go. Let it go, so we can move on."

Charles reached over and wiped the tears from Aja's face. "Come on, I didn't mean to get you all depressed. You've been through enough. Let's talk about this later."

Aja nodded.

"I have some good news," Charles continued. "You remember that story I was talking to you about? The one about the four Rockets players that my boss didn't want me to do but you encouraged me to fight for? Well, I won a Peabody Award for it."

Aja's spirit brightened. Charles had worked hard on that story. At one point, he had even doubted it was worth doing, which was unusual for him, but Aja had pushed him to proceed. "That's great, Charles. You deserve it. But, ummm, what's a Peabody Award?"

Charles proudly stuck his chest out. "It's only one of the most prestigious journalism awards out there. It's higher than an Emmy."

"That's wonderful."

"I'm pretty excited," he said. "We have an awards ceremony next month and I was hoping you would be my date."

Aja smiled for the first time since Eric's death. "I would be honored." Her heart still felt heavy when she thought of her brother, but being with Charles, she couldn't help but feel she had reason to be happy.

Thirty-eight

The beads of sweat trickled down Charles's body, hanging on desperately before finally plunging off his chest. Aja didn't blame them. She could see why sweat would want to linger on his chiseled physique. Charles was so sexy, she could just stare at him all day.

And it seemed like that was what she had been doing. They were in the small, upscale gym at his apartment. This gym was better than the one Aja worked out at on a regular basis, but for as much as Charles had to be paying to stay here, Aja figured the gym should be top of the line.

Charles had been working out for more than an hour. Aja worked out with him for about thirty minutes before she sat on a bench across from him, sipping on her Evian water and treating her eyes to the pleasure of surveying her man at work.

Aja had tried to put the idea of a visit with her father behind her and focus all of her attention on making things work with Charles. She was so grateful that God had sent him back into her life. He had been her rock in the two weeks since Eric's funeral. She had moments when she'd sink into severe depression. Roxie had been there for her, but with a young son, there was only so much she could do. But Charles—he had practically moved in, waiting on her hand and foot. He wasn't overbearing, though. He would let her have her moments, then step in at just the right time to comfort her. He'd even stepped up to the plate with Jada, calling every day to make sure she was holding up okay.

"What are you sitting over there lost in thought about?" Charles said after setting down the ninety-pound weights.

Aja seductively licked her lips. "Oh, just admiring the scenery."

Charles grabbed a towel off the towel rack and wiped his face. "Come with me back in the steam room and I'll give you something to look at," he said with a mischievous grin.

"Don't tempt me."

Charles eased over to Aja, then reached out and grabbed her hand. He pulled her close to him and began kissing her passionately. Aja didn't mind the sweat as it sank into her own clothes.

"Damn, would you two get a room?"

Aja and Charles stopped kissing and laughed at Roxie, who had just appeared in the doorway.

"Hey, girl," Aja said as Charles released her from his embrace.

"Don't hey me. Why aren't you two ready?" As usual, Roxie looked awesome in a black sleeveless turtleneck and some black boot-cut pants. They were going to a book release party for one of their college friends and the attire was dressy casual.

Aja looked at her watch. "It's just six o'clock. The party doesn't start until eight."

Roxie crossed her arms and leaned against the wall, irritation evident on her face. "No, it starts at six. And I promised Pat we would be on time."

"You told me eight."

"I did not," Roxie protested. "I said six."

"I'm going to let you two hash that out," Charles said, grabbing his gym bag. "I'm going up to the apartment to get dressed." He glanced outside. "Where's Brian?"

"He's in the car waiting on you two."

"How'd you know we were in here?" Aja asked.

"That crusty old neighbor of Charles's let me in and told me you two had come down here to work out. Nosy-ass. What if I was Charles's other woman or something?"

"Mr. Jacobs knows I wouldn't have another woman." Charles leaned over and kissed Aja again. "I'm going on up." He grinned at Roxie. "Did I ever thank you for hooking me up with this beautiful woman?"

Roxie rolled her eyes. "Only a million times."

Charles laughed and headed up to his apartment.

"Charles makes me sick," Roxie joked. "Is he always like that?"

Aja grinned and started heading out of the gym. "All the time."

"That shit would get on my nerves." Roxie followed Aja out.

"That's what you say. But you know Brian is just as sweet."

"Yeah, but not sickening sweet. Damn."

"Well, it's not sickening to me. I happen to love it."

"I bet you do," Roxie groaned. "I'm going to go get Brian since it looks like it'll be another hour before you two are ready."

"Okay, we'll hurry. I'll leave the door unlocked so you two can come on in." Aja darted up the stairs.

"And don't be stopping and doing no freaky stuff," Roxie called out after her.

"We'll try," Aja laughed. "It won't be easy, but we'll try."

There had to be more than 150 people. Aja was excited for her friend. Her book, *When Loved Ones Lie,* had been out for less than a month and already it had hit the *Essence* best-seller list.

"Pat, I'm so happy for you," Aja said. She was standing with Pat and Roxie by the table of Pat's books.

"I know," Roxie remarked. "I don't know how you find time to write a book. I barely find time to sleep."

"Girl, you have to make time. But thank you for coming out and supporting me," Pat said.

"You know we have to be here to represent," Roxie said. "And you know I had to come see your man. I still can't believe you are engaged to old nerdy Lydell."

"You know Lydell?" Aja asked Roxie.

"Yeah, I told you I went to elementary school with him. He was the biggest nerd in town," Roxie laughed. She glanced over at Lydell. "But, Lord, he sure did turn out fine."

"You have to excuse her, she's always talking about how fine somebody else's man is," Aja laughed.

"That's all right. I know my baby is all that," Pat said. "But speaking of all that, Aja, girl, I am still tripping over you getting with Charles Clayton."

Aja looked at Charles standing across the room, laughing with a group of guys. "I know. I still have to pinch myself sometimes."

"And the thing is," Roxie interjected. "He loves her dirty drawers."

Aja beamed as she watched Charles theatrically tell a story. Her mood quickly changed, though, when she saw the tall, sultry woman slithering up to Charles.

"I don't believe this," Aja mumbled.

Roxie and Pat turned to see what Aja was looking at.

"Can you believe this tramp?"

Pat looked confused. "Are you talking about Candace?"

"You know her?" Aja asked.

"Yeah, that's my new attorney. She handled the contract for

my book." Pat paused. "Oh my God. Is the Charles she's always talking about being madly in love with *your* Charles?"

"Yes, that's *my* Charles." Aja's blood was boiling. Candace had on a red, slinky dress that dipped down her back, stopping just above the split in her behind. She leaned in and hugged Charles. He didn't return her hug, but that didn't stop her from running her hands over his butt.

"Awww, hell naw," Roxie said, starting toward Candace.

Aja grabbed Roxie's arm then took a deep breath. "No, Roxie. This is my battle. I got this."

Roxie looked surprised, then stepped back. "Handle your business then, girl," Roxie said with a smile.

Aja handed Roxie her drink. She felt like a new woman. A stronger woman. Candace had punked her once, but she'd be damned if it would happen again.

"Oh no, please don't start any drama at my party," Pat whispered as Aja began walking toward Candace.

"Don't worry. My girl's got class," Roxie laughed.

Aja walked with confidence. Charles was visibly uncomfortable at the way Candace was clinging to him. The other men in the group, however, were looking on in awe, surveying her from head to toe.

"Damn, look at that ass," Aja heard one of the men whisper. She ignored the comment, walked over to Candace, and gingerly removed her arm from Charles. Aja tightened her grip before dramatically dropping Candace's arm. Candace looked taken aback, then quickly regrouped and smiled.

"Well, Charles, I see you're still slumming."

Aja and Candace stared each other down. Charles tried to intervene. "Candace, don't start. Would you leave her alone?"

Aja held up her hand, cutting Charles off. "Baby, I can handle Candace." Charles looked surprised, but stepped back.

"Don't tell me you're still upset over that little prank?" Candace said.

Aja glared at her nemesis, but didn't respond. As it stood, only Roxie, Pat, and the few guys standing with Charles knew what was going on. Aja didn't want to ruin Pat's day, but she was not about to let this hussy shame her again. "You would want to back up off my man."

"Ohhhh, fighting for your man. How noble," Candace said.

"She doesn't need to fight for me. I'm hers," Charles interjected.

Aja swung her head toward Charles. "Baby, I said chill. I can handle this bitch."

Charles backed down.

"But I'm a good bitch, aren't I, Charles? That's what you used to tell me in the heat of the moment, isn't it?" Candace turned toward Aja. "Does he still talk dirty when he's making love? He used to love to talk dirty to me. I guess it was an escape from the prim and proper facade he's forced to put on every day."

It took every ounce of strength Aja had not to lunge at Candace and pound her head into the floor. "Wouldn't you like to know what he does when he makes love now?"

"Oh, sweetheart, been there, done that. I've had him, so I know."

"*Had.* That's the operative word. I *have* him. Present tense. And you just can't deal with that."

Candace's arrogant smile began to fade. "If I really wanted him, trust me I would have him."

"If that's what you have to tell yourself to sleep at night, then so be it." Aja stepped up in Candace's face. "But until you get him, you need to back the fuck up off my man before I grab that cake knife over there and slice up your pretty little face. And don't let my kind face fool you, I can get real ghetto if need be."

Candace gasped. Aja thought she heard a small cheer from Roxie, but right now all her attention was focused on the woman standing in front of her. Candace tried to compose herself but everyone could tell her confidence had been shattered.

"Oh, so now you want to get all bold. You weren't saying that when you thought I was carrying his child."

Aja could've let the comment get to her, but if she didn't know anything else, she knew Charles was hers. All hers and only hers. "I'm through talking to you, Candace. I would advise you to get your pathetic, desperate ass out of my face and away from my man before that three hundred dollar outfit you're wearing ends up ripped to shreds on the floor."

Charles stepped up beside Aja, wrapping his arm around her waist. "Candace. You can play all the games you want. But the bottom line is, I don't want you. I will never want you. No amount of conniving and throwing yourself at me will make me feel otherwise. You aren't half the woman Aja is and if I were you, I would turn around and walk out of here while I still had some dignity left."

Candace looked around at all the people staring at her. Several other people had stopped talking and were looking at them like they were waiting for a catfight to break out. Roxie casually strolled up behind Candace, leaned in, and whispered, "Pick your face up off the floor, bitch, and get to stepping."

Candace rolled her eyes, huffed, then spun and stormed out. Everyone watched her leave.

Pat stepped in, breaking the uncomfortable silence. "Ahem, that was our entertainment for the evening. And if you liked that, you'll love the drama in my book, *When Loved Ones Lie,* which can be purchased for $14.95 at that table right over there in the corner."

Several people laughed as the crowd of spectators began dispersing.

Roxie hugged Aja. "Girl, I didn't know you had it in you."

Aja smiled as Charles squeezed her hand. "I didn't either."

"That's my baby," Charles said. "First she put my mother in her place, now Candace." He leaned in and kissed her. "She's just a regular little whippersnapper."

"Whippersnapper?" Roxie said, looking back and forth between Aja and Charles. "Oh my God, you two were meant for each other."

Aja and Charles laughed as Roxie walked off, shaking her head.

Thirty-nine

The migraine was in full effect now. Aja ignored the warning label and popped another Advil—her fourth in the last three hours.

"You're going to overdose," Charles said as he adjusted the bow tie that perfectly matched his tuxedo.

Aja grimaced as the pill struggled to slide down her throat. She gagged, then ran to the bathroom and stuck her mouth under the faucet. She relaxed and closed her eyes as the water washed the pill down.

"I'm starting to think overdosing would be better than having to go through with this evening." Aja wiped the dripping water from around her mouth, then walked back into the bedroom. She eyed Charles as he primped in the mirror. The sight of him brought a smile to her face. They had picked up where they'd left off, and their relationship had never been better. They'd spent almost every day of the last month together. She had tried to put Troy out of her mind and be the type of woman Charles deserved. Facing her demons had given Aja a newfound strength. And she was determined to do things differently this go round.

"So, do I look okay?" Charles asked.

Aja nodded her approval. Charles looked spectacular in his Armani french-cuffed tuxedo. His hair was freshly cut and his skin glistened—the effect of a rigorous skin-care regimen. Charles was sure to dazzle the crowd when he stepped onstage to give his acceptance speech for the Peabody Award for Outstanding Sports Reporting. "You know you look spectacular."

"So do you."

Aja sighed thoughtfully. "Yeah, well I need to down a few more pills to prepare me for this evening."

"Come on now, it can't be that bad." Charles kissed Aja on the forehead and walked into the kitchen. "You act like you have to spend the evening with Attila the Hun."

"Close," Aja muttered.

"I heard that," Charles called out from the other room.

Aja sat down on the edge of the bed. She so did not want to endure this evening. Of course, she wanted to be there for Charles, but she just couldn't bear the thought of having to spend the entire evening with his mother.

"Why can't your mother come with someone else tonight?" Aja whined.

Charles reappeared in the doorway and leaned against the door frame. "This means a lot to me. This night is special and I want the two special women in my life to be there sharing it with me. Besides, you two really need to get to know each other. I think once she knows you, she'll see what I see and fall in love with you just like I did."

Aja contemplated making a smart remark, but she knew how much putting forth an effort meant to Charles. They'd already had this argument countless times and Charles wasn't budging.

"Sweetheart, please don't make this any more difficult,"

Charles said. "If I didn't have to be there early, you know I'd never leave you alone with her."

Aja inhaled. Charles never asked her for anything. He was always giving and she was always taking. It was about time she did something for him. Besides, if she was going to be with him, she would have to learn to deal with his mother.

"Fine," Aja mumbled. "But please tell me I don't have to go to Galveston and pick her up."

Charles smiled and grabbed his cufflinks off the dresser before heading out of the room again. "Of course not. Her next door neighbor, Mr. Brinkley, was heading this way and offered to drop her off."

Aja lay back on the bed and closed her eyes. The doorbell caused them to pop right back open.

"That's probably Mother right there."

"Oh my God, no!" Aja jumped up and looked at the alarm clock. "What is she doing this early? It's just five o'clock. The ceremony doesn't start until seven."

Charles just shrugged as he walked toward the door. "That's just the way my mom is, she has always liked getting places early." Aja made her way into the living room while Charles opened the door. "Hello, Mother."

Mrs. Clayton looked just as stunning as her son. Her silver hair was immaculately swept up into a bun on the top of her head. Her pearl floor-length gown looked like it cost more than Aja made in an entire month. A brown mink wrap draped her shoulders.

"Hello, my darling wonderful son." She stuck her cheek out for Charles to kiss, which he did.

Mrs. Clayton turned her attention to Aja, who had followed Charles out of the bedroom. "Aja, how are you?"

Aja almost fell over backward. *She got my name right.* "I'm fine, Mrs. Clayton." Aja managed a small smile. "You look absolutely beautiful." Maybe this evening wouldn't be as bad as she thought.

"I'm sure you'll look beautiful too, as soon as you change into your outfit for the evening." Mrs. Clayton's eyes made their way up and down Aja's body. Her nose was turned up in disgust.

Okay, maybe it will be as bad as I thought.

Charles quickly jumped in. "Mother, Aja is wearing what she has on. And I happen to think it's beautiful."

Aja tried to hold her head up high and forced a smile. She thought she was looking rather cute. She had on a strapless mauve Vera Wang dress that hugged her body up top, then draped out into a beautiful flowing bottom.

"Besides," Charles continued, "I picked that gown out and specifically asked her to wear it."

Mrs. Clayton glared at her son, most likely trying to determine if he was being honest. "You picked that out?"

"I sure did."

Aja wanted to jump in and ask Charles why he was lying. She and Roxie had picked out that dress and Charles didn't have a single thing to do with it. But he looked like he did not want to get into a long, drawn-out argument, so she just let the comment slide.

"Well, okay. If Ajax wants to look like she's going to a pajama party, then that's fine with me."

"Mother, please. You know her name is Aja."

Mrs. Clayton wobbled past Charles and over to the sofa, where she eased herself down. "That's what I said, isn't it?"

Charles sighed heavily. Aja felt bad for him. This was his big night and having to play referee was taking its toll. "Baby, it's okay." Aja walked over to Charles and rubbed his back. "Don't let any of this stress you out. Your mother and I will be fine." Aja tried to feign a smile.

"Really?" Charles asked hopefully.

Hell, no, Aja wanted to say. "Yes, really."

Charles looked over at his mother, a haughty expression on her face. "I'm sorry to do this to you," he whispered. "I just want her to get to know you."

"Don't apologize. I can handle it. I've had a whole bottle of Advil, remember?" Aja smiled. "Now, you get going. We'll see you in a little bit."

Charles stroked her hair gratefully. "I love you for this, you know that, right?"

"You better."

Charles lightly kissed Aja, then made his way over to the sofa where he kissed his mother on the cheek as well.

"Mother, please behave," he said.

"Don't I always?"

Charles gave Aja an apologetic look, then headed out the door. Aja stood at the door with her back to Mrs. Clayton. She inhaled deeply, then turned around. "Can I get you anything?"

"No, I'm fine." Mrs. Clayton clutched her purse tightly. "I'll just sit here until you're ready."

"Well, can I turn on the TV or something?"

"I don't watch that garbage—except for Charles, of course."

Aja stood for a moment, an awkward silence hanging in the air. "Okay then. I guess I'll just go finish curling my hair."

"Hmpph. You sure are comfortable here," Mrs. Clayton muttered.

Aja sighed, then decided to ignore the comment. She went back to Charles's bedroom and began curling her hair.

"You sure are comfortable here," Aja mocked as she maneuvered the hot curling iron around several strands of hair. "Hell yeah, I'm comfortable here. This is my man's place." Aja felt her fury building. Why did that woman have to be so ornery? And what the hell was that "Ajax" about? "Ouch!" Aja jumped after burning her ear with the curling iron. "Calm down," she told herself. She gently placed the iron back on the counter. "Tonight is special. Don't let her ruin it." Aja stared at her reflection in the mirror. Her image seemed to be speaking to her. *You stood up for yourself before. Do it again. Go in there and give that woman a piece of your mind.*

The thought was tempting, but Aja knew how much Charles loved his mother and he would be genuinely hurt if the night didn't go as planned. He had been so good to her, enduring her emotional baggage and never asking for anything in return. He was her dream come true and she needed to make an effort to have a better relationship with his mother, even if it killed her.

Aja took another breath, said a quick prayer, and walked back into the living room.

Mrs. Clayton was still sitting on the sofa, her back straight, poised like she was about to take a family portrait.

"Why do you have a problem with me?" Aja softly asked.

Mrs. Clayton ran her eyes up and down Aja's body, a stoic expression plastered on her face. She hesitated before speaking.

"Charles is all I have." Mrs. Clayton's voice had lost its usual confidence. She sounded surprisingly defeated. Even her eyes drooped as if the realization that her son was a grown man was finally setting in. And for the first time since meeting her, Aja felt a tinge of sympathy for Charles's mother.

She walked over and sat in the armchair across from Mrs. Clayton.

"I don't want to take Charles away from you. I *couldn't* take Charles away from you. He loves you too much. But I love him too. You know your son. There's room enough in his heart for both of us," Aja said.

Mrs. Clayton swallowed. She seemed to be fighting back tears. Aja was shocked. You couldn't have paid her to believe she would ever see this side of Mrs. Clayton.

"I know I need to let Charles go," Mrs. Clayton responded, her voice wavering. "My husband, God rest his soul, always told me I babied him. But that is my baby. He has a big heart and I don't want him hurt."

"I won't hurt him."

"You already have."

Aja flinched. Maybe she deserved that one. She had wondered if Charles told his mother about their breakup, but she guessed she had her answer now.

"I was the one Charles came to when you left him," Mrs. Clayton continued. "I watched the sadness and pain in his eyes. Pain that was multiplied because he didn't even know why you left him—at least that's what he told me."

Aja didn't know what to say. She hated that Charles had told his mother. She had enough strikes against her as it was. But then, why wouldn't he tell her, especially considering how close they were?

"I was relieved when he first told me," Mrs. Clayton continued. "I was hoping that he'd get over you quickly and move on. So imagine my surprise when he told me you two were back together."

Aja struggled to keep her composure. "I'm sorry. I was confused. I come from a background where you don't put a lot of faith in relationships," Aja responded.

"Well, we come from a background where you do. My Charles is a good man. Are you a good woman?"

Aja lowered her eyes. Was she a good woman? She had enough drama to fill a lifetime of soap operas. She had let her distrust lead her into the arms of another man. Charles brought so much to the table. What did she bring? Aja reflected on Mrs. Clayton's words. Normally, she would have let those words get to her. But standing up to Candace had given her the confidence to demand respect, even from someone like Charles's mother. And her resolve seemed to be strengthening.

Aja slowly raised her head. Her eyes were glossy, yet full of a newfound confidence.

"Yes, I am a good woman. And I will make Charles happy."

Mrs. Clayton glared at her. Aja matched her gaze, drawing strength from the piercing stare. Mrs. Clayton's expression softened. Not much, but enough for Aja to notice.

"Nobody's ever talked to me like you do."

Aja didn't know if that was a compliment or an admonishment. She decided to play it safe and kept a blank expression.

"I don't ever want to disrespect you, but I love Charles and we're together now. I hope that you will learn to accept that."

Mrs. Clayton sighed heavily. "I guess I can learn to accept it. That doesn't mean I have to like it."

Aja took a deep breath. This was going to be a long journey. "Okay, Mrs. Clayton. I can't do anything about that. I hope for Charles's sake, in time, you'll learn to feel differently. I'm going to finish my hair. Give me fifteen minutes and I'll be ready to go." Aja stood and began making her way to the bedroom.

"You can have ten minutes, then I'm calling a cab. I don't want to be late."

Aja kept her back turned. She wanted to scream. "Fine. I will be ready to go in ten minutes." Aja continued toward the room.

Mrs. Clayton stopped her. "Oh, and Aja . . ."

"Yes?" Aja turned around and bit her bottom lip. Getting along with this woman was going to be a lot harder than she had thought.

"My baby likes you. A lot. So I guess I can try to like you."

Aja was dumbfounded. Was she hearing things? Mrs. Clayton still refused to smile, but a huge grin swept across Aja's face. It wasn't much, but Aja could tell just by the look on Mrs. Clayton's face that giving her a chance had taken great effort.

"Your baby loves me, so maybe one day you can love me too," Aja gently said.

"I don't know about all that," Mrs. Clayton quickly responded.

Aja stood with a huge smile plastered across her face.

"Well, don't just stand there looking like a Cheshire cat. Go finish combing your hair. It looks horrible," Mrs. Clayton snapped.

"I'll be ready in five minutes." Aja felt like she floated into the bathroom. She was on cloud nine. All she could think of was how happy this little truce would make Charles.

"And for his special report, 'Rockets Revealed,' the Peabody for Outstanding Sports Reporting goes to Charles Clayton with KTKR, Channel 13." The announcer held up the gold statuette as Charles stood and made his way to the podium. The audience erupted in applause.

Aja was beaming with excitement. She glanced over at Mrs. Clayton who looked like a proud mother hen. Roxie and Brian sat on the other side of Aja, along with some people from Charles's station.

Everyone rose to their feet clapping until Charles finally accepted the award.

Aja felt like crying. But this time, from joy. Charles had put a lot of work into that story, which chronicled the lives of four Houston Rockets players from boyhood to the NBA. He had won three Emmys before, but this was his first time winning the prestigious Peabody Award.

"Thank you." Charles's voice quieted the audience, and they began easing back into their seats.

Charles gave a quick speech then cleared his throat. "Before I go, I have to thank the special person in my life who encouraged me to fight to get this story told. Aja James, will you please stand up?"

Aja looked around nervously. What was Charles doing? She hadn't expected to become the center of attention. She felt frozen in her seat.

"Girl, stand your ass up," Roxie whispered.

Aja eased out of her chair and forced a small wave at the crowd. She was going to get Charles for this. Aja tried to slink back down in her chair but under the table Roxie hit her in the leg. "Don't sit down yet," Roxie muttered.

What is going on? Aja wondered.

"Let me first apologize to everyone," Charles continued. "I have talked with Jim and the other organizers of tonight's event about this and they've given me the go-ahead, so I'll ask that you bear with me for just a minute."

Charles cleared his throat again, then began walking toward Aja. The spotlight followed him as he made his way back to the table.

Aja turned toward Roxie, a bewildered look on her face. Roxie just shrugged and started stirring her coffee.

Charles stopped in front of the table and kissed his mother on the cheek. She gave him a reassuring smile as he handed her his award. Charles turned toward Aja and looked her straight in the eye. The room was silent and all eyes were on them.

"Charles, what are you doing?" Aja whispered.

"Shut up, girl. You talk too much," Mrs. Clayton hissed.

Charles quickly shot his mother an admonishing look before turning back to Aja. He gently took Aja's hand, then eased down on his left knee.

When the reality of what he was about to do set in, Aja felt her heart begin to race.

"Oh my God," she muttered.

Charles ignored the trembling that had suddenly taken over Aja's hand.

"Aja, you satisfy me mentally, emotionally, and spiritually. I believe God has a divine plan for all of our lives. And a special person He wants us to share that plan with. Someone to complete our purpose on this earth. You are my completion." Charles reached in his jacket pocket and pulled out a small box. He opened the box to reveal a glistening three-carat pear-shaped diamond ring. "Aja Jenine James, will you marry me?"

Aja paused, letting the words sink in. Was this really happening?

"Ahem," Roxie let out a fake cough and Aja snapped back to reality.

"Yes! Yes, Charles, I will marry you." Aja pulled Charles up toward her and threw her arms around his neck." He squeezed her tightly.

Aja ignored the oohs, ahhs, and awwws coming from the crowd. She ignored Roxie's giggling next to her. She ignored the thunder of applause vibrating through the room. She focused all her attention on the man in front of her, letting the tears of joy finally flow freely down her face.

Forty

It was a long drive to Conner Correctional Facility. Aja still couldn't figure out how she ended up in the car on her way to see her father. Although it had been well over a month since her father called, it seemed like just yesterday that she was lamenting to Charles about how she would never go visit him. She needed to be off somewhere making wedding plans, not on her way to prison to see her father. Yet here they were. In her heart, though, Aja knew it was time. She had to face her demons. Her future with Charles depended on it. That's the one thing she had gotten from her two sessions with her psychiatrist. Aja had finally scheduled an appointment and actually gone twice, on two back-to-back days. She liked the elderly white man who was helping her work through her problems. He told her she was harboring pain that kept her from moving forward. Of course, she already knew that, but he had been helping her talk about it and that was making a world of difference. He, too, had suggested she visit her father.

She'd shocked Charles last week when she told him she wanted to go see her father.

"I never thought this day would come," Aja sighed.

"What?" Charles looked over at Aja in the passenger seat.

"I just said, I never thought this day would come."

"I know, but it's time."

"Yeah, yeah, yeah, as you've constantly told me since I first met you." Aja stared out the window. Was she making a mistake? She hadn't seen or talked to her father in thirteen years.

Aja thought about Jada and the joy she had after receiving their father's letter. She didn't remember anything—why she was the way she was.

"Maybe that's best," Aja muttered.

"What do you keep mumbling about over there?" Charles asked.

Aja shook her head. "Nothing. Just revving myself up for this."

Charles reached across the armrest and took Aja's hand. "Just know that I'm here by your side every step of the way." Aja gave a faint smile. She was skeptical about this whole visit thing, but she felt she could make it through with Charles by her side.

Once they arrived at Conner's, it took another hour to actually check in, get frisked, and all that other stuff they do to prison visitors before they are able to actually go back to the visiting room.

"Follow me." The guard led them through a long, musty hallway and into a large room with tables. The room was a flurry of activity. All across the room loved ones were reuniting. Some were crying. A few looked angry. Kids were running all over the room. A wide array of emotions were displayed. Aja didn't know how she would react.

"You can have a seat right there. He'll be right out." The guard pointed to a table in the far right-hand corner. Charles nodded at the guard, took Aja by the elbow, and led her to the table.

"You okay?" he asked after he saw the nervous look on Aja's face.

"Yeah. Thanks for coming with me today." Aja grabbed Charles's hand and squeezed it tightly.

He leaned over and lightly kissed her on the lips. "Now where else would I be?"

"I know. It's just I know I've been really difficult and all, but . . ." Aja stopped talking and stared at the doorway. There he was. He looked a whole lot older, but there was no mistaking him. The little flab that used to surround his stomach looked firm and muscular. His black, short-cropped Afro and beard were now peppered with gray. There were bags under his eyes and a few more wrinkles across his sandpaper-colored face. But other than that, Gerald James looked the same as he did thirteen years ago.

Gerald walked to the back of the room where Aja and Charles were sitting. "Hey, pumpkin," he said with a grin.

Aja sat with a stunned look on her face.

Charles tried to break the awkward silence. He stood up and shook Gerald's hand. "Hi, Mr. James, I'm Charles."

Gerald took Charles's hand and shook it vigorously. "Charles Clayton, nice to meet you. I've caught you on the tube a couple of times doing the NFL games, but I don't get a whole lot of TV time around here." Gerald let go of Charles's hand and sat down across from Aja. Charles sat down as well. Aja still didn't move.

Gerald's eyes scanned his daughter. "You blossomed into one beautiful young woman. You look just like your—" Gerald caught himself. Aja shot him a look like she dared him to mention her mother.

"Anyway, thank you for coming," he continued. "You can't even begin to imagine how much this means to me. Did you get any of my letters?"

Aja clutched her purse tighter, still unable to say a word. She couldn't bring herself to open her mouth.

"Umm . . ." Charles cut in. "Understandably, Mr. James, Aja is a little nervous about all this." He turned to Aja. "Baby, I'm going to give you two some time together." He got up to go, but Aja grabbed his arm.

"No, I want you to stay," she said without taking her eyes off her father.

"I don't mind, Charles," Gerald said. He looked at Aja. "But nervous? Why would my pumpkin be nervous?"

"Would you stop saying that!" Aja snapped. "I stopped being your pumpkin thirteen years ago!"

Gerald looked hurt. "You know I would never hurt you." He stared at his daughter as tears welled up in his eyes.

"I never thought you'd hurt Mama either." Aja's words were cold and calculating.

Gerald looked down at the table. "Aja, like I told you, your sister, and your brother in my letters, I'm sorry. I am so sorry. I never meant to hurt her. When your mama pulled that gun out, I knew she would never use it. Just like I knew I'd never use it. It was an accident. An accident that I have regretted every single second since it happened." Tears streamed down Gerald's face as he continued. "Did you know your brother came to see me?"

"What? When?" Aja responded. Eric had never mentioned a desire to talk to their father, let alone to come see him.

"About three years ago. Right when he moved back home. I think things were getting serious with his girlfriend and I guess he was trying to put the past behind him and move on. Only it didn't work. The visit didn't go too well. He had so much hate. I told him then that hate would kill him. I told him!" Gerald pounded the table. For a moment Aja felt a tinge of sympathy. It quickly passed.

"Eric died because he didn't want to be like you." Aja felt tears forming under her eyelids, but she refused to let them fall.

"Don't you think I know that?" Gerald cried. "Don't you think that's tearing me up? I know that Eric is dead because he had my temper and it destroyed him! I know that Jada's in that place because of me! I know that my family is in turmoil because of me! If I could turn back time so I'd be the one that died that night, I would!"

Aja felt the hardness in her heart start to weaken. "Why? Why did you do it?"

Gerald wiped his eyes. His voice cracked as he spoke. "It's a question I have asked myself for the last thirteen years. Why? The only answer I can come up with is that I loved you all so much."

"What kind of crazy answer is that?" Any sympathy Aja was starting to feel quickly dissipated. "Getting drunk and killing my mother is your definition of love?"

"That was an accident. What I mean is that I wanted to be the perfect father, the perfect husband. When I lost my job and couldn't find another one, I felt like a failure."

"Lots of men lose their jobs. They don't become alcoholics who kill their wives."

"Please let me finish," Gerald said. He took a deep breath and continued. "I used to love the light in my kids' eyes when I came home with an armload of gifts. When we could do stuff together. Do you know Jada wanted a birthday party and I couldn't even give that to her? We were about to lose the house. When your mother and I married, we talked about how we couldn't wait to get to a point where she could be a stay-at-home mom. When she had to go back to work, she was crushed. But she never let on. And that crushed me. Everything we had was gone and I didn't know how to handle it, so I started drinking. First just beers all the time, then the hard stuff. Before I knew it, I was an alcoholic. Only I didn't realize it. And I refused to listen to anybody. I felt like a failure and I drank more. Things got worse and worse between your mama and me and I was scared of losing her, so I drank more. I was drunk that night."

"No kidding," Aja snidely remarked. Nothing he said could change the past.

Gerald ignored Aja's sarcasm and kept going. "I was drunk but I still would've never intentionally hurt her. I don't know. It was just stupid. I got mad when your mama pulled out that gun, even though I knew it was the only way she thought she could stop me, to scare me. Between my anger and being drunk—well, things just got out of hand."

Aja was speechless.

Gerald continued talking. "I couldn't get your brother to forgive me before it was too late. I'm begging you to forgive me and let it go."

Aja paused, then stood up. "I came to see you like you wanted. Now please don't bother me again." Aja turned to Charles. "Can we go now?" Aja started walking to the door.

Charles didn't protest. He stood up. "I'm sorry, Mr. James. It's just going to take some time."

"I know. Thank you for convincing her to come."

Charles nodded and darted off behind Aja who was already summoning the guard to let them out.

"I love you, pumpkin," Gerald called out. "You can hate me for the rest of your life. But I'll always love you!"

Aja didn't turn around. She let the prison doors slam on the sound of her father's voice.

Forty-one

Aja didn't have much to say on the drive home from the prison. Part of her was mad at herself for even thinking that visiting her father was a good thing.

She rolled down her window and stared outside as they sped down the highway. The countryside was beautiful. Aja loved the smell of the outdoors. They passed a cotton field that reminded Aja of the stories her father used to tell her about growing up in Mississippi. They were stories she loved hearing, back when she loved her father so much it was unbelievable. Those days were long gone, though. She didn't even feel like he was her daddy anymore, just Gerald.

"I'm sorry I got upset. I guess I just wasn't ready to face or deal with him."

Charles nodded without saying anything. They spent the next twenty minutes riding in silence. The only noise was the whir of the car as they whipped down the highway.

"It's still early. I bet I know what can cheer you up," Charles finally said. "Let's go see Elise and the baby."

Aja smiled. That sounded like a great idea. Elise was staying with her mother. Her parents had actually moved to Houston three months before Eric died. It was a good thing they did, because Elise's sister lived in a small one-bedroom apartment with her two kids. It would have been a madhouse if Elise had to go there. Aja had talked to Elise almost every day since the funeral. Elise was still reeling from Eric's death. Sometimes Aja thought Elise wished she had died that night. But Madison kept her going. That little girl was probably the only reason Elise willed herself to live that night. "That sounds wonderful." Aja leaned over and softly kissed Charles's cheek. "I knew there was a reason I liked you."

"Like? Just like?" Charles playfully responded.

"Did I say like? I meant love." Aja kissed Charles's neck. "Adore . . . desire . . ."

"Hey, hey!" Charles weaved to the side of the road. "You're going to make me have a wreck. Besides, in your infamous words, you don't want to start nothing you can't finish."

"Okay." Aja grinned and leaned back in the seat. Her anger at her father was starting to evaporate. Suddenly she felt herself enjoying the countryside, watching Charles as he mimicked the singers on the radio. He had a way of singing every song, even when he didn't know the words, that made Aja laugh—anything that could make her laugh after leaving her father was good.

"So what do you think?" Aja said when they finally pulled into the city.

"Think about what?"

"My father."

Charles paused. "Honestly? I think he's really and truly sorry."

Aja didn't respond. Surprisingly, she agreed. Although the visit didn't go well, the one thing Aja did get out of it was that Gerald was sorry. But was sorry enough to heal the hurt?

"You know Charles, I don't understand how a man goes from one extreme to another. From a loving father to a raving monster."

"I can't condone anything your father did, but I think you've blocked out all the good stuff. There was good stuff, wasn't there?" Charles kept one hand on the steering wheel and reached over with the other hand to gently caress Aja's arm.

She reluctantly nodded.

"Do you think it's possible you can ever remember that sometimes, instead of all the bad stuff?"

"I don't know Charles, I just don't know."

Charles nodded again as he pulled into South Park, the neighborhood where Elise's mother and father lived. Elise's parents had bought the house from a distant relative when they retired last year. They had spent months fixing it up and had finally moved in.

"Wow, I can't believe they actually live over here." Charles's nose was turned up in disgust.

Aja glanced at all the garbage that littered the streets and the men hanging out on the corner with bottles of liquor in their hands.

"Are you being a snob?" She smiled at Charles.

"No, it's just, they moved here from out of town. You'd think they would have picked a nicer neighborhood."

"Well, they got a good deal on the house. And Elise's parents are just down-home people. Besides, I know lots of people who grew up in this area with no problems. And not everybody wants to live in the suburbs."

Charles just shook his head as he parked his car in the driveway behind Elise's mother's 1988 Cadillac. Aja laughed as

Charles pulled the handle to make sure his door was locked, looked around nervously, then checked the handle again.

"Your car will be safe."

Charles gave her a look like he wasn't too sure.

Aja laughed and walked in the house. "Hey girl." Elise was sitting in a recliner, covered with a blanket. Aja bent down and hugged her. "Where's my niece?"

Elise smiled the saddest smile Aja had ever seen. A deep, mournful smile. Her eyes were swollen and her hair looked disheveled. "Hey, guys. Madison is in the back with my mom." Elise looked up as her mother made her way into the living room. "Oh, here she comes now."

Elise's mother walked in holding Madison in her arms. Pearl Wooten was a burly woman in her late fifties. She had a jovial look no matter what mood she was in. She loved her daughter like crazy. She had liked Eric but hadn't been too pleased with the fact that he'd never had a real job. Still, she stood strong by her daughter's side at the funeral.

"Hey, Mama Pearl." Aja leaned in and tightly hugged Elise's mother. She had met Pearl and her husband, Eli, on several occasions when they came down to visit Elise and her sister, Valencia. "Mama Pearl, this is Charles."

"Pleased to meet you, ma'am." Charles extended his hand.

"Everybody gives Mama Pearl a hug." Pearl reached over and hugged Charles with her one free arm. "Nice to meet you too. You just make yourself at home." She handed the baby over to Aja.

"You wanna go to your auntie?" Pearl said. She ruffled the little curly black hairs on Madison's head and turned to Elise. "Will you be all right? I'm tired, but I have to go to the store. I'm supposed to bake a cake tonight for usher board meeting and I'm all out of eggs. Your father is out playing golf somewhere and I don't know when he'll be home."

"I'll be fine, Ma," Elise responded. "You want me to go to the store for you?"

"Why don't I go?" Charles cut in. "It'll give you two ladies and the little one here time to bond, and you, Mrs. Wooten, can get some rest."

A huge smile crossed Pearl's face. "Why thank you, darling. That would be so nice." She reached in her bra and took out a five-dollar bill.

Aja and Elise snickered at the embarrassed look on Charles's face. Pearl didn't pay them any attention. "I need one pack of extra-large eggs and a little bottle of vanilla flavoring. And make sure you check to see that those eggs ain't broke. I can't stand to pay good money for no cracked eggs. My husband, bless his heart, he never checks. It just drives me crazy."

Charles laughed. "Yes, ma'am. Be right back." He kissed Aja lightly on the lips. "You want anything?"

"No thanks."

After Charles left, Pearl smiled and turned to Aja. "He's a keeper. Handsome and fine too. Y'all goin' make some pretty babies."

Aja chuckled. "No babies anytime soon."

"Well, I don't know what you waiting on. You goin' be too old in a minute." She kissed Madison on the head. "Granny goin' go lay down for a minute. I'm sho' tired."

Elise waited until her mother left the room before turning to Aja. "So let me see it!"

Aja grinned and held out her hand.

Elise leaned in and peered at the ring. Her eyes widened. "Dang, check that out. Now why couldn't I get your brother to give me one like that?" Aja watched as the smile slowly left Elise's face.

"He loved you so much," Aja softly said as she noticed Elise's eyes watering up.

"I know. And I loved him." Elise took a deep breath. "But I'm not going to cry anymore. I have to be strong. That's what he would want."

"Yeah, he'd want us both to be strong." Aja rubbed Madison's back. The infant had laid her head on Aja's shoulder. Her tiny hands were firmly grasping Aja's shirt. "How are you holding up, really?" Aja could tell when she talked to Elise last night that things weren't too good. But now, seeing her confirmed it.

"I'm making it. I have good days and bad days. I'm just glad Mama is here. She's taking real good care of both me and Madison. So don't worry about me.

"Anyway, I'm glad you said yes. Charles is a good man and you know good men are hard to find." Elise's smile faded again. "Eric was a good man. He just didn't know it." She shook the thought away. "Here I go again talking about Eric." She nodded her head. "But he did have a good heart."

"I know. I just wish I could've helped him realize that," Aja said.

Elise's look turned serious. "Aja, that wasn't your job. What happened to you guys was beyond your control. Eric used to always gripe about how protective you were. I understand you were doing what you felt you had to do, but he's gone. Maybe now you can move on."

"That's what I'm trying to do." Aja sat down on the couch across from Elise. The baby had fallen asleep in her arms. She looked lovingly at her niece.

"She is getting so big."

"I know. It seems like she gets to wear her clothes only once or twice before she outgrows them."

Aja struggled for something to talk about. She had never been at a loss for words with Elise, but now she didn't know what to say. "I saw my father today," Aja finally said.

Elise's ears perked up. "Oh yeah? How did it go?"

"Not very good. He says he's sorry and all, and I actually believe him, but I don't think I'll ever be able to forgive him. He's the reason Eric isn't here today." Aja really didn't want to get into a discussion about her father, but somehow it just popped out.

"No, Aja, the fact that Eric couldn't forgive your father is the reason he isn't here today. I will always love Eric. But I'm going to tell you that boy had a stubborn streak in him."

Aja laughed. "Who are you telling? He was one of the most stubborn people I know. Only he didn't think so."

"Yeah, it's that stubbornness that kept him from getting help, dealing with what happened, and most importantly, forgiving and moving on. Don't let that happen to you," Elise warned.

Aja looked down at Madison. The infant was absolutely beautiful. Aja ran her fingers across the baby's cheek.

"You can go lay her down on my bed." Elise pointed toward the back.

Aja gently got up and walked down the hall to the back bedroom Elise had claimed. She laid Madison down, moved the pillows out of the way, grabbed a baby blanket draped across a chair, and placed it over the infant. Aja turned the light out and eased the door shut.

When she made her way back into the living room, she noticed Elise staring off into space. Aja didn't know what to say to her—she definitely felt her pain. If anybody came close to loving Eric as much as Aja did, it was Elise. Aja thought about what

Elise had just said. Maybe Elise had a point, because God knows she was tired of being angry. Aja knew she'd never be able to forget, but maybe she could forgive. That's something she was going to really think about.

Aja summoned up her strength, forced a smile, and walked back in to try to cheer up Elise.

Forty-two

"The parole board said yes!" Aunt Shirley was screaming into the phone. "Your daddy's coming home!"

The news hit Aja like a rock. She sat in stunned silence. Sure, she knew it was a possibility, but never in a million years did she think it would actually happen. Her father was going free. Thirteen years. He served thirteen years for killing her mother and was now about to walk away like it never happened.

"Baby, I know how you feel about it. I know when you went to see him, it didn't go too well. He told me," Aunt Shirley said after Aja didn't respond. "Like I've been telling you for years, that's still your daddy. Ain't nothing you can do or say can change that. It was a horrible accident brought on by a horrible time in y'all's life."

Aja sighed heavily. She didn't want to hear this song and dance. She had heard it so many times before. Aunt Shirley continued anyway. "You need to forgive him. He has been a miserable man. I don't think he's forgiven himself. God's forgiven him, but he hasn't forgiven himself. You need to do that. Aja, are you there?"

Aja hesitated, but didn't answer.

"You think about what I'm saying, okay?"

"Aunt Shirley, I gotta go."

Aunt Shirley continued on, ignoring Aja's attitude. "I am going to have a little something at the house because it will be a glorious day when Gerald comes home. It sure would be nice if you were there."

"Auntie, I don't know if I'm ready for that."

"No time like the present to get ready."

"But—"

"I won't take no for an answer."

Aja wanted to argue, but she knew with Aunt Shirley it was futile. As a teenager, she had spent many days arguing for an extended curfew or to go somewhere. They were arguments that she never won. Eventually, anyone who ever argued with her aunt just gave up. Her domineering personality always won out. The best thing would be to say she'd be there and then just not show up. Better to deal with Aunt Shirley's anger after the fact than listen to her pleading lectures beforehand.

"All right, Aunt Shirley, I'll see what I can do."

"No, you won't. I'll *see* you there," she firmly declared. "And feel free to bring your friend Charles." Aunt Shirley hung the phone up before Aja could say anything else.

Aja didn't care how good Aunt Shirley had been to her, this was one request she simply could not honor. She'd rather die than celebrate her father's release.

Aja picked up the laundry basket of clothes she had been carrying before she stopped to answer the telephone. She walked to her utility room and began sorting the clothes. Thoughts of her father clouded her mind. *How can I ever forgive him?*

Aja stuffed clothes into the washing machine. "Would you want me to forgive him?" She found herself talking out loud. She would give anything to hear her mother's voice. She started the washing machine and walked back into her bedroom.

For some reason, Aja's eyes made their way to her closet. She walked over, opened the closet door, and pulled out a large shoebox from the back. Inside were all the letters and cards from her childhood—everything that was special. Aja riffled through the box until she came across a letter on light pink stationery. It was from her mother, written when Aja was fifteen and away at camp. Aja started reading:

My Dearest Aja,

I am so proud of you. You are the light of my life. It's amazing watching the young woman you have become. I know whatever it is you choose to do in life, you will excel. You have a desire like something I've never seen. If I had the power to create from scratch the type of daughter I wanted, I would create you. No changes. Just you.

I know things aren't good at home right now, the problems with your father and I. But we're going to make it through this. Your father is a good man who has fallen on hard times. The devil is hard at work on him. And right now, it appears the devil is winning, but in the end God will emerge victorious. You've got to believe that. You know it wasn't always like this. That's why I'm going to stand by him as long as I can. I'm staying for my family, because I promised your father for better or for worse.

Things will get back to normal. Please don't be angry with your father for the things he's doing to our family. We just have to be strong. I'm counting on you as the oldest to help me be strong and to understand why I'm staying.

*Well, I just wanted to say hello and let you know everyone
misses you and we can't wait for you to come home.*
   Love always, Mama

That was written in July 1984—four months before her
mother died. Aja wondered if her mom knew there was a possibility things would turn out the way they did. Aja remembered
how Eric had called her at camp that summer, hysterical after
their parents had had another fight. That was the first time Aja
saw how angry her brother could get. Sure, he got mad when
they were growing up, but nothing like that day. He had been
screaming uncontrollably, talking about killing their father if he
ever touched their mother again. He was also mad at their
mother because she wouldn't leave. Eric had even tried to call
the police, but his mother had stopped him, begging him to let
her handle the situation. Aja's mood turned sad at the memory.
She chided herself for being off at camp, frolicking in the woods
with her friends while her little brother and sister were going
through all that.

   Aja folded the letter and gently placed it back in the box.
She continued digging. It had been years since she had gone
through that box. She smiled as she crossed some of the items.
A letter from her first boyfriend. Pictures of her high school
friends. She stopped when she came across an oversize card,
given to her on her twelfth birthday. It had a big red rose on the
front and said "To Daddy's little girl." Aja tossed it aside and
continued digging. She noticed how everything in the box was
a reminder of good times with her father. Aja slowly began
looking at card after card. Birthday cards, congratulation cards,
cards for good grades, for making the honor society, and just-
because cards. Her father loved giving cards, primarily because
he knew Aja liked receiving them. *What happened to the man who*

gave me all these cards? Aja held the stack of cards in both hands. These were the good times Charles was asking about, the times she had forgotten.

It was then Aja decided that while she wouldn't make any promises, she would go to the party. She wouldn't celebrate, but she would be there.

Forty-three

Aja tightly grabbed Charles's hand. She had reservations about coming to this party, but she knew she needed to. Besides, she owed it to her aunt to at least try. They were approaching the entrance to Aunt Shirley's house. Charles reassuringly squeezed her hand. Aja managed a weak smile and walked in. The room was filled with activity. There had to be close to thirty people there. Most were relatives, a few were family friends. Some of the faces looked vaguely familiar. With so much going on, no one actually noticed Aja and Charles enter. Aja was grateful for that—the last thing she wanted was attention. Everybody knew how she felt about her father, so she figured they'd be watching to gauge her reaction.

After they made their way farther into the house, Aja noticed her father standing in the corner talking to several men. She recognized one of the men as Terry, her father's best friend when she was growing up. Terry spotted Aja first and pointed her out. Gerald slowly turned around and his eyes met Aja's. He said something to his friends, then came walking over to Aja and Charles.

"Hey there. I'm so glad you made it." Gerald had a huge

smile across his face—one of those free-at-last smiles. Gerald reached out and hugged Aja. She let go of Charles's hand, but kept her arms at her side, not returning his hug. "Shirley said you would be here. I was skeptical." Her father grinned, not noticing the fact that his daughter failed to hug him back.

"I'm here for Aunt Shirley," Aja dryly said.

Gerald paused. "Long as you're here." He turned to Charles. "And how are you?"

"Just fine. Nice to see you, Mr. James. Congratulations on coming home."

"Thank you, thank you, thank you. It feels so good to be free."

Aja wanted so bad to say something sarcastic, something about him being free while her mother was dead. But something inside her told her to just let it go.

"Shirley put her foot in this food. I can't tell you how good it is not to have to eat creamed mush." Gerald was so excited. Aja couldn't stand to see him so elated. She had to fight to keep her comments to herself. She knew if she was to ever move forward she'd have to get over the bitterness.

"Well, looky here. It's a regular family reunion." Luther appeared out of a back room and patted Gerald on the back. "Ain't you just happy to see your daddy?" he asked Aja.

Aja didn't respond. She didn't feel like dealing with Luther.

"And if it isn't the TV guy." Luther stuck his hand out. "How you doing, Charles Clayton? I'm Aja's cousin Luther."

Charles shook his hand. "Nice to meet you. Aja's told me a lot about you."

"Don't believe none of it. I'm innocent!" Luther slapped his leg and cracked up laughing. Nobody else laughed, but that didn't really seem to matter to him. "Hey, man, can you send me a shout-out on the news?" Luther said after he caught his breath.

"We can't really do shout-outs."

"Can't you just do a little one? Or throw me up a peace sign and I'll know it's for me."

Charles laughed. "I'll see what I can do."

"Right, right. I'll be looking for it." Luther turned to Gerald. "So, unc, have a beer with your favorite nephew." He held up a bottle of Busch.

The expression froze on Aja's face. Gerald looked at the bottle, then quickly said, "Now, Luther, I told you I don't touch that stuff no more."

"Awww, come on, unc. One beer ain't never hurt nobody."

"He said he doesn't touch the stuff anymore," Aja stiffly remarked.

Charles gently grabbed Aja's hand and squeezed it to try to keep her from getting riled up.

"Damn, my bad. I'll go get you some apple juice then," Luther sarcastically said.

"Don't worry about it, Luther. I'll get my own juice when I'm ready."

"Well, excuse me then. I guess I'll just mosey on over here where I'm wanted and maybe get me some of Mama's sweet potato pie."

"Yeah, that'll be a good idea," Aja snapped. "Go somewhere where you're wanted."

"Grrr . . . down girl," Luther growled at his cousin. He laughed and walked off.

"So, you don't drink anymore?" Aja asked her father.

"Well, when you get locked up, you have to go cold turkey," Gerald gently said. "But even if I had access to all the liquor in the world, I wouldn't touch the stuff after what happened."

Aja didn't reply. Her eyes glossed up as she fought back tears. She heard Roxie's voice in the back of her head, chastising her for always crying. She took a deep breath and vowed not to let a teardrop fall from her eyes.

"Well, I'm not going to take up all your time here. I just wanted to say thanks for coming," Gerald said.

"Glad to be here," Charles responded. Again, Aja remained silent.

"I don't know about being glad to be here," Aja whispered when Gerald left.

"I think you handled it very well."

"I'm trying."

After cordial greetings and introductions to a few other people, Aja and Charles made their way into the kitchen. Aunt Shirley was standing over the table, putting out another bowl of macaroni and cheese.

"Hey baby," she said excitedly when she noticed Aja. "I'm so glad you're here!" She wiped her hands on her apron. "And this must be your little friend."

"He's not exactly little," Aja laughed. Aunt Shirley was one of those jolly types who could make a bad mood disappear just by her presence. She had dimples and bright eyes. Her thin black hair had sprinkles of gray.

"You know everybody's little to me," Aunt Shirley chuckled. She was right. She was almost three hundred pounds and wasn't even thinking about losing weight. She reached out and took Charles into a big bear hug, which Charles quickly returned.

Aja scanned the table. It looked like Aunt Shirley had cooked for an army. There was a huge ham smothered in pineapples, turkey and cornbread dressing, a bowl of turnip greens, cole slaw, hot water cornbread, green beans and potatoes, fried okra, corn on the cob, buttermilk dinner rolls, and every kind of pie imaginable.

"Dang, Auntie, you think you got enough food?" Aja asked.

"It ain't every day that my little brother gets to come home." Aunt Shirley noticed the smile fade from Aja's face. "It means a lot to your daddy that you're here. And it means a lot to me too. How you doing with it?" she asked.

"Oh, I guess I'm doing okay," Aja said as she picked up a piece of okra and popped it in her mouth. "It's not easy, but I'm trying to do like you said and put the past behind me. Especially now . . ." Aja paused and looked at Charles, "Especially now, that I'm getting married."

"What!" Aunt Shirley shrieked. "Lord have mercy! When did this happen? And why didn't you call me right away? My Aja is getting married!"

Charles grinned. "We wanted to tell everybody in person."

"You're goin' be part of the family. Praise Jesus!" Aunt Shirley hugged them both again, and then grabbed them each by a hand. "Come on here," she said as she led them back through the swinging kitchen door and into the living room.

"Hey, everybody," she yelled. "I have an announcement to make." The room slowly grew silent as everyone turned their attention to Aunt Shirley.

"As you know," she continued. "We've gathered here today to welcome my brother back. But we're also celebrating something else."

Aja looked down nervously. Aunt Shirley still had Charles by one hand and her by the other. "Aja and Charles are getting married!" she announced.

The room grew noisy again as everyone started clapping and extending their congratulations. Aja blushed. Charles was used to such attention and stood proudly as people started approaching them.

Over the congratulatory noise, they heard Luther yell, "So you goin' let Uncle Gerald give you away?"

Aunt Shirley was standing right next to him when he said it. She popped him on the back of the head.

"What? I was just asking a damn question," he said as he rubbed his head.

Aunt Shirley hit him again. "Don't be cussing in my house."

Luther rolled his eyes and grumbled. "I'm too damn old to be getting hit."

"What? What you say? I'll pop you again," she threatened.

Luther didn't respond. He just kept rubbing his head, then walked over and flopped down on a chair in the corner like a kid who had just broken his mother's favorite lamp.

One of their younger relatives walked over and stuck his tongue out at Luther. "Ah-hah, you got the mess knocked out of you," the seven-year-old teased.

"Get outta my face." Luther kicked at the boy, who took off running, still laughing.

Aja was mulling the question Luther had asked. She had never thought about that. But Gerald was looking at Aja like he was really hoping for an answer. *I hope he doesn't think he's walking me down the aisle.*

Aunt Shirley stepped in and broke the awkward silence. "That's something you don't even need to be worrying about right now. We came here to celebrate."

Thank God she stepped in. Aunt Shirley knew how much was too much and the thought of Aja's father giving her away was just too much.

"Well, I wanted to share the good news. Now back to the party!" Aunt Shirley shouted. "And y'all better get in that kitchen and eat up the rest of that food." She patted her hips. "Because if you don't, you know I will."

As everyone scattered and went back to doing what they were

doing, Gerald made his way back over to Aja and Charles. "Congratulations," he said.

Charles put his arm around Aja. "Mr. James, I'm going to do my best to make your daughter very happy."

"I know you will. I don't know much about you, but I can see how much you love my daughter." Gerald took Aja's hands. "And Aja, I'd love to give you away. But more than anything else, I just want to be there."

Giving me away, no way. With a weak smile she responded, "An invitation, I think I can manage." The other part, her father would just have to understand.

Epilogue

This was a day Aja never would've imagined. She sat on a blanket under the towering oak tree at Lake Houston. This time next month, she would be a mother. Just one month after she and Charles got married, Aja found out she was pregnant. The good thing was she didn't have to wonder who the father was. She was still extremely ashamed of her indiscretion and had wanted on more than one occasion to clear her conscience and tell Charles about her night with Troy, but Roxie had convinced her that some secrets were best left buried. The more Aja looked at Charles, the more she believed Roxie was right. Charles was an understanding man, but that's something Aja wasn't sure he would be able to get over.

They'd already agreed on the baby's name—Eric Paul. Aja was ecstatic when they found out they were having a boy. She didn't hesitate in coming up with a name, and luckily, Charles thought it was a great one.

Aja lovingly watched Charles play with Madison. Gerald and Jada sat at the picnic table, while Elise sat across from them. It had been two years since Eric's death, but Elise had never returned to her usual, vibrant self. She still had a hollow look in her eyes, like a part of her was missing. She hadn't dated anyone and showed no desire to do so.

Aja closed the book she had been reading, pulled herself up, and walked over to the table.

"Daddy says he will take me to the movies next Saturday," Jada exclaimed.

Aja gave a small smile. She was still having a hard time dealing with her father, but for Jada's sake she had made the effort.

Gerald had started visiting Jada almost every day after he was released from prison. His visits had sped Jada's recovery along at an amazing rate. The doctors said she would probably be ready to leave the home in the next year. Although she'd probably never be like other twenty-one-year-olds, she could lead a normal, healthy life and like it or not, Aja thought, Gerald was to thank for that.

"That's nice, Jada," Aja told her sister.

"Sure would be nice if I could take both my girls to dinner and a movie," Gerald said.

Aja's eyes met her father's. She saw the apologetic look, the plea for her to give in just a little bit. She had been trying so hard to forgive her father. While she would never feel the way she used to, she had made tremendous progress, and was finally at a point where she felt she could give just a little bit.

"We'll see," Aja said.

Gerald smiled. "That's good enough for me. It's more than I could've ever asked for."